Praise for DDC Morgan…

"With each new book, the Calloway Series is developing into a tour de force of British noir – a must-read…"

"A terrific addition to the English Mean Streets school…"

"A brilliant piece of post-war noir…"

"A gem of a find and highly recommended."

"As I read, I had that feeling that I haven't had since I read chandler for the first time."

"I literally couldn't put this down and read the whole thing in under 24 hours."

"A fantastic read, stylishly written."

"Exciting, gripping and enjoyable - what more could you want!"

This edition first published 2023

ISBN: 978-1-914475-57-3

10 9 8 7 6 5 4 3 2 1

www.Fahrenheit-Press.com

F 4 E

Cover Design & Manuscript Typesetting by www.SkullStarStudio.com

Pills & Soap

By

DDC Morgan

A Reg Calloway Mystery

Fahrenheit Press

Also available from Fahrenheit Press

- *Blood & Canvas*
- *Rope & Canvas*

To my son and daughter.

ONE

When the phone rang, Calloway sat bolt upright in the old iron bed. The sheet clung to his back. It was soaked with sweat. He'd been dreaming again, the dream from the war.

He looked at the clock. It was one in the morning. The shrill bell of the phone pierced his skull. He wanted to ignore it, go back to sleep, hope this time he wouldn't dream.

He crossed the cold linoleum floor in his bare feet and picked up the receiver. Old Arthur, the night watchman, was panting down the line.

'You'd better get down here,' he said.

Calloway dressed and pulled a comb through his hair. He tugged a mackintosh over his big frame as he descended the stairs that led to his attic room, slamming the door behind him. There were no neighbours to wake. The rest of the three-storey factory building was empty this time of night.

The air in the street was damp. The starter motor of his car rasped through the silence before the engine spluttered into life. The drive took less than ten minutes. The road was dark and empty.

As the studio loomed into view, Calloway saw the cause of old Arthur's panic. Young women hobbled over the cobblestones in their heels. They looked distressed. They wore low-cut evening gowns showing plenty of cleavage. Their bare shoulders glowed white against the soot-black brickwork of the old brewery buildings that were home to Centurion Pictures. Rich-looking men bumbled around them, confused and indignant. The women were eighteen, nineteen, twenty-one at the most. The men were forty-plus. They were mostly overweight and bald, squeezed into expensive dinner suits, some with lighted cigars still in their pudgy hands.

Calloway pulled up, killed the motor and eased himself out of the small car. Fire engines appeared ahead of him, their bells drowning the distressed cries of the party guests as they stumbled through the studio gates. He spied Arthur in the crowd.

'It was the guvnor's car,' the old boy said.

The guvnor was Sidney G Spelthorne, head of Centurion.

'Blown sky high.'

He was gasping for breath, the tarry phlegm of the chain smoker bubbling audibly in his chest.

'An explosion?' said Calloway.

The old man nodded, struggling to speak over the chatter of his dentures.

'Must have been. Blew the glass of my hut right in. If I hadn't had my head down, the shards would've cut me to ribbons.'

Sleeping on the job, thought Calloway. He let it pass.

'Was Spelthorne in the car?'

Arthur shook his head.

'He was still at the dinner. Soon as the blast went off, his men shuffled him off the studio floor and up to his office. He's inside there now. There's blokes minding the door.'

Arthur was trembling with shock. Calloway pulled a hip flask from his pocket and pressed it into the night watchman's bony hand.

'Sit in my car and have a nip of that. I'll call you if I need you.'

The old boy complied. Calloway pushed through the fleeing bodies and into the studio courtyard. Spelthorne's Bentley burned brightly. The fuel tank had ignited in the blast and flames now lapped around the twisted metal of its mutilated bodywork. There were expensive cars either side, damaged but not yet on fire. In moments they would be.

The firemen had dismounted their tenders and were now urging the crowd back. Their oilskin over-trousers gleamed black in the light of the flames, and the silver buttons on their heavy wool tunics glistened like tiny stars. Two of them rolled a hose through the gates towards the burning motor and signalled to their colleagues to start the pump.

Revellers were still emerging from the big double doors of Studio A, amongst them musicians from a dance band clutching instruments to their chests. Calloway pushed his way towards the doors. The best he could do was to help get everyone off the premises. He stopped dead as a fleeing body slammed into his. It was a woman, dressed to the nines like the others, her makeup smeared and her platinum hairdo unravelling. As their shoulders collided, a small lamé clutch purse fell from her hand onto the cobblestone yard. She glanced down at the purse, hesitated, then fled. It seemed odd to Calloway. He slipped the purse into his pocket, looked around, but she was gone.

The scene inside Studio A matched the chaos outside. The room had been dressed for a gala, draped in rich red velvet with gilt trimmings. Inside this opulent shroud was a mess of upturned chairs and tables, shattered wineglasses and wine-stained tablecloths. The dance band stage had been abandoned like a sinking ship, strewn with bent and tangled music stands and big black instrument cases left open like empty lifeboats. It was the wake of a three-hundred-strong stampede fleeing the boom of the explosion, memories of the Blitz still all too clear in their minds.

Calloway ushered a dozen stragglers out through the doors. The women were blind drunk, stumbling knock-kneed as their male companions led them away with an outward gallantry that to Calloway seemed little more than an excuse to paw at their curves. From behind one of the upturned tables he heard a groan. A man lay on the ground clutching a champagne bottle which dripped its contents between the fleshy lips of his open mouth.

'On your feet, pal,' Calloway shouted down to the man on the ground, who responded with an inebriated giggle.

'I think I'll just stay here a little while longer chum, if it's all the same to you.'

He then began to sing a dance band hit, holding the dribbling neck of the bottle like a microphone. Calloway planted his heavy leather shoe into the reveller's fleshy backside with such force the man jumped to his feet and staggered towards the doors. Calloway had no time for drunks. He didn't much like being called chum either.

He left the studio and doubled timed across the courtyard towards the main gate. The firemen had cleared the area and were training hoses onto the flaming car. The car was a mess, its bodywork splayed, its windows shattered and its paintwork bubbling. Only the personalised number plate seemed to have survived intact: CP1.

Passing through the gates Calloway saw an ambulance crew handing out blankets to the evacuees, who now perched on the kerb or leaned against the big boundary wall smoking and swigging from wine bottles they had grabbed as they fled.

From the end of the street he heard the metallic clang of police car bells. The cars screeched to a halt ahead of the guests that filled the road. Two big Wolseleys and a Black Maria. They disgorged uniformed flatfoots who set about looking important without really knowing what to do. The fire crew and the ambulance had the scene under control, the firemen training hoses on the last of the flames that burned stubbornly around the melted tyres of the blown-up car. Calloway spied Sandy Phelps, Chief Inspector at Hackney Central, who was giving orders with an air of authority that obviated the need for a plan. He recognised Calloway and strode in his direction adjusting his peaked cap as if he meant business.

'Well this is a right bloody mess,' Phelps said. He nodded towards the dinner guests. 'Who are these swells, and where'd all the skirt come from? I'm guessing it's not their wives.'

The young women had formed their own group, talking nervously and sharing cigarettes. They seemed relieved to be away from the men.

'The annual Producers Club dinner,' said Calloway. 'The boss throws a party once a year for the money men. The girls are bussed in from the charm school.'

Phelps frowned, not understanding. 'Charm school?'

'The Centurion Company of Stars, if you want its official title. A hot house for starlets.'

'So how come I don't recognise any of them?'

'You might call their duties largely ceremonial. Once in a blue moon they get a couple of lines in a B picture.'

Phelps gave a grunt in acknowledgement.

'Were you here when the car went up?'

Calloway shook his head. 'I was stood down for the night. The boss brought in private security for the event.'

'To make sure the guests keep their hands off the merchandise?'

Calloway scoffed. 'I rather think that's the whole point of the evening.'

'Show the money a good time, eh?'

'It seems to work. This place is churning out quota quickies like there's no tomorrow.'

With the fire extinguished and the site made safe, the firemen had dropped the air of urgency. They clumped around in their gum boots, loose limbed and relaxed, reeling up the hose and stowing away their equipment in lockers on the side of the fire tenders. Phelps's men set up a cordon around the burned-out cars. Some worked the crowd outside, taking names and addresses while sneaking looks down the dresses of the women.

'Where's your boss now?' said Phelps.

Calloway nodded towards a three-storey wing that adjoined Studio A. It was Centurion's administration building. Only now he noticed half its windows had shattered.

'Holed up in his office. Third floor.'

'We'll need to talk to him, but it can wait. Any idea what caused the blast?'

Calloway shrugged.

'Faulty engine? A discarded fag perhaps?'

Calloway doubted either. A blast enough to shatter two dozen windows suggested more than an engine fire.

‘I’ll get a forensic team over tomorrow. Can you secure this place overnight?’

‘I don’t think that’s beyond me. I’ve got keys to the gate. They came with the job, funnily enough.’

‘Alright, alright. No need for that. We’ll get the folk outside packed off home. You lock the place up. I’ll put a couple of lads on duty outside and we’ll be back in the morning.’

‘It is the morning,’ said Calloway.

‘Then we’ll be back when you’ve had a shave. You look like a sack of shit.’

The chief constable turned on his heels and went back to ordering his men around. Calloway rubbed the stubble on his chin. Phelps had a point. He needed to clean up, but that would have to wait. He crossed the yard to the administration block and climbed the three flights of stairs. The anteroom where Spelthorne kept his secretaries was empty. The door to his office was shut. Two goons stood sentinel. They wore dinner suits that looked more expensive than they did. One smoked a Wills while the other perched on a desk, leafing through last month’s Picturegoer.

‘Who are you?’ the smaller of the two demanded. He tossed the magazine onto the desk. His pal pinched the fag between his thumb and forefinger and drew hard on it with tensed lips.

‘Calloway, studio security.’

The big goon smirked and blew smoke in Calloway’s direction. ‘A fat lot of use you were then.’

‘I could say the same about you. Tonight was your lookout.’

The big goon bristled. ‘Wind your neck in.’

Calloway let this ride. ‘I need to see Spelthorne.’

The smaller goon grinned. ‘He’s not at home to callers.’

He’s at home to someone, thought Calloway, judging by the sounds from behind the door. Spelthorne was calming his nerves with some female help.

‘Enjoy listening, do you?’ Calloway said.

He left them to it. One of the goons muttered ‘prat’ under his breath.

The courtyard was empty now. The fire tenders’ engines

rumbled in anticipation of departing, as the crew mounted and took their positions in the cabs. The fug of the burned-out Bentley hung in the damp air. Water from the fire hoses had spread over the cobbles and collected in pools which reflected the neon light from the illuminated studio sign. A quiet had descended.

Calloway pulled out his old gun-metal cigarette case and lit a Navy Cut. In the calm of the moment, the woman who had dropped the purse flickered into his consciousness. The face was wrong somehow. The woman was dressed the same as the others, she wore the same shoes and had the same hair, but the face didn't fit. It wasn't a charm school face. Those girls all had a look. Spelthorne handpicked them and he definitely had a type. High cheek bones and watery blue eyes with lips just full enough to pout. Redheads and blondes, and only delicate brunettes. Nothing too bold, nothing that smouldered. Spelthorne liked a hint of vulnerability, with just the promise of something more. Girls who looked like they would yield, then ignite. If they didn't have the look when they joined the Company of Stars, they had it when they came out. The woman who ran into Calloway was different. No one owned that face.

The two constables Phelps had stationed outside helped Calloway pull the big iron gates closed. They slid the bolts into the ground and Calloway locked up. Spelthorne and his boys could use the tradesman entrance if they planned to leave anytime soon. He told the coppers that the boss was still inside. They seemed uninterested and grumbled something about a waste of bloody time.

Arthur was asleep in the car, the hip flask still in his hand. Calloway drove him the half mile to the prefab he shared with his wife. She was awake when they pulled up, her hair tied up in a frayed and faded snood, a drab housecoat cinched around her old bird-like frame.

'I've been so worried,' she said.

Arthur put a mottled hand on her shoulder and explained that everything was alright. He was calm now. The shock had passed. He offered Calloway tea, which Calloway declined.

'Funny old night, eh?' the old man said.

Calloway had an inkling the coming days would be funnier still, but he didn't feel much like laughing.

TWO

There were two of them in Calloway's office. Both plain clothes. One was smoking a pipe. He'd been there long enough to fill the ten-by-ten-foot room with sickly sweet smoke. His colleague flicked through yesterday's Daily Sketch, which Calloway had left on the plain utility desk the previous day. Vice gang boss gets eight years, the headline read. A mugshot glared from the page, a criminal face straight out of Centurion's casting office. Both men rose as Calloway entered. The one with the newspaper glanced at his watch.

'Half day, is it?'

It might have been a joke, but he wasn't smiling. 'It was a late night.'

The electric clock on the wall said it was nearly ten. Calloway had overslept. The clock ticked like a termite to remind him.

'You show-business types need your beauty sleep, eh?'

Calloway ignored this. He crossed the small office and opened the metal window. A dirty mist blew in on the breeze and mingled with the pipe smoke. It was a small improvement. Calloway gestured to the men to sit and did the same. He leaned forward in the swivel chair and laid his big fists on the ink-stained desktop.

'And you are?' he said.

He knew they were police, but they weren't the usual sort. In his line of work he was used to visits from regular coppers. They turned up when things got nicked and looked bored. These were keen types. Straight backed and serious. They had an almost military demeanour.

The pipe smoker flashed a warrant card. 'Special Branch. I'm

DI Belcher, this is DS Bryant.'

Calloway opened his battered cigarette case. He'd carried it all through the war and it showed. Every dent and scratch told a story. Some were stories he wanted to forget. He lit a Navy Cut and blew more smoke into the small room.

'You here about last night?'

'Tell us what happened.'

If they were Special Branch, they'd be here because of the explosion. In the no man's land between regular policing and MI5, Special Branch stomped around in their oversized boots. Explosions were very much their business. Belcher refilled his pipe and sucked audibly to light it. Calloway hated pipes. His old commanding officer smoked one. That relationship didn't end well. He decided not to like DI Belcher, at least for the moment.

'The boss threw a party. Someone flicked a dog-end under his Bentley. It went up like a Roman candle.'

Belcher and Bryant exchanged glances. Belcher leaned forward.

'We doubt that very much.'

Calloway doubted it too. In the studio courtyard he'd seen men in white coats picking over the debris of the burned-out car. They weren't looking for dog-ends.

'We're you at the studio when the explosion happened?'

Calloway shook his head. 'There were private security guards on duty. It was a special event. You'll need to speak to the boss about that. What are you boys going to be doing here?'

This was his turf. He wanted them to know it.

'We'll check what's left of the car for fingerprints and tool marks, see if we can get comparisons. We can forget footprints. We're told there were more than three hundred guests on the premises.'

Calloway nodded.

'We'll need to interview witnesses,' said Belcher, 'so we're going to be hanging around here for some time yet. If we get anything useful from the interviews in terms of a suspect, we'll get an artist in to do sketches.'

Belcher changed tack. 'What's in production here at the moment?'

'You a film fan, DI Belcher?'

The detective inspector gave a small, grudging smile.

'I like a good western, seeing as you ask.'

'That figures. Good guys versus bad guys and a right old punch-up at the end, eh? We don't make those here. No room for the horses.'

Calloway paid little attention to what Centurion produced, save for the information necessary for his job. But he answered the question.

'At Studio A it's a family melodrama. Studio B is some thriller or other.'

'Tell us about the thriller,' said Bryant. He had crossed to the window and was watching the forensic men beetling around the blackened carcass of the Bentley.

'Moonlighting for Picturegoer?'

Belcher sighed and dug into the bowl of the pipe with a matchstick. 'Just answer the question, Calloway.'

Belcher's pipe was really irritating Calloway now. Not just the stomach-turning fug. It was the ritual of smoking, like some signifier of confident manhood. It said authority and surety far too loudly.

'It's called The Rebel Gun, I believe, although the title might change. They often do. About two assassins on the run.'

Bryant turned away from the window and looked Calloway in the eye. He had a flattened nose and a scar running through his upper lip. Done a bit of boxing in his youth, Calloway surmised. He looked the sort.

'IRA assassins,' Bryant said. It wasn't a question.

'Sounds like you know more than me. I think there's a republican thread running through the plot, yes. I don't pay much attention to the productions themselves. No call for it in my line.'

'Who are the writers?' asked Bryant. He was leaning against the filing cabinet. Calloway gestured for him to shift. He opened a drawer and rifled the files, then pulled out a hundred-page document in a manila cover.

'Cedric Dryden and Michael Balfour, according to the shooting script. They write social dramas mostly.'

Belcher stopped sucking the pipe. 'Social dramas? Communist sympathies would you say?'

Calloway shrugged. 'I wouldn't know. The likes of me don't move in their circles. But we don't start many revolutions here. That would be bad for Mr Spelthorne's business. I'm pretty sure he's not a communist.'

Calloway stifled a yawn. He'd not slept well. He'd been turning the events of the previous night over in his mind. It had kept him awake. He kept seeing the face of the woman who had dropped the purse. The woman whose face didn't fit the charm school mould.

'Keeping you up, are we?' said Bryant. Belcher asked, 'Do you have a list of the cast and crew?'

Calloway nodded. He always asked for a list so that he knew which stars would be on set. The bigger the star, the bigger the crowd around the gates. Autograph hunters, kids mostly, but less-salubrious types too. The obsessives. The creeps. The ones you had to keep an eye on. He took another file from the cabinet and passed it to Bryant, who ran a finger down the list, raising his eyebrow when he saw a name he recognised. There were two male leads. Both were name actors. A veteran and a pretty boy. The female lead was an unknown. Not from the charm school. She'd come from the theatre. She was Dryden's suggestion. He didn't like the charm school girls, apparently.

'We'll take this, if that's okay.'

Bryant had already unclipped the list from the folder and was slipping it into his inside pocket.

Then he asked the question he'd clearly been waiting to ask. 'Which part was Terrence McCaffrey due to play?'

Calloway knew the name. A jobbing character actor and a handful. He'd been asked to escort McCaffrey off the premises when he'd turned up to Spelthorne's office, stinking drunk and spoiling for a fight. He'd taken a swing at Calloway then regretted it. Calloway's fist had added a little more character to his face. That was a couple of months back. He'd not been seen since.

Calloway shrugged in response to Bryant's question. 'I'm head of security, not the casting director. How should I know?'

Bryant bristled. He stepped forward, squaring up.

Belcher cut in. 'Cut the act, Calloway. We're immune. And we've handled bigger than you.'

'Much bigger,' Bryant added. Calloway was deciding not to like Bryant too. He leaned back in his chair and peered down at the burned-out car. The forensics men were packing away their kit. A uniformed copper at the gate was waving through a glaziers' van. There were two dozen windows to mend.

'Am I a suspect? You think I flicked that fag butt under the boss's car?'

Belcher laid the pipe on the scorched Bakelite ashtray. 'No, but you're being a pain in the neck. We know the difference between an accidental fire and a suspicious explosion. So do you. Don't pretend otherwise. You're also savvy enough to know that when something explodes at a studio that's making a film about republican gunmen, that's too much of a coincidence for us to ignore. We've looked you up Calloway. Ex-Intelligence Corps. Field security background. Stop playing the dumb night watchman.'

Calloway conceded the point. 'What's your interest in McCaffrey?'

Belcher and Bryant ignored the question.

'When did you last see him?' said Belcher.

'A few weeks back. He'd been to see the boss.'

'What about?'

'A role, I assume. From his demeanour I judge he didn't get it.'

'A role in...' Belcher glanced at the cover of the folder on Calloway's desk, 'The Rebel Gun?'

'Possibly.'

Calloway worked the timings backwards in his head. The picture would already have been cast by the time McCaffrey visited Spelthorne. Shooting had already started. It was unlikely

McCaffrey's beef with Spelthorne would have been over a casting decision.

'Do you know where we could find him?'

Calloway shook his head. He knew McCaffrey wasn't under contract to Centurion. 'I can check with casting. They should have a file on him. Why the interest?'

'You know better than to ask,' said Bryant. His scar showed white against his tensed lip.

'Oh I think we can cut Calloway a bit of slack,' said Belcher. 'He used to be a copper, of a sort.'

Calloway shrugged. 'I was Military Police until 1940, when field security was transferred to the Intelligence Corps.'

'You see Bryant, a former Redcap. A brown-job copper.'

Bryant gave a grudging nod. Belcher pulled a file from his case. He passed it across the desk to Calloway. It had McCaffrey's name on it. Calloway flicked through it.

Belcher continued. 'This McCaffrey is on our watch list. A known republican sympathiser with some high-powered friends. See that photo?' He gestured with his pipe to a shot of McCaffrey seated at a dinner table next to a well-dressed man, guests at what appeared to be a gala dinner. 'It was taken last year in Chicago. The other man is Martin O'Driscoll, a well-known fundraiser for Irish republican causes in the United States.'

Calloway closed the file and passed it back. 'So you suspect McCaffrey of blowing up the boss's car.'

'I'm not saying that. But you can see how it looks. Your studio is making a film about the IRA, a republican sympathiser has a beef with the boss whose car is blown sky high a week or so later. Smells a bit, doesn't it?'

Not as much as that bloody pipe, thought Calloway. 'Last time I saw McCaffrey, he couldn't plant one foot in front of the other, let alone plant a bomb. I was stationed in Belfast in the thirties. I've known a few of the boyos in my time. That clown McCaffrey doesn't fit the mould.'

'Then I'm glad you're just a glorified night watchman and not the investigating officer on this case.'

'Why don't you speak to McCaffrey? If he's on your watch list you must have his address.'

'We have his address. He's just never there.'

'Party animal,' Bryant chimed in with a sneer.

'We were hoping you might tell us his regular haunts.'

'I wouldn't know. I don't move in the same circles. He's a film star. I'm just a glorified night watchman.'

Belcher passed Calloway a card. 'Find out, then call me.'

Calloway nodded without enthusiasm. He held the door open for the two detectives.

'Centurion Pictures will do everything it can to assist in your enquiries, Detective Inspector,' he said, like he'd mislaid his sincerity.

As the two detectives turned to leave, Bryant leaned forward and spoke quietly into Calloway's ear.

'You should go back to bed, son,' he said. 'You look tired.'

THREE

The casting office was down a long corridor at the rear of the administration building. The door was open. A man and woman sat at adjoining desks arguing. The man was in his late twenties with a weak face and too much forehead for someone his age. He wore a tweed sports coat with leather buttons and a yellow cravat, the kind horsey folk wear. The woman was pushing forty and not to be messed with. Buttoned tightly into a pre-war two-piece, with wiry greying hair that was devouring the pencil she kept in it. She gave off an aura of elegant hostility. She held a short tortoise shell cigarette holder between her teeth as she spoke to the young man opposite her.

'Jack Warner?' she said. 'Far too long in the tooth, darling.'

'But the part calls for an everyman,' said the young man. 'They don't come more every than Warner. He's the nation's father figure.'

'The part calls for a romantic. Warner can't do romance, unless you think a peck on the cheek and a bunch of daffs on Mothering Sunday counts.' She impersonated Warner, '"There you go, Ma, picked 'em from me garden",' then switched to a matronly cockney, '"Bless you, Jack, you aaare thoughtful." No, no, no.'

The young man thought for a moment, tapping his teeth with the barrel of a fountain pen.

'Jack Hawkins then. He can turn on the suave when he wants to.'

'Too gruff. Too military,' the woman said. 'At his best when barking orders on a ship.'

The young man made a plaintive face. 'Stanley Holloway?'

'Oh Fuck off, Tony!'

Tired of being ignored, Calloway cleared his throat and rapped on the open door.

The woman looked up, irritated by the interruption.

'And you are?' she said.

'Reg Calloway. The everyman that looks after security.'

The woman removed the lunettes from the bridge of her nose and looked Calloway up and down. Her hostility ebbed away.

'You know what? You might just do, darling. Can you act?'

'Only tough, when the role calls for it. Usually when I'm throwing someone out of somewhere they shouldn't be.'

The woman replaced the lunettes and leaned back in her chair. 'The screen tough-guy type. That might work. Can you do romantic?'

'Tried it once. Didn't work out.'

She smiled. 'Poor, poor you. Now come and sit over here,' she said, her tone softening even more. She patted an old stacking chair next to her side of the desk. 'Tell Marjorie how she can help.'

Calloway sat then immediately wished he'd stayed standing. He felt foolish. Like an oversized lapdog. The woman called Marjorie leaned into him and whispered, 'Is it about this explosion business? It's the talk of the studio this morning. Tongues haven't wagged this much since Stewart Grainger threatened to punch Sidney G's lights out for goosing Jean Simmons.'

Calloway's responded with his habitual stone face. 'Last night's incident is in the hands of the police. The studio will be helping them with their enquiries in any way it can.'

'Pah!' she said. 'That sounds like a press statement from the publicity office. Did Ivor tell you to say that?'

Ivor Cole was head of the publicity department. A slick-haired, fast-talking type who carried a lot of clout at Centurion. Calloway shook his head.

'I managed it all on my own.'

'You clever boy.' She removed the lunettes on the bridge of

her nose and looked him up and down again as he sat awkwardly in the chair. 'They're shooting a thriller in Studio B. I'm sure they could find use for another heavy. You should have a go, darling. The camera would love that lantern jaw of yours.'

She took his chin in her hand and turned his head from side to side as if examining an object d'art she was considering purchasing from Portobello Road. The man called Tony tossed his pen onto the desk and let out an irritated sigh.

'I'm sure the gentleman came here for something other than your personal amusement, Marge. Put him down.' He turned to Calloway. 'What is it you want, squire?'

Calloway was grateful for Tony's intervention. Marjorie had a way about her that was uncomfortably engaging.

'Do you have a file on an actor called Terrence McCaffrey?' he said.

Marjorie looked quizzical. 'Tearaway Terry? What would a fine upstanding man like you want with that reprobate? Has he been a naughty boy? Oh do tell.'

'Just a routine enquiry,' said Calloway.

Marjorie rolled her eyes. 'You're sounding like a press statement again.'

She took a long draw on the cigarette holder and placed it in the ashtray, then stood and crossed the room towards a battered grey filing cabinet that stood in the corner. Calloway followed her with his eyes. Somehow he couldn't help it. Opening a draw, she rifled through the tightly packed hanging files.

'Mason, McGoohan, McCaffrey, here he is.'

She passed Calloway the file and as he reached to take it, their hands brushed. Calloway pulled back his hand too quickly and Marjorie noticed. She raised an eyebrow. Her painted lips twisted into a predatory smile. He returned to the stacking chair and leafed through the file, which held only a few typed sheets, with a portrait of McCaffrey paper-clipped to the inside cover. He was younger in the photo by a good ten years. When Calloway had ejected him from Spelthorne's office, he'd looked older and wearier, his face puffy from drink and his jet black hair peppered with dry, wiry streaks of grey.

'Is this his current address?' Calloway said. It was the fifth address listed in the file, the previous four struck through with a red pen.

Marjorie glanced over his shoulder. 'Yes, if he's not been kicked out already.'

'Bad payer?'

'Hellraiser.'

'And where does he raise hell when he's not at home?'

The young man Tony piped up. 'Where doesn't he? The Mandrake, The Gargoyle, The French, The Torino, The Swiss. But mostly you'll find him in the Feldman Club. He loves bebop.'

'Where's the Feldman Club?' asked Calloway.

'One hundred Oxford Street, in a hell hole of a basement with a soundtrack to match.'

Marjorie peered at the young man over her glasses. 'Tony doesn't believe in jazz,' she said, like it was an accusation.

'Neither do I,' said Calloway.

The room darkened as two studio hands passed the widow carrying an oversized panel of painted scenery. Calloway looked out towards the rolling green hills and brooding purple sky as it passed. The Irish film, he guessed, suspecting the scenery had been used many times over to evoke anywhere from Hungary to the Hebrides.

'It's like sitting in a railway carriage,' said Tony to no one in particular as the scenery rolled past.

Marjorie leaned into Calloway and whispered again, 'I hear old Terry stabbed Sidney G with a letter opener and got a punch in the kisser for his trouble.'

'No one stabbed anyone,' said Calloway.

'But he still got punched. Was that you, you big brute?'

'It generally is,' he said.

She looked distracted for a moment, as if turning something over in her mind. Something about him.

'Don't worry, darling, he probably didn't feel it. I heard he was roaring drunk at the time.'

'Does he usually throw his weight around when he doesn't get a part?'

Marjorie corrected him. 'Oh, he got the part alright. Third from top billing in The Rebel Gun. He just didn't keep it. They'd been shooting for a fortnight when he got the news he'd been dropped.'

'Why was that?'

Marjorie shrugged. 'Search me, luvvie.' She winked and held out her arms. 'That's an invitation by the way.'

Tony scoffed. 'Stop it Marge. You're incorrigible.'

She patted Calloway's leg. 'I'm only teasing, darling.'

Calloway rose to leave. In the yard outside the window he saw three young women in costume hurrying towards Studio A. Extras, he imagined, and late by the looks of them. As he watched, the face of the woman flickered into his consciousness, the woman that had dropped the purse the previous night, the one who seemed more afraid of him than of the explosion and the burning car.

'Do you keep files on the Company of Stars?' Calloway asked.

'The charm school girls?' Marjorie looked disappointed again. 'Oh really, Reg. Is that what you came here for? A telephone number? Has someone caught your eye? I suppose I shouldn't be surprised. We get a steady stream of chaps through here looking for the same thing. But frankly, Reg, I thought you'd be above such a thing.' She wagged a finger. 'A man of your age too.'

He was not yet forty but six years of war had aged him, like most men of his generation. He looked fifty and worn out, with thinning hair and a pale complexion, a less corpulent version of the producers at last night's dinner, although age didn't seem to have stopped them taking more than a professional interest in the charm school cohort.

'One of them dropped her purse last night and I need to return it. I don't know her name. I only have a face to go on. If I could see their file portraits, I could identify her.'

'Lost property?' Marjorie sounded suspicious. 'Alright, I believe you, but we can't help you here. The charm school has its own office, at the back of an old gymnasium in Islington. It's where they teach the girls deportment and RP. But beware of Rene on the front desk.' She pronounced it re-nee. 'A veritable Cerberus at the gates.'

As Calloway headed for the door, Marjorie looked at her watch and said, 'It's nearly noon, darling. Would you care to join me for lunch? The canteen toad-in-the-hole is more than passable. My shout. I'll even bring Tony along as a chaperone.'

'For me?' Calloway said.

Tony cracked a smile and nodded. 'Believe me, Mr Calloway, she can't be trusted.'

'Afraid I'll have to decline,' said Calloway. 'Explosions on my watch tend to upset my social calendar.'

Marjorie had risen from her chair and was checking her make-up in a compact mirror. Satisfied, she snapped the compact shut and said, 'You're forgiven. But I'll make sure there's a next time.'

FOUR

Calloway returned to his office. It reeked of Belcher's pipe smoke. He lit a Navy Cut to take away the smell, then reached down to his desk drawer and pulled out the purse the woman had dropped. It was a lamé clutch purse with a gold clasp. He snapped it open and emptied its contents onto the linoleum desktop, then laid the contents out in a neat line. A lipstick, a powder compact and mirror, a silk handkerchief with lipstick stains, a ten-bob note, some loose change and a tortoise shell propelling pencil.

There was a knock at the door and a woman in her early twenties entered. One of Spelthorne's secretaries. She had the Centurion look. A redhead with blue eyes and lips just full enough to pout. She stood in front of Calloway's desk with her hands clasped in front of her and spoke as if to a script.

'Mr Spelthorne says he'll see you in his office.'

She spoke with the plumminess of a suburban girl trying to sound sophisticated.

Calloway gathered up the items on his desk and put them back in the purse, then locked it in his desk drawer. He followed the secretary as she clip-clipped on her heels down the echoing corridors towards the lift. Calloway slid back the lift's cage door and stepped into the small panelled carriage behind her. It was just big enough to take the pair of them, with Calloway's own big frame wedged into one corner, the secretary into another, with an inch of space between them.

'Tight squeeze,' she said, her arms crossed tightly across her chest. He pressed himself harder against the sides of the lift carriage.

The lift opened onto a well-lit corridor leading to the office he'd encountered Spelthorne's goons in the night before. Three secretaries sat at small desks: a blonde, a brunette and a redhead. Spelthorne had hired one in every colour. The brunette was typing, the redhead was on the telephone and the blonde just looked bored. Four different perfumes fought for mastery of the air supply in a fug of femininity. The roomed smelled like the ground floor of a department store. The secretary at the typewriter paused her typing and told Calloway that Spelthorne would only be a moment. She asked him to take a seat. Calloway sat on a studio couch and picked up a film magazine from the coffee table. That new young actor Dirk Bogarde gazed out from the cover looking perfect. Calloway had never seen his movies but he somehow looked familiar. He read the Bogarde article. He'd no interest in the show-business flannel, but the young actor's war record caught his eye. Intelligence officer, photographic interpreter, Normandy, Holland, Germany. The same theatres of war as Calloway. Both of them in intelligence. Then a paragraph that stopped him abruptly as he read. It mentioned the camp. The camp Calloway and his section had discovered. The actor claimed to have visited it in 1945.

'Nothing has very much really mattered to me after that experience', the quote read. 'When you've seen twenty thousand bodies in a heap, just lying in the sun like wax, you begin to wonder what life is.'

Calloway had been first man into that camp. His section were used to being first in, but never to anything like that. It had changed him for ever, in the way it changed so many others that had seen those places first-hand. He fought down a painful memory. The secretary's voice brought him back to the present.

'He'll see you now,' she said.

Calloway knocked and entered. Spelthorne's office was darker than the airy anteroom that led onto it. The walls were papered in a deep green flock, with wall lights like miniature chandeliers dangling from gold fittings. A pair of plum-coloured velvet curtains hung down to the floor, looking incongruous next to the metal-framed industrial window that overlooked the studio courtyard. There was a drinks trolley beside the window so overloaded with bottles it looked like it might crash through the parquet into the offices below. It was a night-time room, somewhere you'd smoke cigars and swill scotch around crystal glasses. Calloway's shoes sunk into the deep-pile rug until it tickled his ankles.

Spelthorne sat at a desk that was almost as big as his car. He ignored Calloway while he busied himself with papers. He went through a repertoire of expressions as he read them. Satisfaction, concern, disbelief, surprise. The expressions said he was an important man. Calloway by implication was not. He waited in silence, looking at the framed photos on the office wall with bored disinterest. Spelthorne had met a lot of people and liked being photographed. The people were old, male and important, or young, female and beautiful, but no other combination of those qualities. Calloway thought about clearing his throat to signal his presence, but Spelthorne would be waiting for that. It would just be a cue to look at the paperwork some more. He stood at ease and waited. After a few minutes Spelthorne spoke without looking up from his desk.

'Are you the security Johnny?' His accent sounded London Italian.

'Calloway, sir.'

'New, aren't you?'

'Three months now.'

'Good at your job, would you say?'

'I believe so, sir.'

Spelthorne glanced up from his paperwork. 'Then why was my Bentley blown to kingdom fucking come in the car park of my own studio?'

He rose from his desk and crossed the room to the drinks trolley. He wasn't a tall man, but he was powerfully built, with a broad chest, short arms and stocky legs. He was balding, with a prominent forehead creased with worry lines, his remaining hair heavily oiled and combed back behind his ears forming wiry tufts that tickled his shirt collar. His nose was flattened against his oval face, his top lip thin and mean, his bottom lip fat and moist. He wore a crisp white shirt, a silk tie in a Windsor knot with narrow braces holding up his impeccably cut flannel suit trousers. He poured a large slug of what looked like whisky from a cut-glass decanter and dropped in two ice cubes from a silver bucket. It was shaped like a barrel with a gold horseshoe on the front.

'Well?' he said, turning to face Calloway.

'The police suspect terrorism.'

'I know that. I spent half the morning with them. I'm asking what you were doing last night when you were supposed to be stopping things blowing up.'

Calloway looked him in the eye and spoke without apology. 'I was asleep, sir.'

The veins on the side of Spelthorne's bald head pulsed visibly. He looked like he could kill someone. Someone like Calloway.

'On my payroll?' He spat the words. Calloway felt saliva on his chin.

'On my own time,' said Calloway. 'There were private security on duty for the event last night. I was stood down.'

'By who?'

'By you, sir.'

Spelthorne's nostrils flared.

Calloway continued. 'I received a memo from your office three weeks ago, setting out the arrangements. My men cleared the car park for the VIP cars as instructed, then handed over to your men.'

Spelthorne looked less like he could kill someone, just hurt them in places the bruises wouldn't show. It went with his reputation. They say never ask a producer how he financed his first film. Actually, they only said it about Spelthorne.

The studio boss returned to his chair and sat. He'd calmed down. He kicked back and loosened his tie, then swallowed half the whisky in a single gulp.

'It's the last thing I fucking need. My investors are shitting bricks. This kind of thing doesn't inspire confidence, now does it? And the production in Studio A is all over the fucking place. It's over time and over budget. Broken cameras, broken lights, spoiled film. I buy new equipment but it still manages to break down. Same in Studio B. They can't look after the stuff either. Then all this business.' He waved a hand towards the courtyard where the police were still busying around. 'I had to sack that big Mick from the gunmen film and pay him off, then cast the new fella, so that's more time and money.' He knocked back the rest of the scotch and poured himself another, shaking his head. 'I've hired a bunch of cowboys.'

'Perhaps you should make a western,' said Calloway.

Spelthorne shot him a look. 'Don't be smart with me son,' he said. Then he laughed. 'Yeah, maybe you're right.'

Spelthorne glanced over at the framed photos on the wall.

'I met John Wayne once. His real name's Marion. Didn't like him. All mouth, and about as tough as my old mum. Actually mum could handle herself pretty well, so that's not a good comparison.' He nodded at the drinks trolley. 'Help yourself. You probably need one as much as I do. It's been a rum old couple of days.'

It was early, but Calloway did as invited. Spelthorne perched his generous backside on the windowsill and looked out over the courtyard. The last of the police were climbing into a van, gesturing to the commissionaire at the main gate to open up. Spelthorne swilled the ice around his glass.

'Do you think he did it?' he said.

'He didn't strike me as the type,' Calloway said. 'And it's not an easy thing to do. You need the materials, and you need to know that you're doing. You can't just go into an ironmonger's and buy a stick of TNT. I don't know McCaffrey but I doubt he's going to go to these lengths just to get even with you. He's an actor, a bon viveur by all accounts. Why would he care that much?'

'The police reckon he's connected,' said Spelthorne.

'To the IRA? It's not their MO. Centurion's not a symbol of British authority.'

'But he's a sympathiser. That's why I sacked him.'

'How did that come to light?'

'He was doing an interview, something Ivor had set up to promote the picture. The journalist asked what he thought about the Irish problem. McCaffrey started mouthing off. Saying how he'd always supported the republican cause and that the IRA were freedom fighters not terrorists. Ivor had his work cut out getting that one buried. He bought off the journalist with some dirt about a starlet at a rival studio. That and a night on the town with a charm school girl. Ivor arranged that.'

Spelthorne crossed the room and took a cigarette from a silver box on his desk.

'I had to sack McCaffrey,' he said, lighting up. 'He was a liability.'

Calloway swigged the scotch. It made him lightheaded, on top of the sleepless night.

'Then what happened?' he asked.

'You were there. He tried to kill me.'

'He waved a letter opener at you.'

'One man's letter opener is another man's shiv,' said Spelthorne, sounding like he spoke from experience. 'Where is he now?'

'The police say he's gone awol from his flat.'

'On the run?'

'On the lash is more likely. Special Branch wants me to find out his regular haunts. I've just been down to casting to see what they know. He likes jazz apparently.'

Spelthorne drew hard on the cigarette. Calloway felt light lighting up too, but this wasn't the moment.

'Find him for me,' said Spelthorne. 'Tell him I want to talk to him.'

'This is a police matter,' said Calloway.

'It was my studio, my car and my party. It could have been my fucking hide spattered all over Hackney. This is my business and if that half-cut Mick is behind it, I want a word with him.'

He looked at Calloway. 'A friendly word, naturally. Before the police get their hands on him.'

Calloway took another gulp of the scotch. It gave him time to think. 'Wouldn't this be better handled by your private security people?'

He meant the goons that were minding Spelthorne's padded door the previous night.

'Franco and Giordano? They're just gorillas in dinner suits. Don't get me wrong, they have their uses. But I've heard about you...'

He grappled for the name. Calloway supplied it.

'Calloway, yeah. Intelligence Corps, weren't you? I bet you've felt a few collars in your time. This should be right up your street.'

Spelthorne was right, but it was a street Calloway tried to avoid. In his years in field security he'd interrogated German prisoners. He'd earned a reputation for not sticking to procedure. Once his adrenaline started flowing, the Geneva Convention became more of a guideline than a rule. Sometimes prisoners got hurt. He wasn't proud of it. He blamed war but knew there was more to it. He had a short fuse. It was best not to be around once you'd lit it.

Calloway shook his head. 'It's not the kind of work I signed on for.'

Spelthorne waved his hand dismissively. 'A hundred quid says it is.'

Calloway turned to leave.

'Wait,' said Spelthorne. 'Let's call it double or quits.'

'Meaning?'

'I give you two hundred quid to find the Mick. If you refuse, you quit.'

'I quit?'

'Well, not exactly. I fire you, for letting someone plant a bomb under my car.'

Spelthorne offered up his hands. 'I mean it doesn't look good, does it? You being my head of security.'

Calloway's stomach knotted. He felt nauseous. It may have been the lack of sleep or the scotch he'd just tipped down his throat onto a breakfast of phlegm and Navy Cut. More likely it was the threat of losing his job less than six months after he'd left the last one. That had ended when he'd agreed to moonlight for his former boss as a snoop. It felt like he was about to make the same mistake.

'Here's a hundred in advance,' said Spelthorne, pulling cash from his wallet. 'That's yours to keep. You get the next hundred when you bring me McCaffrey.'

Spelthorne could read the reluctance on Calloway's face.

'Like I said, I only want a friendly chat with him.'

Calloway could imagine Spelthorne's idea of a friendly chat. It would probably involve Franco and Giordano and not much chat.

Calloway folded the sheaf of crisp white fivers and put them into the inside pocket of his jacket.

'There's a good boy,' said Spelthorne with a wink. He sat back in the chair, stretched and sighed. 'Christ I'm tense,' he said.

He craned his neck until the sinews showed though his pudgy skin. 'I need to loosen up. All this stress can't be good for a man, eh Calloway?'

He pressed the palms of his bloated hands together in a half-hearted attempt at calisthenics, then wove his fingers together and cracked his knuckles.

'I really need to loosen up,' he repeated to himself, nodding like he'd just decided how. He leaned forward and pressed the buzzer on the intercom on his desk. 'Send Miss Hope in,' he said into the device. Spelthorne was the type that never said please.

There was a knock at the door and the bored-looking blonde secretary entered. Unlike the others, she wasn't from the Centurion mould. She was five foot five in heels with the kind of body advertising agencies use to sell corsets, her cashmere sweater stretched taught and the seams of her skirt looking ready to snap like overwound violin strings. She had the air of someone who already knew why she had been summoned, with a rigid smile and eyes fixed on an imaginary point in the middle distance.

‘Would you like me to take a letter Mr Spelthorne?’ she said like she was trying to sound keen. Calloway noticed she had no pen or notepad.

Her boss nodded then said to Calloway, ‘You can go.’

Calloway crossed the room and opened the padded door by its ornate gold handle. Before he’d closed the door behind him, he saw Spelthorne taking off his tie and getting comfortable on the couch.

FIVE

Oxford Street, past midnight. Calloway had worked his way through the list of bars and clubs that Tony in casting had reeled off. He'd met piss-heads, poets and ponces and plied them with drink. They'd talked about themselves. He'd talked with tarts who recited their repertoire of sickly small talk for the price of a gin-and-It. He'd even been propositioned by a merchant seaman in full drag, which was a first for him. Everyone knew McCaffrey but no one had seen him. There was one dive left on the list. The Feldman Club.

Calloway stood outside the anonymous doorway in the light of the restaurant windows beside it. A neon sign above the restaurant said Mac's in bright red letters. Through the windows, a tired kitchen hand swept beneath tables and upturned chairs. Calloway entered the side door. The sounds of jazz oozed up from the basement. Halfway down the grubby linoleum stairs a woman in a black sweater with a red neckerchief sat behind a hatch reading a Penguin edition of Homer's Odyssey. She was twenty at most with short black hair and a fringe which looked home cut. She made Calloway buy membership. It cost him five shillings. She said, 'If you want to drink you need to bring a bottle.'

'I can live without a drink,' he replied, wondering where he was supposed to buy a bottle in the early hours of Sunday morning. She shrugged and returned to her paperback. He continued down the stairway. A heavy black door at the bottom held back the nerve-shredding sound of saxophones. As he pulled the door open, a wall of heat hit him. It reminded him of stepping onto the airstrip in Palestine in forty-five, after an eight-hour flight from the chill of a Baltic morning. Only this heat was damp, the dampness of two hundred sweating bodies crammed into the low-ceilinged space. The room was vibrating. Bebop bounced off the ceiling and ricocheted off the dripping walls. A mixed race crowd had formed a circle to watch a young couple jitterbug. The boy wore a powder blue zoot suit with a gaudy spiv's tie and slip-on shoes worn rough from dancing. The girl wore a loud print dress cinched tight by a red leather belt. Her hair was piled high above her face, a corral necklace swinging in time with her moves. The crowd watched intently, studying their steps. White youths stood side by side with young black men who smoked cigarettes and pipes, dressed in the same heavy wool suits as the Caribbeans Calloway had seen on the newsreels arriving at Tilbury docks. Calloway pushed through the crowd. A young woman blocked his way. She was leaning against a column and nodding in time to the music. She dressed like an art student, studiedly shabby. A pungent plume of smoke rose from the Gauloises she held between slender fingers with chewed-down nails. He recognised the smell from the bars in Normandy whose grateful owners had poured him and his comrades weak red wine to toast their liberation. She held the cigarette packet in her other hand in full view, in case anyone doubted her avant-garde credentials. He tried to push past her.

'Loosen up, big man. Listen to the band,' she shouted over the noise, her eyes directing him to the stage. She spoke in faux American, but her home counties roots showed through in perfect vowels. Calloway looked towards the stage. Six white men with hair en brosse played with intensity. Sweat-sodden shirts clung to their skinny young frames. Calloway's unease at the sound they created showed on his face. The young woman misread his expression.

'Okay, so it's not Club Eleven, but at least the cops haven't closed it down,' she shouted.

'Why did they close Club Eleven down?' Calloway shouted back.

She stared into his eyes and took a long draw on the

Gauloises, this time holding it between her thumb and forefinger, then mouthed reefer as she blew smoke into his face. She looked him up and down and laughed.

'You don't dig jazz, do you?'

'I dig the German romantic composers.'

She scrunched up her face as she thought about this.

'That's okay,' she said, offering him a cigarette from the decorative French packet. 'Square, but okay.'

'You've just written my epitaph,' he said, taking one from the pack and accepting a light.

'So why are you here? You're not a cop, are you?'

He thought of DS Bryant and shook his head. 'I failed the IQ test. I scored too high.'

'I'm glad,' she said, and laughed again. She noticed he was empty-handed. 'You need a drink,' She reached for a slender wine bottle from the shelf behind her.

'It's German. Like your taste in music.'

She picked up a used glass and shook the dregs onto the sticky wooden floor before pouring him some wine. He ignored the lipstick on the rim and took a sip. The wine was as warm as the room.

'I'm looking for a friend,' he said. 'A big bebop fan. He's an actor. Terrence McCaffrey.'

One of the saxophonists on stage stood to take a solo. The woman whooped and clapped her hands. Without taking her eyes off the band she shouted, 'The table in the corner, to the left of the stage. He practically lives there.'

Calloway drained the wine and nodded his thanks before losing the dirty glass and pushing his way to the corner. McCaffrey sat alone, lost in the music. He had the same trance-like expression the young woman had. Calloway pulled up a chair and sat at his table. It jolted McCaffrey into awareness. He recognised Calloway.

'Did you come here to hit me again?' he said, in a soft Irish brogue.

'Will you give me cause to?'

'Not after last time. I had three loose teeth for a fortnight.

What brings you here? You don't strike me as the bebop type.'

Calloway looked towards the stage. The saxophonist had finished his solo. Now it was the trumpet player's turn. The sound pierced Calloway's skull like a dentist's drill.

'I'm more the Mahler type,' he said.

McCaffrey raised a thick black eyebrow. 'A man of culture,' he said. 'A quality not usually found among studio henchmen.'

'You'd be surprised,' said Calloway. 'We studio henchmen are an unpredictable lot.'

McCaffrey laughed. 'You can say that again. I didn't see that right hook coming.'

'That's because you were blind drunk.'

McCaffrey held up his hands. They were big and work-worn. The actor had had a real life before show business.

'I'd just been sacked,' he said, 'for my beliefs.'

Calloway played dumb. 'What beliefs are those?'

'I'm an Irishman, Mr Calloway. Ireland is a divided country. I believe it shouldn't be so.'

'So not typecast then?'

'On the contrary,' said McCaffrey. He pulled a cigarette from a gold case and lit it with a Zippo. 'Apparently it's alright to play a republican but not to be one.'

'So you turned up drunk at the studio to give Spelthorne a mouthful.'

McCaffrey drew hard on the cigarette and nodded. 'I was in full swing when my jaw collided with your fist. That's quite the hammer you've got there.'

'You were threatening the boss with a letter opener.'

McCaffrey laughed. 'Assault with office equipment? That's quite the offence.'

'It was shaped like a dagger.'

The Irishman gave a grudging nod. 'Fair point. But I'd never have used it.'

McCaffrey was talking now. Calloway pushed him. 'So instead you put a bomb under Spelthorne's Bentley. Did your republican friends provide the explosives?'

'That explosion? If you suspect me then you're a bigger fool than you look.'

'Special Branch suspects the IRA. They're guessing you had a hand in it.'

'Oh, Special Branch is it? I must have made the big league.' McCaffrey shook his head. 'They're barking up the wrong tree. It wasn't a bomb. Not on the mainland.'

'They've done it before,' said Calloway. He remembered the bombing campaign in thirty-nine and forty. The S-plan, they called it. S for sabotage. The IRA blew up power stations, pylons and public lavatories. Then they started bombing tube stations. It caused a handful of deaths and a lot of panic. By the time the Luftwaffe arrived that September, everyone forgot the S-plan. It was small beer compared to the Blitz.

'That was then,' said McCaffrey. 'They've more to worry about at home. Their priority is the border right now.'

'You seem well informed.'

'I follow current affairs.'

'Closely, by the sound of it.'

'I won't deny I've met a couple of the boys. Show me a Tyrone man that hasn't.'

'More than a couple I'd say. Word has it you've been fundraising for the boyos in America.'

'Now who told you that? Special Branch was it?'

'They showed me your file. You take a good photo.'

'I'm a film star, Calloway. I always give 'em my good side.'

'I saw photos with you and a man called Martin O'Driscoll.'

'Ah, Martin. He's an old friend.'

'He's Sinn Fein's bagman in Chicago.'

'Did Special Branch tell you that too?'

Calloway looked up. A man had approached the table looking like he was about to join them. Six foot, slender and black. His suit suggested African not Caribbean.

'Now then Mr Calloway. I'd like you to meet my lawyer. This is Mr Ndungu,' said McCaffrey.

'Please, call me Paul,' the man said, shaking Calloway's hand. 'It's true, I am a lawyer. Well, law student at least. But I don't represent this reprobate.'

He'd brought a bottle of wine, already uncorked. McCaffrey picked up his glass and pointed it in Ndungu's direction. The young law student filled it, then poured a glass for Calloway and himself.

'Reprobate, he calls me. And this from the man that lured me into the darkest corners of London to listen to ungodly music at unholy hours.'

'I gave you jazz, Terrence. You should thank me.'

McCaffrey gave a small bow. 'I am forever in your debt, sir. Now Calloway here, he's more the romantic composers' type.'

'We'll have to convert him,' said Ndungu.

'Don't waste your time,' said Calloway. 'Someone already tried that.'

McCaffrey gave Calloway a knowing smile. 'From the tone of regret in your voice, I'd hazard a guess that someone was a woman.'

'Not a bad guess,' said Calloway, taking a sip of the wine. It was colder and better than the glass the student girl had offered him. 'I didn't come to talk about jazz,' he said.

McCaffrey turned to Ndungu. 'Mr Calloway here thinks I'm a terrorist.'

Ndungu laughed. 'You are certainly forthright in your views, Terrence.'

'Forthright enough to plant a bomb?' said Calloway.

It never hurt to stir the pot. McCaffrey rose from the table. 'Don't talk shite, Calloway.'

He headed towards a door marked lavatory. When he had gone Calloway said to Ndungu, 'How did you meet Terrence?'

'He was giving a talk at the university. Something about Ireland and Africa under the yoke of British colonialism.'

'A good talk, was it?'

'Poorly argued, but beautifully spoken. Afterwards a few of the students came here. Terrence has been a regular fixture ever since.'

Calloway looked towards the stage where another saxophonist was soloing. 'He must actually like this music.'

'This music?' said Ndungu. 'You make it sound distasteful.

Come on, Mr Calloway. Listen to that saxophone. Pure poetry.'

'It's a mercy it doesn't have a smell,' said Calloway.

Ndungu let out a roar and slapped Calloway hard on the back. 'I like that,' he said. 'I'll use that line.'

'You're welcome to it. Was Terrence here last Saturday night?'

'Are you testing his alibi?'

'He hasn't given me one.'

'Then I will,' Ndungu said. 'Yes, Terrence was here and I was with him. From around ten until they threw us out.'

'When was that?'

'Three in the morning, give or take.'

'And then?'

'I put him in a taxi. He'd had a good night and was, let's say, unsteady on his feet. What is all this? Bombs, terrorists, what is it you think my friend is mixed up in?'

'Someone blew up my boss's car. Thankfully he was pawing a young actress at the time so was nowhere near.'

'That's shocking.'

'The bomb or the pawing?'

'I could make a case against both, if the client so wished.' He poured Calloway another drink and smiled. 'At least I might, if I wasn't studying company law.'

'Your friend Terrence had a flaming row with my boss a few days earlier. He threatened him. He had just been sacked from a role in a film about the IRA. He's a known republican sympathiser who, according to the police, raises money for the cause in America. The boss didn't like this.'

'And you've put all of this circumstantial evidence together and found Terrence guilty, or near as dammit.'

'I haven't,' said Calloway. 'I can't say the same for the police.'

McCaffrey returned to his seat shaking water off his hands.

'Bad-mouthing me to my friend, Calloway?' he said. 'Shame on you. So the question is, do you believe your friends in the Special Branch, or do you believe me?'

'They're not my friends.'

'You seem to care what they think,' said Ndungu.

'I care about a bomb going off on my watch. For what it's worth, I don't think you or the fanatics you rub shoulders with planted it.'

'May I ask why?' said Ndungu.

'I was army intelligence. I spent time in Northern Ireland. I know a thing or two about McCaffrey's friends. The MO doesn't fit. The IRA bombs factories, utilities and military targets, or civilian targets that will cause disruption, not film studios and certainly not for something as trivial as their pal losing a part in a picture.'

'So why the grilling, Calloway?' said McCaffrey.

'This is a friendly chat. You'd know if you were getting a grilling.'

'I'll take your word for it. When were you in Ireland, may I ask?'

'I was posted to Belfast in 1935 with the Military Police.'

'You were there for the riots?'

Calloway nodded.

'Your republican friends caused a lot of trouble.'

'So you stamped your size ten boots all over them, like a good occupying army.'

'We tried to maintain order.'

'With a fleet of armoured cars training their Vickers guns on innocent civilians. I bet that was a proud day.'

'We kept a lid on it.'

'That's the problem, Reg. When you keep a lid on things, the pressure builds up.'

Calloway knocked back the wine in his glass. The band was playing a new number. The noise assaulted his senses.

'I'm not totally immune to the problem. I saw the other side of the story too. I watched a Protestant mob going house to house, kicking out Catholic families. The mob threw their furniture into the street and burned it.'

'And did you try to stop them?'

'Our orders were not to intervene.'

'So you obeyed them.'

'I was a soldier.'

'Then may your God forgive you,' said McCaffrey, raising his glass. 'Why did you come looking for me?'

'Special Branch wants to know your regular haunts.' Calloway didn't mention Spelthorne's double or quits proposition. 'You have a habit of being out when they call.'

'It's a habit I've cultivated, believe me.'

'What are you going to tell them?' said Ndungu to Calloway.

'He can tell them that Terrence Patrick McCaffrey doesn't give a flying fuck,' said the Irishman.

Calloway rose to leave. 'It was a pleasure to meet you, Paul,' he said. He turned to McCaffrey. 'For what it's worth, you may want to lose yourself for a while.'

'Thanks, Calloway. I might just do that.'

Ndungu pushed the half-full wine bottle across the table towards McCaffrey.

'I must leave too,' he said. 'I have an exam first thing on Monday morning. I need to study tomorrow. I'll walk out with you, Mr Calloway.'

They pushed their way through the mass of sweating bodies. The dancing couple were jitterbugging with fury, the boy flinging the girl around dance floor effortlessly, like she was part of him. The crowd loved them. They clapped and cheered. Some copied the couple's moves. When Ndungu and Calloway had made it to the relative quiet of the stairs, the law student said, 'Terrence is no terrorist. He's a passionate republican and a hot-headed orator, but candidly, I get the impression he's playing at it. He doesn't have the stomach for killing.'

'How can you be sure?'

'I'm from Kenya. I've seen first-hand the carnage of the Mau Mau and the violence of the British response. Terrence is not in that league.'

'His fundraising work in America seems to be real.'

'I'm sure it is. And I'm sure he knows people. Perhaps there's no difference morally between facilitating a struggle and actually taking part in it. But in Terrence's case, it's an act of naive enthusiasm, not sedition.'

The street outside was deserted, save for the odd taxi whose diesel engine tick-ticked through the hush as it passed. The pair walked south through Soho. It was quieter now, its pubs closed, its shops dark, the only signs of life being the warm and enticing glow of red lights in windows of flats above and the footsteps of the furtive callers plucking up the courage to ring their doorbells. As they turned into Broadwick Street, there was a shout from behind.

'Where'd you think you going?'

There were three of them. None of them looked more than eighteen. They wore high-cut trousers and long sports jackets over check shirts with greasy hair piled up on their heads. They were looking at Ndungu, who kept walking.

'Ignore them, Reg,' he said.

'Perhaps you didn't hear me,' the youth said, gobbing into his fingers and flicking spittle in their direction.

Calloway turned to face them. 'Alright, lads. That's enough.'

Ndungu spoke softly, 'Leave them be, Reg, please. It will only aggravate them. Nothing will be gained.'

'We'll see about that,' said Calloway. He leaned in towards the leader of the three and lowered his voice to a whisper. 'You need to calm down, boys. Go have your fun somewhere else.'

The lead youth looked to the others for encouragement.

'Or else what?'

Calloway grabbed his ear, digging his fingernails into the soft flesh, and pressed his face against the boy's.

'Or else I knock seven shades of shit out of the lot of you.'

Ndungu stepped forward and took Calloway's arm.

'Let's go, Reg. These boys are really not worth the trouble.'

'Who asked you.' said the leader.

Den grinned, then jumped. A blade flashed in his hand under the streetlight. A cut-throat razor. Calloway shifted his weight and stamped hard on the boy's shin. He grabbed his arm and smashed his hand against the lamppost. The blade fell. Calloway kicked it into the gutter. A second boy lunged towards him, his fist raised. Calloway tripped him, pushed him onto the pavement and kicked him in the stomach. From the corner of his eye he saw Ndungu take a punch to the side of the face. A boy slap, no force behind it. The lad squared up for a second punch. Ndungu balled his fist and landed an undercut beneath the boy's jaw with a crack. Ndungu had done some boxing. As the boy reeled, Ndungu grabbed his lapels and threw him to the ground. Ndungu winced. His hand bled. The boy had razor blades sewn under his lapels. Calloway kicked the boy on the ground as a police whistle shrilled from the street corner.

'Scarper,' the boy called Den shouted, before turning on his heels. The other two scrambled to their feet and followed him into the darkness. Ndungu fumbled with a handkerchief to bandage his hand. The copper approached him, his truncheon raised. The copper shouted at Ndungu.

'Stay right where you are.'

Ndungu froze. The copper was rattled. His voice trembled. Without taking his eyes off Ndungu, he said to Calloway, 'Are you alright, sir?'

Calloway stepped in front of Ndungu to face the policeman, who was no older than the boys who'd just run off.

'Put it down, son,' he said. 'He's not the attacker, he's the victim.'

The copper looked confused. 'Then who are you?'

'I'm his friend,' said Calloway.

This seemed to throw the young copper completely. Calloway watched the little cogs in his brain working overtime. Calloway explained, 'We were jumped by three lads,' he nodded at Ndungu's hand. 'They had razors.'

Calloway pulled his own handkerchief from his pocket and helped Ndungu bind the wound.

The cogs in the young copper's brain finally clunked into gear. He turned to Ndungu.

'Are you alright, sir?' he said, sounding not quite apologetic enough.

'I'm fine,' said Ndungu. 'No harm done. Just a nick.'

The copper fidgeted, looking for an excuse to leave.

'I'll go to the police box on Regent Street. Put a call out to all cars. See if we can pick the boys up.'

Ndungu waved the suggestions away with his good hand. 'Please don't go to any trouble constable. It was just high spirits.'

The copper eyed him suspiciously. 'If you say so, sir.'

Ndungu spotted a passing cab and flagged it. When he and Calloway were in the cab, he said, 'There was no need for that Reg.'

'The lad pulled a razor,' said Calloway. 'I'd say there was every need.'

'It doesn't help.'

'Are you sure? You're not lying in the gutter with your belly sliced open, are you?'

'They'll do it again. To someone else. And now they've got a score to settle. Your intervention has solved nothing.'

'You'd have just stood there and taken it?'

'We have a saying in Kenya: only scratch where you can reach.'

They sat in silence until the taxi pulled up outside an address in Maida Vale, a tired stucco-fronted house with an array of doorbells beside its peeling black door. Ndungu stepped out of the taxi into the street.

'It was a pleasure meeting you, Reg,' he said. His face said he meant it. 'Go easy on McCaffrey. Under all that bluster is a good man.'

SIX

A young man in a shawl-collared cardigan and cavalry twills shouted at Calloway.

'You're standing on my mark, love!'

He held a clipboard as a statement of his authority. Assistant director or some such, Calloway guessed. He'd still not figured out how it all worked. He stood on a set built to look like an Irish inn, at least in the imaginings of a set designer who'd quite possibly never crossed the Irish Sea. It looked nothing like the Belfast bars Calloway had drunk in as a Redcap in the mid-thirties. Those were Victorian palaces, panelled and glazed to excess. This place looked more like an American tourist's idea of a pub in what they would no doubt call the old country. Fake beams, low ceiling and tiny windows looking onto a backdrop painted to look like distant heather. Calloway stepped off the mark, an X chalked onto the concrete floor presumably marking the spot where one of The Rebel Gun's stars was to stand. Around him, technicians busied themselves with lighting and cameras and microphones on booms that resembled Bofors guns. He walked towards the edge of the stage, treading carefully to avoid the dolly tracks that cut across his path. At the end of the track, two technicians, one in tweeds, the other in a brown store coat, were digging around in the metal bowels of an opened camera.

'I don't bloody believe it,' the technician in tweed said. He was clearly the senior of the two. 'Same problem as last time. Grit in the workings.'

'But this one's new isn't it?' said the man in the store coat, taking one of the four pens clipped to his breast pocket and prodding it gingerly into the workings of the camera.

'Yep, arrived from Studio Equipment Co. on Friday. We tested it on delivery. Had it open and everything. It was clean as a whistle.'

For some reason unknown to Calloway, the man in the store coat leaned forward and sniffed at the workings.

'And it's been sitting here all weekend?' he said.

The man in tweed nodded and looked upwards, as if expecting to see a hole in the roof and a cloud of grit threatening to rain again from the sky above.

Calloway cut in. 'Is this the same trouble that's been affecting the equipment these past few weeks?'

Startled, the man in the tweeds looked him up and down. 'You heard about that?' he said.

Calloway nodded. 'Spelthorne's been ranting about it.'

'Ranting?' said the man in the store coat. 'I'll say he was. You should have heard where he threatened to stick my pen.'

He reddened at his own reference to the unnamed orifice.

'Sorry, squire, I don't believe we've met,' said the man in tweed, frowning at Calloway.

'Reg Calloway. Head of studio security. Our paths haven't crossed up to now.'

'Security, eh?' said the man in tweed, with a hint of suspicion. 'And what might this have to do with studio security?' The implication being that this was a technical matter that was beyond the ken of a glorified night watchman. To Calloway, everyone on the studio floor was a self-important technocrat. They reminded him of the REME boys from his army days, the ones who treated you like you'd broken your field radio on purpose and behaved like they were paying for those replacement valves out of their own pocket.

'I take a professional interest in anything irregular,' Calloway said.

He figured that by looking into the broken equipment, he might at least find something to keep Spelthorne at bay on the McCaffrey matter.

'How many times has this happened?'

'This is the third time we've found grit in a camera in the last three weeks.'

'And then there's the water in the lights,' his colleague chipped in. 'Taken us over a fortnight to dry them out.'

'Very real risk of electrocution, you see,' the tweed man said, as though Calloway couldn't have worked that out for himself.

'Very real, I'm sure,' said Calloway. 'What's the cost of the damage?'

The man in tweed shook his head and tutted. 'It's not about the cost of the damage, it's about the cost of the time. A delay to shooting is an expensive business. You can't just stand the cast and crew down. They still need paying. And some of the cast will be contracted on other films afterwards. It throws everything out, you see.'

Calloway saw, funnily enough. He said, 'So, all this damage. Too much to be put down to chance?'

The tweed man shook his head grimly. 'Search me, squire. All I know is I've never seen anything like it in twenty years in the trade.'

His pal echoed, 'Nothing like it. Twenty years,' as he fiddled with the pens in his breast pocket, evening out the spaces between each, as though the gesture might bring some order to the situation with the lights and cameras.

'What type of grit is it?' said Calloway.

The man in tweed looked incredulous. 'What type of grit?' he said. 'I know my cameras chum, and my lights, but an expert in grit I am not.'

Calloway gestured towards the bright red fire bucket that hung on the wall a few feet away from them. 'That type of grit?'

The tweed technician looked over towards the bucket full of sand. 'It could be, I suppose,' he said, sounding reluctant to acknowledge the possibility.

'And you first discovered this latest incident today?'

'This morning, yes. We were double checking before loading.'

'And the other times?'

The store coat technician perked up. 'Mondays,' he said. 'The grit in the cameras and the water in the lights. We found out on a Monday.'

'And the equipment had been fine the previous Friday?'

Both men nodded.

'Who's on set at the weekends?' Calloway asked.

'No one,' said the man in tweed. 'The studio's dark at the weekend.'

'Apart from the cleaners,' said his colleague. 'They come in Saturdays. They're not allowed on set though, in case they move anything about.'

'Continuity, you see,' said the tweed man.

Calloway saw, again. He knew about the cleaning staff. It was his commissionaire's' job to let them through the gates.

'They clean the canteen, the offices, the lavs, that kind of thing,' said the tweed man. 'They're meant to do a quick spruce up around the stages, although sometimes they don't bother.' He shook his head. 'Some Mondays I've had to empty the bins myself.'

Calloway tutted.

'A man of your qualifications too,' he said.

Not knowing which way to take this, the tweed man returned to examining the eviscerated cameras, while his colleague withdrew a pen from his pocket and started to poke around some more.

Calloway returned to his office. He took a big lever arch file from the shelf and laid it on his desk. The file held copies of personnel records. He turned to the section on cleaning staff and read down the list of names. There were eleven in total. Against each name was written the days of the week on which they worked and the times of their shifts. Four worked weekends. He took out the small black police notebook from the inside pocket of his suit jacket and noted the four names and their contact details. Addresses only. None had telephones. As he snapped the notebook shut there was a tap on his open door. Marjorie from casting stood in the doorway in a trench coat that looked old enough and dirty enough to have fallen at The Somme. She spoke with the tortoise shell cigarette holder gripped between irregular teeth to one side of her mouth.

'You snubbed my lunch invitation so I'm trying again. Join me for a scotch and soda in the Star and Temple?'

'Will Tony be my chaperone?'

'He's taking his mother to the Empire. Another of those ghastly Huggetts pictures. So it'll be just you and me.'

She gave him a sly wink. 'Go on, live dangerously.'

He'd spent six years living dangerously in places like Normandy, Arnhem and the Ardennes. He reckoned he could risk a scotch and soda with Marjorie and whoever might have died in her trench coat. He wasn't one for company, not normally. But some evenings he felt the need to fill the big empty space in his soul with conversation. Occasionally, something more. It could never replace what he'd lost. But sometimes a distraction was enough, even in the unlikely form of the lady from casting with the pencil still stuck in her hair.

SEVEN

The Star and Temple was the remaining half of a pair of buildings, its mirror image levelled in the Blitz leaving only a flank wall of bare brickwork. It had the bottle green glazed brick frontage that characterised half the pubs in the neighbourhood. Inside it was cosy, with ornate tiling and dark wood panelling beneath a nicotine-brown ceiling. A gaggle of drinkers had already gathered. Storemen from the Lipton's tea warehouse talking football and politics. A couple of technicians from the studio talking shop, one sketching a scene on a beer mat. Two old retainers still in their heavy black coats, staring at the rows of dominoes in front of them. At the bar, a small man in a market trader's apron held court. He spoke loudly, like someone who spends his days shouting for a living. Two off-duty bus conductors nodded along with his rhetoric. A drayman from the Truman's brewery shook his head and looked doubtful.

Marjorie knew the landlady, a small, dark-haired woman with tired eyes and a face full of sadness. They exchanged pleasantries. There was a framed photo behind the bar, Calloway noticed. A signaller in uniform. Little more than a boy. The kind of photo with only one meaning: dead or missing in action.

Marjorie ordered two large scotch and sodas and insisted on paying. Calloway accepted but felt awkward. In his world, the man always paid. Not that he had much opportunity to these days. He seldom socialised. The landlady took the big white pound note from Marge and dispensed change from an ornate till which resemble the gilded sarcophagus of a tiny emperor.

There was an empty table by the window with a bench seat and a couple of bent wood pub chairs. Marge laid her coat and bag on the bench and slid alongside. Calloway sat in the chair opposite her. He wasn't playing lap dog again.

Two men entered the pub. One noticed Marjorie. He was in his sixties, tall and straight backed, wearing a clerkly suit with shiny elbows and a faded bowler hat. He managed to look dapper in spite of his frayed shirt cuffs.

'Alright young Margie? How's your mum?' he asked cheerily.

'Not so bad, Mr Franklin. Her sciatica comes and goes, you know how it is. Nice of you to ask though.' She'd dropped the theatrical RP, Calloway noticed.

Mr Franklin said, 'Send her my regards,' then looked Calloway up and down before adding, 'and be a good girl' with a wink. He joined his friend at the bar.

Marjorie rolled her eyes.

'I'm thirty-nine and he still talks to me like I'm eight.'

'So you're a regular here?' said Calloway.

'You sound surprised,' she said and he was. 'What were you expecting? A trip down to the riverside at Kew Bridge in Daddy's MG?'

She waved the idea away. 'I grew up round here. I've known this place since my mother used to send me in to tell my father his dinner was on the table.'

'Seriously?' said Calloway.

'Don't let the studio accent fool you, love. I've cultivated that over many years. Believe me, Marjorie Moss didn't start out speaking that way.'

'Ashamed of your roots?'

She looked around her. 'Never ashamed. I just knew that if I wanted to get on in this business, I needed to sound the part. We're all at it, love. You won't hear many genuine accents on the Centurion lot.'

'Apart from Spelthorne's.'

She laughed. 'Ah yes, apart from Spelthorne's. That accent's genuine. It's his name that's not.'

Calloway had figured as much.

'So what is his name?'

'Search me, darling. Something Maltese and ending in 'i' I suppose. Like everyone else born in Saffron Hill.'

Saffron Hill, nestled between Hatton Garden and Farringdon Road, once a wretched, stinking place immortalised by Dickens as the site of Fagin's den, now one of London's Maltese and Italian quarters.

'And what about you, Reggie? Sounds to me like you've taken trouble to lose whatever accent lurks beneath that overtone of grammar school respectability.'

'You said yourself, we're all at it,' he said.

'But you're not from round here.'

'I live round here. But it's not home. No pits, no working men's clubs, no chapel on Sundays.'

'Son of a coal miner?'

He nodded. 'And you? What was your father, when he wasn't drinking his wages in here?'

She gripped her lapels like a music hall comedian. 'Morris Moss, hatter and tailor,' she said, adopting the local accent and taking a small bow. 'We lived over the shop on Bethnal Green Road.'

'Shame he couldn't make you a new raincoat,' said Calloway, nodding at the stained and crumpled mackintosh on the bench.

'He's long dead, Reg, poor old boy. And I'm wearing that mac because I'm going somewhere later where it's advisable not to wear your best schmatta.'

Calloway tried to imagine a date where a dirty raincoat would be de rigueur.

'I like it here,' he said, looking around the pub, which had filled up since they sat down.

Marjorie nodded in agreement. 'You can only hang around film people for so long before you go crazy with all the pretension.'

'And this from the woman that calls everyone darling.'

'You've got me there,' she said, laughing. 'Of course, you'd never put on airs like that. You strike me as ever the pragmatist. The big stoic brute that keeps everything in order for the rest of us flakes.'

She took a sip of the scotch. Her lipstick left a perfect now on the rim of the glass.

'What made you take the job?' she said.

'I walked out of the last one.'

She looked intrigued and leaned forward across the battered pub table.

'Do tell,' she said, almost in a whisper.

'I got too close to the people I worked with.'

She leaned back against the bench seat. 'Then I shall keep my distance.'

'You've no need,' he said.

He didn't want Marjorie to keep her distance, at least not at that moment. He was enjoying the company. It didn't often happen.

'I won't make the same mistake twice,' he said. But he already had. He'd taken Spelthorne's shilling, or at least succumbed to the threat of its removal. There was a part of him that wasn't stoic, or a pragmatic. There was a part of him that was a bloody fool.

'And before that?' she said.

'Army. Thirteen years. Military Police then Intelligence Corps. Field Security.'

Marjorie's interest was piqued. 'Intelligence Corps,' she said, 'Were you now? Tell Marjorie all about that. It sounds awfully exciting.'

'Anyone who says war is exciting is a psychopath or an idiot.'

And there were plenty of both. Calloway had met his fair share. Public school types with something to prove. The ones who used words like dash and elan to describe the senseless rush into a melee of blood and screaming. Or the brawlers, the ones who treated combat like a Saturday night punch-up. And the trophy hunters. The sick bastards.

'It was rough work,' he said. 'We'd often go in first, or close as dammit. We'd grab enemy files, take prisoners to interrogate, round up collaborators from local towns and villages. Establish order.'

'Interrogation?' She rolled the r's and savoured the word. 'Were you a smooth talker Reg? Did you charm them into giving away their secrets?'

There was nothing smooth about Calloway. Others may have played good cop, as the yanks call it. He had used menace, coercion and the threat of brutality. Sometimes the threat was fulfilled. He had a reputation for it among his section. Some of his comrades gave him a wide berth. Others stuck with him as a good man to have around. His old CO compared him to an oversized terrier sent in after the hounds to finish the job. It was a good description.

'I was a bastard,' he said. 'A right rough bastard. Not something I'm proud of.'

After the camp he had tried to change. He'd realised he was little more than a secret policeman. Not so different from the butchers who ran that place. And he had met someone there. A prisoner. A woman. A woman who had changed him in the few precious, all too short weeks he had known her. She hadn't changed him completely though. And when he'd lost her, the brute inside him had stepped right back into the space she left in his soul.

Calloway downed his scotch with a thirst he'd not come in with.

'Can we change the subject?' he said.

Marjorie had seen the change in him. Calloway felt she was reading him. He clearly fascinated her, but she said, 'Gladly.'

He bought them two more drinks. When he was back at the table, Marjorie said, 'So the chat in the canteen is that the IRA blew up Sidney G's car for sacking Tearaway Terry from The Rebel Gun. They say Terry is a sympathiser.'

'The police seem to think so.'

As a subject changer this was hardly light relief.

'And you don't?'

Calloway shook his head. 'McCaffrey's a clown. The IRA are serious boys. They're not going to deploy an active service unit on the mainland because one of their pals got his cards. The police reckon he's a fundraiser for the cause in America and that might be the case. But the IRA's not going to put on a firework display and draw attention to the fact. They operate in the shadows and strike where it hurts. Military targets, civil disruption. Spelthorne's Bentley is an irrelevance.'

'Who do you suspect then?' she said.

'It's a police investigation. It's not my job to suspect anyone.'

But in his mind he saw the face again, the face of the woman who'd fled from the scene. The dolled-up Cinderella who'd drop the purse. For an instant he thought about describing the woman to Marjorie. She seemed to know everyone. He dismissed the thought.

'And what about you, Marge?' Do you have a past?'

She laughed. 'We all have our stories, darling. Some of them are even true.'

'What's yours? Truthfully.'

'I grew up three streets from here. One of three girls. We lived three to a room over the shop. As I said, my father was a tailor.' She corrected herself, 'Hatter and tailor. Mother was a cleaner at a bank in the city.'

'How did you get into the film business?'

'You make me sound like Sam Goldwyn. I'm just a little old casting girl in Spelthorne's tin pot little studio.'

'You've got an office with your name on the door.'

'So have you. Aren't we both important.'

She took a packet of Capstans from her handbag and offered him one. He leaned in to accept a light. Her closeness in that moment felt good.

'When I was eight my mother signed me up for Brady Club,' she said. Calloway looked quizzical. 'It's a youth club for Jewish kids. I was one of the first girls to join. They put on club shows. My mother pushed me to the front whenever they were casting. She was convinced I had talent.'

'And had you?'

'Oh I've got many talents, luvvie.' She gave a mischievous grin. 'Sadly acting isn't one of them. But I tried. Tried and failed, and in the process I found myself on the fringes of the film world. One thing led to another and within a few years I was Marjorie Moss, casting director, spinster, and a great disappointment to her mother.'

She took a small bow, then looked at her watch. 'And with that,' she said, 'I need to leave.'

She seemed to notice the small look of disappointment on Calloway's face. She picked up her coat, hung her bag over her shoulder and said, 'Fancy making a night of it?'

'Won't your date mind?'

She laughed. 'Oh, he'll mind alright. That's the whole point of you coming.'

EIGHT

They walked through the late autumn evening towards Dalston. As they walked, they were joined by others, like a crowd heading to a football match, but without scarves or rattles. Working men, some still in their overalls, store coats and aprons. Clerkly types too, and women home from shop work or cleaning. One woman holding a baby. Some people Marge clearly knew, and they exchanged nods of recognition, although they didn't speak. By the time they had reached the corner of Kingsland High Street they were among perhaps fifty men and women, walking as a group with a clear sense of purpose. As they turned the corner into Ridley Road, Calloway heard the distorted crackle of an amplified voice and the rumble of a collective response.

At the far end of the street a crowd had gathered. In front of them was a platform draped in union jacks and flanked by two big Tannoy speakers. The speakers were blasting out the words of the man at the microphone. Sharply dressed in a grey suit with blonde hair and a long, chiselled face, he spoke with intensity to the two hundred people gathered in front of a cordon of grim-looking stewards. The stewards dressed uniformly, although not in uniform. They wore grey suits, with black shirts and white ties. The closer Calloway got to the platform, the better he could make out the speaker's words. Nationalist rhetoric. Aliens in our midst. Britain for the British. His followers cheered. But others heckled. They shouted 'fascists out' and 'never again'. The hecklers started to shove; the supporters shoved back. Faces tensed. Words were spat not spoken. The anger was palpable. There were more supporters then hecklers, but the balance changed when the mob of fifty or so that Marge and Calloway walked with arrived.

'Who is he?' Calloway shouted into Marge's ear, gesturing towards the speaker on the platform.

'Jeffrey Hamm,' she replied. 'Leader of the British Union.'

Hamm shouted his words now, so that his voice could be heard above the din of the crowd. Nationalistic vitriol poured from him. His brow furrowed, demonic eyes beamed from his face, the sinews in his neck stretched as if they would snap at any moment.

'The aliens waxed fat in the black market, while our boys died in a pointless war!'

Calloway and Marge were pressed together by the mass of bodies now jostling each other. 'You believe in all this?' he said, nodding towards Hamm on the platform.

Marge laughed. 'Hardly, darling. I rather think those aliens he's ranting about include me. Come on,' she said. 'There's someone I want you to meet.'

She pushed forward and Calloway followed. They got closer to the front and Marge stopped. A well-built man in a blouson jacket and a brown trilby that had seen better days stood with his back to them, facing the stewards. Marge tapped his shoulder and he turned to face Calloway.

'Hello Reg,' he said, with a mischievous smile.

Johnny Suskind. Sergeant Johnny Suskind, Parachute Regiment, Sixth Airborne Division. At least that's what he was last time Calloway had seen him. Big, tough, fearless Johnny Suskind, who could fire a PIAT from the hip. Big Johnny, who'd taken out the crews of two Flak 88 guns singlehandedly. Earned himself a DSM. Tasty with his fists too. Regimental boxing champion three years running. Slammer Suskind, the Hackney heavyweight. A good man, but never to be messed with. Johnny turned back to face the platform, nose to nose with the stewards. He shouted 'Fuck off you fascists' in their faces. The stewards bristled. They stood their ground, challenging the crowd to have a go.

Hamm raised his fist and hollered. He spat his hatred into

the crowd, sweat dripping from his hairline. Johnny Suskind turned back to face Calloway and spoke into his ear.

'You're in my wedge, Reggie. The first wedge. When I give the signal, we push forward and tip the platform over. The second wedge moves in and smashes up the Tannoy. Then it's free for all. Crack as many fascist heads as you can. If you hear a referee's whistle, it means police. That's the signal to scarper.'

Calloway looked around. Half a dozen other men had been listening to Johnny's instruction. They nodded acknowledgement. Suskind said, 'On three,' then counted down with his fingers until they formed a clenched fist. On three he shouted, 'Go, go, go!'

The six-man wedge surged forward. Calloway's instinct took over. He went in with them. It was a reflex, the conditioning of six years of war. The collective consciousness of military men. They grabbed the platform by the nearest plank and heaved. The Tannoy crunched and crackled. Hamm toppled. The stewards kicked off, fists flailing. Some had slipped on brass knuckles. Others drew coshes. Johnny's wedge fought back. They were unarmed but they were fearless. Seasoned fighters by the look of them, with little regard for their own safety. They served up bloody noses, broken ribs and bruises. Calloway spied Marge among them. She was tearing up copies of a newspaper called East London Blackshirt, a dozen at a time.

The whistle sounded. Johnny shouted, 'Here come the Chuter Ede bus company. Job done folks, time to leave.'

Calloway looked back. Police disgorged from Black Marias. Fascists lay on the ground nursing wounds. Hamm was gone. The platform was in pieces, the banners ripped, the fascist papers torn. Suskind's mob were bloodied too, but they walked tall as they quick-stepped down the street, away from the scene. Calloway and Marge walked with them. Calloway's knuckles hurt. One hand bled. The fracas was a blur in his memory, but clearly he'd used his fists. There it was again. The short fuse. The hair trigger. The quickness to violence, the nature barely suppressed. And the memory. The memory of the camp. What he'd seen. What he'd lost. When Suskind's wedge surged forward, Calloway had needed no encouragement. Hamm and his band of thugs were the same bastards he'd fought for six years to defeat. Only this lot were British. And they'd lost no time in regrouping after their wartime internment. He put the wounded fist to his mouth and licked it clean of blood. Somewhere on the ground behind them was a fascist missing his front teeth. Not a great look for Britain's answer to the master race.

He felt Marge's arm slip into his as she walked beside him.

'Not the date you imagined, eh Reg?' she said.

They regrouped in the Star and Temple. Johnny Suskind and his crew took over a couple of the tables and the landlady gave them drinks on the house. She pulled a dozen pints from the tall, ceramic-handled beer pumps which stood like sentinels along the polished bar top.

'It's good to see you, Reg,' Johnny said.

'You too, Johnny. And something of a surprise.'

'I bet,' said Suskind. 'You've got Marge to blame for that.'

Marjorie raised her pint glass and winked at Calloway.

'You boys are well organised,' Calloway said. 'That was like a military operation.'

'Course it was,' said Johnny. 'Hardly surprising, seeing as we're all ex-servicemen on our commando.'

'Commando?'

'We're the front line.'

'Front line of what?'

'Suskind pulled a pamphlet from the inside of his blouson jacket and pushed it across the table. The cover read The 43 Group Fights Fascism Today with 43 inside the Star of David.

'43 Group, eh? I counted more than forty-three back there.'

'We were just forty-three when we started.' He downed half his pint in one then said, 'It started spontaneously. A few of us ex-services lads were having a drink in a pub up near Hampstead, when we clocked Jeffrey Hamm and his boys setting up a podium on the heath opposite. We went over to have a gander. They were selling copies of Britain Awake and ranting on about 'aliens'. Meaning us. Us lads were all British, born and bred, and proud of it. We'd all fought for this country, in the paras, the infantry, the Raff, even one lad with the merchant navy on the Arctic convoys. Then one of the lads just went for it. He said, 'I'm not having this', and started pushing through the crowd. The rest of us followed like we were some kind of unit. The old military state of mind,' he looked Calloway in the eye with admiration. 'I saw that in you today,' he said. 'We banged some heads together, tipped over the podium and sent Hamm and his boys packing. They were scrabbling around, gathering up what was left of the podium and their papers and stuffing them into their little van, shouting, 'We'll get you fuckin' Jewboys. You wait and see.' We were buoyed by it. We'd done something, you know. Achieved something. We'd stood up to the fascists right here in our hometown in the same way we'd stood up to them at El Alamein, or in Normandy, or crossing the Atlantic. And we knew if we carried on others would join us. If we got organised, we could win. We started meeting regularly at Macabi House, that's a sports club where Jewish ex-servicemen hang out, and people kept turning up, volunteering themselves, or their services and skills. Men and women. Mostly ex-services. Cabbies offered us transport, printers offered to print our leaflets. Now there's about five hundred of us.' He gestured towards the other men at the two tables. 'My lads are the commandos. We do the rough stuff. But we've got a headquarters on the Bayswater Road, that's where the planning and decision making happens, and an intelligence section which finds out when and where the fascists will be speaking next, or where they're printing and distributing their literature.

'How do you gather intelligence?' said Calloway.

'Looking and listening obviously,' said Johnny. 'But the most effective gen comes from our undercover boys and girls.'

'Undercover?'

Suskind looked around him and lowered his voice.

'I know I can trust you, Reg, so I'll tell you. We put group members into fascist organisations, and there are plenty of them, believe me. The Union Movement, The Order of St George, The Gentile-Christian Front. We use Aryan-looking Jews. They join up and act like they believe in the whole fascist ideology. They become really committed. They spout the anti-semitic bullshit and even fight with 43 Group members at rallies. It's not pretty work, Reg, believe me. But they do it for the cause. And clearly, all the time they're feeding gen back to group headquarters.'

'Sounds like a very effective set-up,' said Calloway.

'Oh, it is. But the trouble is, the undercover boys and girls can only do it for so long before their tumbled, or before we withdraw them when things are getting too risky. Frankly Reg, we're running out of group volunteers that can pass for fascists. We need more non-Jewish members. That's why Marge tapped you up. She's one of our recruiters.'

Calloway turned to Marge. 'So I've been played.'

Marge gave him a devilish smile. 'I guess so, luv' she said. 'But I enjoyed the game.'

There was an awkward moment. Suskind cut in.

'Marge told me about this ex-services type working security at her studio. Reckoned he had potential. She's got a good instinct, Marge has. When she told me your name, well, it seemed like a shoo in. I know you Reg. I know how you think. I know what you saw.'

Calloway and Suskind were both Sixth Airborne. Suskind was there the day Calloway's field security section was sent to reconnoitre a barracks that had been spotted in aerial reconnaissance photographs. The barracks turned out to be the camp. Johnny knew this. He'd seen the effect it had on Calloway when he rejoined the unit.

Suskind downed the rest of his pint. He looked Calloway in the eye. 'I want you in the group, Reg. I want you to help us crush British fascism, for good this time.'

Calloway had never been one for joining in. He kept himself to himself, mostly. The times he didn't were the times he found himself in trouble. Like his last job. He thought up a reason to decline.

‘I’m not political,’ he said.

‘Nor are we,’ said Suskind. ‘We’re anti-fascist but we’re not partisan. The group’s got members of every political leaning.’

He tapped the 43 Group leaflet on the table in front of Calloway. ‘This isn’t about politics. This is about humanity. You of all people know what fascism can do. You’ve seen it. Politics ain’t in it. It’s down to us, Reg. The government’s refusing to do anything about it. Chuter Ede the Home Secretary won’t stop the meetings. They’re perfectly legal, you see. That’s why the police show up when we kick off. The fascists have effectively got police protection, while us protesters are treated like criminals.’

‘And the Labour government’s allowing this?’

Suskind nodded and took out a crumpled packet of Woodbines from the pocket of his blouson jacket. He offered one to Calloway and Marge.

‘That’s about the size of it,’ he said, as the three of them shared a light. ‘There are individual Labour MPs who speak out. And the local councillors are generally on our side. Good sorts, most of ’em. And the trade unions help by refusing to print the fascist literature. But the government? Nah, mate. They’re sitting on their hands. The group, the communists and the local people, we’re the only ones fighting back. But we need more help. Help from men like you, Reg.’

Suskind downed the last of his pint and set the glass down on the table. ‘Never again, Reg. That’s what we say. Never again.’

Calloway heard the words of the actor in his head.

When you’ve seen twenty thousand bodies in a heap, just lying in the sun like wax, you begin to wonder what life is.

‘I’ll think about it, Johnny,’ he said. ‘No promises.’

NINE

He offered to walk Marge to the bus stop. She may have retained a grudging pride in her origins, but she had long since given up the thought of living in the area where she was born. She was heading west. She slipped her arm into his as they walked.

'I did enjoy our chat, you know,' she said, sounding apologetic. 'It would be nice to do it again.'

'At least until I agree to join your group?'

She gave him a gentle punch on the arm. 'Don't be like that.'

'I'll say to you what I said to Johnny. I'll think about it, provided it's not another scotch and soda with a punch-up for a chaser.'

'Perhaps we can think up another kind of chaser,' she said and kissed him full on the lips. It was a lingering kiss. A kiss with intent. Calloway was taken aback, but not so much so that he wanted her to stop. He fought the urge pull her closer. It was a hard fight, won by a slim margin.

'You're forward, I'll say that,' he said.

Marjorie slipped her arm into his again and they continued walking.

'I like to get off with people, I like to lay their arms,' she said, with poetic cadence. 'I like to be held and lightly kissed, safe from all alarms.'

Calloway laughed. 'Is that from one of Spelthorne's pictures?'

'Good god, no. That's Stevie Smith, the poet.'

'Good, is he?'

'She, darling, she. And yes, she is. She understands women,

which is more than can be said for most male poets.'

'Sounds a bit strong for a lapsed chapel goer like me.'

She looked up at him. 'Darling, that all depends how lapsed you actually are.'

She held his gaze long enough to see him look embarrassed. He was grateful when the bus arrived, and he could carry on his walk alone. But deep down, a part of him wanted to join her on her journey west.

It was past nine when Calloway returned to the tiny cobbled lane off the Kingsland Road. A pea-souper was blowing in from the river which had filled the narrow street with a haze of sour-tasting soot. There was a car parked opposite the entrance to his building. A black Austin 12 by the look of it, although it was hard to tell the colour in the monochrome streetscape. Two men leaned against the car smoking in silence in the half light of a lone street lamp. A third man sat behind the wheel.

People didn't park on Calloway's street. Not at this time of night. They didn't pass the time by smoking in silence either. His 'brown job' copper's instinct told him something wasn't right. There were warehouses further down the street. He had no idea what they held, but it would be something of value to someone, with the black market still thriving and rationing showing no sign of ending anytime soon. But if the three men were there to knock off a warehouse, why advertise their presence so blatantly?

One of the men glanced up at Calloway as he passed the car. He was a brute. Five-eleven and thick-set with a mop of dark curly hair on top of a big misshapen head. He exchanged glances with the other man, who was lean and slight. He wore a cheese-cutter cap pulled down over his fine-boned face. The peak of the cap couldn't quite hide his angelic blue eyes that shone even in the half light. Their clothes were mismatched and shabby, the uniform of working men on their uppers. Blue eyes nodded at Curly, flicking the butt of his half-smoked cigarette into the gutter. Men on their uppers don't flick away a half-smoked fag. Calloway braced himself.

Blue eyes spoke. 'Mr Calloway, is it?'

His voice was low and husky with no discernible accent. Before Calloway had a chance to answer, the brute Curly had him in a body lock. Blue eyes opened the door to the big Austin saloon and pushed Calloway towards the back seat. Calloway struggled. He slammed his head backwards into his assailant's nose, like they trained you in the army. Curly yelped and loosened his grip. Calloway turned and landed a fist on the side of his misshapen jaw, but it was a panic punch with no force behind it. In return he got a kick to the back of the knees from Blue Eyes. As Calloway buckled, the two men bundled him into the car. This time he complied. A cold prodding sensation in his ribs told him it wasn't a good idea to resist. The Colt automatic he could see from the corner of his eye wasn't a thing to be argued with. He sat in the middle, Curly on his right, Blue Eyes sliding into the back seat on his left. Blue Eyes tapped the driver on the shoulder with a worn but slender hand. The driver put the Austin into gear, gunned the engine and turned left towards Shoreditch High Street, then right into Great Eastern Street.

'You boys going to tell me what you want?' Calloway said.

Blue Eyes replied, 'Bernie wants to see you.'

The muzzle of the automatic dug deeper into Calloway's ribs. They drove in silence. They headed west for ten minutes or so, then turned north off Euston Road. Somewhere between Chalk Farm and Kilburn they pulled up alongside the pavement. A prod from the automatic told Calloway to get out of the car. Curly and Blue Eyes got out too. The illuminated facade of a dance hall cast a dim, tobacco-coloured glow over the three of them. The muffled sound of a second-rate dance band banged against the insides of the building's two double doors. Billboards either side advertised dancing to Paddy Paige and his Popular Band, all for three and six. A doorman in a uniform with grease stains on the collar and rings around the armpits gave Curly and Blue Eyes a deferential nod.

'A visitor for Bernie,' Blue Eyes said.

The doorman stood aside to let the three men enter. The decor was deep red-and-gold-painted stucco, scuffed and peeling. Calloway caught the ingrained smell of a half century of dust and the faint odour of disinfectant from the gents. Blue Eyes had by now pocketed the automatic. He guided Calloway up the stairway with an insistent shove. They climbed three twisting flights and entered through a half-glazed door into a small narrow bar room. It was empty and the bar was closed. Calloway guessed it only opened at weekends. The tables had upturned stools on them to allow for cleaning. The cleaning had yet to happen. Calloway felt the stickiness of a hundred spilled pints through the soles of his brogues. Two figures sat in a booth at the far end of the bar room with a bottle of Johnny Walker and three glasses in front of them. One was a woman, forty perhaps, small and slim, with hair dyed a colour blacker than liquorice. She wore a raglan-sleeved raincoat buttoned to the collar. The other was Terrence McCaffrey.

'I'm guessing you're not here for the music,' said Calloway to McCaffrey.

The band was murdering 'Little Brown Jug' from the dance hall below them. McCaffrey looked fearful of Calloway. Perhaps it was the memory of the three loosened teeth. He didn't seem reassured by the presence of Curly and Blue Eyes standing guard over the studio's big security boss.

'For musicians, they'd make very good panel beaters,' McCaffrey said with forced good humour.

'So you're going by the name of Bernie now?' said Calloway.

'I'm Bernie,' said the woman. Her voice was an octave deeper than her small frame implied. If McCaffrey was a Tyrone man, Bernie was from somewhere much further south, Calloway reckoned. She nodded to Curly and Blue Eyes to stand down and gestured for Calloway to join her and McCaffrey in the booth. It was clear who was in charge here. She uncapped the Johnny Walker bottle and poured three glasses. She passed one to Calloway. McCaffrey took another and drank half the generous measure in one mouthful. Beads of sweat popped on his hairline.

'Thank you for coming, Mr Calloway. It's good of you to make the time for us,' the woman called Bernie said, sounding like she almost meant it.

'I generally do when there's a Colt automatic digging into my ribs,' he said. 'I assume this is about the car bomb.'

'Terry tells me you don't suspect him.'

'I'm beginning to change my mind,' he said, looking McCaffrey full in the face.

The woman called Bernie laughed.

'I wouldn't trust Terry with a box of matches, let alone a stick of dynamite.'

McCaffrey managed a weak smile. Gone was the confident, booze-fuelled bon viveur of the Feldman Club. In present company, he was cowed and anxious.

'So who would you trust?' said Calloway.

'The question's irrelevant. Special Branch are barking up the wrong tree.'

'You seem very sure of that.'

'I'm in a position to know,' she said.

'So what's this got to do with me?' said Calloway.

'I've got a job for you,' she said.

'Whatever it is, I'm not in the market.'

Bernie continued undeterred. 'These people Special Branch suspect. Call them friends of mine, if you will. They've no intention of starting a mainland campaign, and they're certainly not minded to indulge in petty vendettas on behalf of gobshite actors who shoot their mouths off.'

McCaffrey gave a self-conscious laugh. Bernie shot him a look that shut him up.

'My friends' priorities are, shall we say, closer to home right now.'

'McCaffrey told me,' said Calloway. 'A border war.'

Her frustration with the loose-lipped actor showed even more.

'I wouldn't know,' she said, meaning she knew full well. 'Let's just say my friends are more interested in the B Specials than B pictures.'

B Specials, the Ulster Special Constabulary. A reserve police force, armed and run on military lines. Calloway had patrolled alongside them in Belfast in the thirties. Loyalist hard men with blood on their hands.

'My friends have no time to be worrying about their friends and relatives in London,' she said.

'Why would your friends worry about relatives in London?' Calloway asked.

'Because sooner or later MI5 will have Special Branch turning over every Irish pub, club and tenement flat from Kilburn to Camberwell looking for a bomb factory that doesn't exist. Innocent people will get hurt, unnecessarily.'

'That's very community spirited of you,' said Calloway. 'But like I said, I'm not in the market.'

He downed the whisky, pushed the empty glass back towards her and rose to leave.

'I know your friends,' he said. 'They bomb cinemas and tube stations. They put innocent people in hospital, unnecessarily. They put some in the mortuary. Sometimes they put bullets through the heads of my former comrades.'

He wanted no part of Bernie and her scheme. He had enough to worry about, with Belcher and Bryant breathing down his neck and Spelthorne threatening him with a regular appointment at the labour exchange.

'Oh, I think you're in the market, Mr Calloway,' she said, slipping a hand inside the raincoat and pulling out a Webley service revolver. It was old and tarnished but no less deadly for it.

'Find out who planted the bomb under your boss's car,' she said to Calloway. 'Then hand them over to the police. I want their investigation brought to a swift conclusion.'

Curly and Blue Eyes appeared again. Curly gripped Calloway's arm and pushed him in the direction of the door. Calloway shook him free and turned back to face Bernie.

'Why me?' he said.

Bernie glanced at McCaffrey, then turned back to Calloway. 'Because you once stood by and watched a family thrown into the street while their possessions burned on the fire.'

TEN

Belcher and Bryant were taking witness statements at the studio. Calloway had given them his office for the morning. Belcher was filling it with pipe smoke. Interviewees hung around the corridor outside, smoking and speculating on what they might be asked. They found it all very exciting, Calloway judged by their rapid, animated conversations. Having provided the Special Branch men with lists of those present at the dinner, at least those that worked for Centurion, there wasn't much for Calloway to do. He left the studio and took a bus along the Hoxton Street. It was a crisp autumn day with an impossibly blue sky and an arc-light sun. Plane trees had shed a layer of golden leaves, which mottled the grubby pavements like freckles on the face of an urchin. The bus windows reverberated with the cries of the barrow boys, like the soundtrack of a Centurion social drama. And the gilt signage above the shop windows behind the barrows glistened in a way that Centurion's painted scenery never could, no matter how skilled the scenic artists.

He jumped off the bus near the corner of De Beauvoir Road and headed towards a small, soot-blackened, municipal-looking building that from its architecture he judged had once been a bright red terracotta. The building was almost black now, but the stone steps were newly scrubbed and the brass work on the ornate doors was polished so it shined. It stood alone among the rubble of what had once been adjoining buildings but were now an alien landscape of jagged bricks, charred timbers and the torn fragments of wallpaper. Half a dozen kids were playing war in the rubble, holding sticks like rifles and arguing over who'd be the Germans. It was a familiar scene, which Calloway had seen in every neighbourhood he'd visited in the few years he'd lived in London since the war. Bomb-site playgrounds had become unplanned amenities, dangerous and rat-infested, but fun. Places for unrestrained Blitz kids with bleeding knees below all-year-round shorts to smash things up.

He pulled open the heavy door and entered.

'You'll have to wait,' a croaking voice said before the door had closed behind him.

Marjorie's description of Rene was spot-on. Cerberus at the gates, minus two of the heads, which she made up for with a ferocious stare and a Park Drive gripped between her teeth like the thigh bone of a tiny man she'd recently savaged. She sat at the front desk in a cloud of tobacco smoke under a sign that said Centurion Company of Stars. This was Sidney G Spelthorne's famous charm school, in reality a former boxing club. Neither the vase of roses on the windowsill nor Rene's Park Drive could mask the ingrained smell of sweat. Through the door she was guarding, Calloway could see a dozen young women in swimsuits and high heels walking in a circle around the old gymnasium. Each one balanced a hardback book on their heads. In the centre of the circle, a middle-aged woman in twin set and pearls sang out instruction in a plummy Scottish accent.

Rene cleared her throat to get Calloway's attention. 'Mr Cole has been delayed.'

She nodded towards a plush sofa in front of the window. 'Sit over there. No gawping at the girls.'

Calloway took a seat as instructed and refrained from gawping. As he leafed through one of the magazines on the coffee table in front of him, he heard the plummy voice sing out, 'Straighten that back, Barbara Bennett. You look like Quasimodo at a swimming gala.'

Through the door to the gym Calloway saw Barbara Bennett's small lips tense with frustration.

Calloway stared at the cheesecake photos in the magazine and tried not to think about Curley, Blue Eyes and raven-haired

Bernie with the raglan sleeves and the Webley revolver inside her coat.

Through the open door Calloway heard the sound of a book falling onto the wooden gymnasium floor echo around the hall. The plummy voice shouted, 'You, girl, pick that up this minute. I'm not surprised you dropped it, shuffling about like a pregnant camel. You're a disgrace the studio, the lot of you.'

'They're for it,' croaked Rene, seeming to enjoy the moment.

Calloway was halfway through an article about an actress he'd never heard of when Cole arrived. He walked through the door with a lightness of step that defied his short but heavy frame. He was mid-forties with a face that looked like the rest of him lunched well. His hair was a swirl of tight black curls, heavily oiled and glistening in the light. His eyes glistened too through the lenses of his modern-looking glasses. He wore a well-cut worsted suit, with a yellow silk tie pinned with a jewel. His pocket square was ironed to a point which poked cheekily upwards from his breast pocket. He crossed the small reception room towards Calloway his hand already extended.

'Sorry, sorry, sorry,' he said. 'You're here, I'm late. All my fault. Have you been waiting long?'

'Long enough to know that Barbara Bennett is for it.'

Calloway nodded towards the old gymnasium. Cole gave a knowing smile. 'Ah yes, the lovely Barbara. Heavy on her feet but built like a goddess. Looks great in a swimsuit, and that's what counts.' Calloway saw him leer slightly before saying, 'Please, please, come in.'

He gestured to a half-glazed office door that led off the reception. It said I. Cole, Publicity in neat gold letters on the reeded glass.

If Spelthorne's office looked like a place where people gambled and drank hard liquor, Cole's at least looked like a place where work was done. There were filing cabinets with manila folders stacked on top, sheafs of photographs strewn across the desktop and a wall of framed publicity portraits, some even Calloway recognised. Cole seated himself behind his desk and gestured to the chair in front. As Calloway sat, the publicist pushed a gold cigarette box across the table and lifted the lid. Calloway helped himself.

'Now I've seen you around the studio. You're the new security fella. What d'you make of that explosion business?'

'The police suspect a bomb. My money's on a stray dog-end and a leaky petrol tank.'

'Shame. A bomb would have made a great story for The Rebel Gun.'

He tapped an imaginary newspaper and pointed to an imaginary headline. '"Fenian plot fails to thwart film mogul's must-see thriller".'

'I thought Spelthorne wanted to play down the republican angle. That's why he sacked Terrence McCaffrey.'

'It's true, he did. And I had the devil's own job keeping it out of the papers.'

Cole thought for a moment, like a sudden thought had piqued his interest.

'But what if it was a bomb?' he said. 'Do you think McCaffrey's capable?'

'Not in the slightest,' said Calloway. 'He seems the type that shoots his mouth off on any subject you care to mention. And I don't doubt his views on Ireland are heartfelt, but a bomb? Not a chance.'

Perhaps he was overdoing it, Calloway thought.

'So why exactly are you here?'

'Something far more prosaic. Lost property. One of your starlets dropped her purse when she fled the Producers Club dinner after the explosion. I want to return it but I don't know her name. I was hoping you might have photos of the cohort I could look at. Or better still allow me to see the girls next door.'

Cole laughed. 'Some of them are girls next door, at that. But that's what the charm school's for. We weed those ones out. Not the Centurion look.'

'But you're making social dramas.'

'Yes, and have you noticed how every tenement in Britain has a beautiful daughter at home?'

Calloway hadn't. He didn't go to the pictures.

'Do these girls really star in films? From what I've heard they don't get more than a walk on part in one of Spelthorne's B pictures.'

'One or two get near the top, but you're right, most don't. It doesn't matter a jot. Their role is to go out among the great unwashed and add a little Centurion sparkle. The folks out there want to believe these girls are stars. They crave glamour in their grey little lives. Look out of the window, Calloway. Tired little people living among amid the rubble. A decade on the ration eating powdered egg and pork brawn. The greatest luxury the poor sods enjoy is an extra rasher of bacon with their Sunday breakfast. The charm school girls take them away from all that. When I take them to a flower show, or a garden fete, or the opening of a swimming pool, that small corner of this worn-down world is lifted out of its post-war drudgery. The women swoon at their frocks, their husbands drool at their pursed lips and pert little arses. Centurion gives them glitz and glamour. You can't get that on the ration.'

'So you're selling empty promises to girls with dreams.'

Cole looked offended. 'Some of them do make it, really.' Then he waved away Calloway's suggestion. 'Anyway, it's not like the idea is original. Gainsborough pioneered the charm school idea by developing their young stars, you know, Stewart Granger, Phyllis Calvert, Pat Roc, then Rank went for it big time with their Company of Youth. But Spelthorne really knows how to work it.'

Calloway thought of the Producers Club dinner and the cohort of young, would-be starlets fastened into their tight-fitting, low-cut evening dresses being groped by middle-aged financiers. He presumed that's what 'working it' meant.

There were raised voices coming from the gym. Deportment class was not going well today.

Cole said, 'You'll never get into the room next door. Rene would chew your balls off and spit them back in your face. That's why Spelthorne hired her. She looks after the merchandise.'

'Then some files perhaps. I could go through them and see if I can recognise the face.'

'Yes, yes of course. We have the Company of Stars Book.'

He reached into a desk draw and dropped an over-stuffed lever-arch file onto the desktop.

'They're all in there. Starlets from the past five years, since Sidney founded the charm school. Photos, vital statistics, biographies, all grossly exaggerated of course.'

He cleared a path through the piles of photos on the desk and slid the file over to Calloway. 'Have a flick through. The Cinderella that dropped her purse could be in there.'

Calloway opened the file. 'How did you get into this business?'

'It was the war,' said Cole. 'I worked for the Ministry of Information, writing scripts for propaganda films. They were appalling, but Duff Cooper took a shine to me and moved me into his press relations group. When the war ended, one of the directors I'd worked with on the films told me of an opening with Spelthorne for a publicist. I had the right skills. Seemed a waste not to use them.' Cole nodded in the direction of the deportment class.

'And the subject matter was far more appealing.'

The door flew open and the plummy Scottish woman in the twin set entered the room.

'Ivor, you absolutely have to speak to those girls. They're the most appalling shower that's ever been through my deportment class. No better than Limehouse harlots, good for nothing but leaning in knocking shop doorways, with not an ounce of class between them.'

Cole winked at Calloway and rose from his chair. 'Time for a pep talk.' He gestured to the file. 'I'll have to leave you to it. If you find who you're looking for let me know.'

When Cole had left, Calloway continued turning the pages. They were full of soft-focus portraits and swimsuit shots. Each girl had a story that Cole had no doubt concocted. He looked at each face in turn. There was a monotony to them. The charm school was a production line. A few pages before the end, one face jumped out. Brunette, not blonde. Finer features, perhaps. Younger by several years. But the eyes were right. The same eyes that had looked up at Calloway on the night of the explosion with the wrong kind of fear. Eyes that had been staring at him in his mind since that night. Her name was Joyce Rose, she was twenty-two and loved horse riding and romantic walks in the country. She graduated from the charm school two years previously. Calloway removed the portrait photo from the file. He slipped it into his inside pocket and left the office, nodding to Rene on his way out.

'You done then?' she said.

She looked indignant and suspicious. 'Tell Mr Cole thanks, but I didn't find her.'

Rene scowled. He got the impression no one was brave enough to tell her what to do.

Calloway caught a bus and retraced his route back to the studio. The sky had clouded over and there was the threat of rain in the air. The neighbourhood looked suddenly depressed. Grim and grey again, with the detritus of the market stalls spattered over the streets.

He nodded at the commissionaire at the studio gates as he entered and walked over to casting. He was hoping to see Marge. He had reason now to ask her about the woman who'd fled the dinner on the night of the explosion. And he had a name to go on. It was hardly a lead, but he trusted his gut feeling. The frightened face fleeing the scene was as good a place to start as any. And he needed a lead because like it or not, he was working for Bernie and her friends, and the only way they were going to take their Webley revolver and disappear from his life was if he got Special Branch a result.

To Calloway's disappointment, Tony sat alone in the office.

'Margie's out I'm afraid. You'll have to content yourself with me.'

The young man sat on his side of the utilitarian partners' desk smoking a French cigarette and leafing through a folder of photographic portraits. He held one up for Calloway to see.

'What d'you reckon?' he said. 'A passed-over major who

claims credit for his sergeant's gallantry?'

'That reminds me of someone I know. He doesn't look like that though.'

Tony tossed the photo back into the file. 'So what can I help you with?'

'What can you tell me about Joyce Rose?' said Calloway.

The name gave Tony a start. 'Joyce?' he said, looking visibly perturbed. He thought for a moment and relaxed a little. 'One of the studio's most promising starlets. Quite beautiful, and a genuinely good actress too. Not typical charm school fodder. Leading lady material. A good friend, actually. We knew each other when we were younger. Our fathers were both French and we used to keep each other company to relieve the boredom of endless social gatherings.'

'French then, not English?'

'Half French. Her mother was English. She was a telephonist at the Granchester hotel. That's where she met Joyce's father. He was the concierge. Of course, she wasn't called Joyce Rose originally. That was Ivor Cole's idea. He wanted to sell her as a typical English rose. She hated the name. She was christened Celeste Leclerc. It suited her far better I always thought. But Cole didn't know her like I did.'

He was quiet for a moment, as if distracted by a pleasant childhood memory. Then he said, 'Why are you interested in Joyce?'

'I think she was the starlet who dropped the purse on the night of the explosion,' said Calloway.

Tony frowned. Lines furrowed deep into his oversized brow. He shook his head. 'You must be mistaken, Mr Calloway. Joyce died more than a year ago.'

ELEVEN

Joyce Rose was found dead in her flat in Bayswater's fashionable Cypress Court. She had swallowed down two bottles of pills with a full bottle of gin the previous evening. The cleaner found her in the morning and called an ambulance, but by that time the young actress had been dead for several hours.

Police had found a large quantity of prescription drugs in the medicine cabinet of her bathroom. They were prescribed by a Harley Street doctor known to dispense medicines quite liberally to London's film actors. The coroner concluded that she had been living on a diet of stimulants and barbiturates. Uppers for the day, downers at night. Witnesses had reported that she had also been drinking heavily for at least six months. In the final months of her short life, Joyce Rose had been far from the gay young girl that supposedly enjoyed horse riding and romantic walks in the country.

Centurion's casting department kept a file on Rose. In fact, it looked more like a scrap book compiled by an adoring fan. Calloway suspected that Tony had compiled it, or at least embellished it following the actress's death. It was a brown manila shrine to a tragic Madonna.

Calloway had made a visit to the cutting room which was next to the casting office, on the pretence of inspecting the window locks. He'd waited until Marjorie and Tony went for lunch in the canteen. He had noticed that they never locked up behind them and that they also didn't lock their filing cabinet. Calloway found the Joyce Rose file and slipped it inside the jacket of his grey worsted suit, before returning to his office which had now been vacated by Belcher and Bryant and smelled strongly of Belcher's sickly sweet pipe tobacco. He threw open a window and lit a Navy Cut.

Clipped to the inside of the file were three press cuttings, all from the Daily Sketch. The first headline read MYSTERY SURROUNDS DEATH OF STARLET. A second headline read ACTRESS'S DEATH WAS SUICIDE SAYS CORONER. Both news reports featured the stock portrait of Rose from Cole's Book of Stars. There was a third cutting with a lengthier article under a headline that read STARS GATHER AT SUICIDE ACTRESS' FUNERAL. There were photographs from the funeral with actors and actresses that Daily Sketch readers would presumably recognise, although Calloway didn't. Jimmy Hanley, two actresses called Hermione and two young unknowns from the Rank charm school, Christopher Lee and Peter Murray. Centurion's official press release on the death was attached to these cuttings, carefully drafted no doubt by Cole to head off any suggestion that being under contract to the studio may have contributed to her state of mind at the time of her death. You'd be forgiven for thinking she was the happiest actress in the history of film making. Much of this messaging made it into the Daily Sketch copy, such was the strength of Cole's contacts in Fleet Street and his ability to influence them. The report instead dwelt on the celebrity of the mourners and the fact that no family were present at the funeral, both her parents having died in 1944, the result of a doodlebug hit on the Granchester Hotel. The remainder of the file was padded out with press coverage from her short but successful career. At least it was successful compared with the other charm school hopefuls, who no doubt spent their days parading around county shows and opening municipal swimming pools. There were fair-to-middling reviews for supporting roles in soon forgotten romances and photos in the gossip pages, mostly pictured with better known stars.

Calloway stuffed the file into his desk drawer and left the office, locking it behind him. As he walked down the corridor,

Bryant appeared, blocking his way. The detective looked at his watch.

'Knocking off already? I s'pose that's what you lot call a day's work.'

Calloway looked at his own watch and said, 'The working day ended an hour ago. I've already notched up an hour's overtime.'

It was just after noon.

'Smart arse,' said Bryant. 'You got that list of McCaffrey's regular haunts?'

Calloway shook his head. 'No one knows where he goes, or at least if they do, they're not telling me,' he lied. 'He's a dark horse, that one.'

'He'll be a shade or two darker when we get hold of him,' said Bryant.

'So that's how you boys operate, eh?' Calloway said, but he was in no position to criticise. 'Does DI Belcher know you talk like that?'

'Just my little joke.'

'Mine was better.'

Calloway pulled out a cigarette and offered one to Bryant, who took it and accepted a light. He mentioned the name of one of the clubs on the list he'd visited.

'He's been spotted there a few times.'

It was the place Calloway had been propositioned by the merchant seamen in the frock. A trip there should keep Bryant busy for a while, he thought.

They exchanged competitive small talk while they smoked, the one-upmanship of males not used to giving ground. Calloway excused himself, left the studio and walked for twenty minutes towards Liverpool Street. The autumn sun was out again, but the sky was a haze of half smog. The streets looked as though they had been brushed with diluted watercolour, blurring the lines of the buildings into an amorphous grey-brown.

As he turned onto Bishopsgate, the buildings grew larger. These were the temples of commerce, the fruits of imperial prosperity, with their classical features and heavy materials. Bold and imposing to inspire confidence in their occupants to invest inconceivable sums for acceptable returns. Not all the buildings had survived the bombings. Some were half-standing ruins of stone, their columns and cupolas protruding painfully from the rubble around them. The overall impression was of an ornate wedding cake that had been trampled underfoot during a fight at the reception.

He took the Central Line to Queensway and then walked the quarter mile to Cypress Court. It was one of those typical pre-war mansion blocks that managed to remain exclusive while lacking any hint of grandeur. It was the kind of block that kept the Crittall Window Company in business. Calloway walked up the shallow travertine steps which led to a set-back entrance under a simple concrete portico. He entered the glazed doors into an ungenerous lobby whose house plants failed to mask an underlying smell of cooking. There was a small counter and behind it a wall of pigeon holes for residents' mail. A bland-sounding orchestra was playing a forgettable tune behind an adjacent door marked Manager. Calloway tapped the brass bell on the countertop and waited. The forgettable tune stopped abruptly and the door opened. A harassed-looking woman old enough to be a Boer War widow said 'Yes?' in that extended nasal tone ordinary folk use when putting on airs. She had cat hairs on her cardigan and biscuit crumbs at the corners of her parched-looking mouth.

Calloway passed his calling card across the desk. 'Calloway, Centurion Pictures. I've come to inspect flat 309.'

He'd found Joyce Rose's last address in the file he'd taken from casting. It was a Centurion flat, one they maintained for stars under contract that were valued enough to warrant special treatment. He'd been surprised that she qualified, having never had the chance to graduate beyond supporting actress to leading lady. The manager put on a pair of spectacles that hung on the chain around her neck and looked at the card. She nodded a series of barely perceptible nods as she read each word in turn. She looked up at Calloway, scrutinised his face for enough seconds to make him uncomfortable - he had no official reason for being there - before looking back at the card and turning it over on in her mottled, arthritic hands. He'd crossed borders with lesser inspections.

Seemingly satisfied, she said, 'I'll fetch the key,' which she took from a neat row of hooks just inside the door of the office.

'Anyone at home?' he said. It occurred to him only now that the flat might be occupied.

The manager frowned. 'No one has lived there since...' she hesitated, unsure of the words to use.

'I understand,' he said.

Calloway took the small cage lift to the third floor. Flat 309 was down a windowless corridor with a well-worn parquet floor that made his footsteps echo off the bare walls. Pink glass wall lights in the shape of clam shells cast a dim glow of ersatz cosiness. The key turned stiffly

in the lock of the highly polished door marked 309 in brass numbers. Inside, the flat was warm and the air dry, a stark contrast to the cold, damp world Calloway tended to inhabit. The communal heating flowed through heavy iron radiators with a comforting gurgle. Though not cold, Calloway warmed himself against hallway radiator just because he could. It was a rare treat.

The hall opened onto a lounge with a large bay window, through which sunlight would have poured were it not for thick net curtains. Instead, the light inside the room was as muted as the pastels of the decor. The lounge was roomy, but not cavernous, giving the impression of understated comfort. A chintz three-piece suite filled much of the space, making it look safe and suburban, while side tables and standard lamps added daring hints at modernism. A door to the right led onto a modern, fitted kitchen, just large enough to prepare breakfast in the morning and perhaps canapés for cocktails in the evening. To the left was a bathroom with bold green-and-black tiling, angular chrome taps and a bath deep enough to drown in. A cork-topped stool with tubular chrome legs stood beside it. He imagined the freshly bathed starlet, her skin pink and smooth, wrapped in the fluffiest of bath robes as she sat painting her toenails. But when he tried to imagine her face, he couldn't.

There was one bedroom, a large room with the same bay window as the lounge, wide enough to take an elaborate dressing table with numerous drawers and mirrors. Ornate perfume bottles like religious icons stood decoratively on lace doilies on top of the dressing table's shining walnut veneer. It was an altar for the worship of beauty. A rose-pink silk eiderdown resembling a giant Turkish delight covered the double divan bed. Matching pillows were plumped like marshmallows. Calloway tried to imagine the woman in Cole's publicity photo lounging on the bed, flicking idly through a film magazine as she waited for her nails to dry. But when he did, it was the face of the woman fleeing the gala dinner. Older, harder, more worldly, no longer the type for those romantic walks that the publicity department concocted for her. A different face and yet the same. He couldn't make it fit. Not in these surroundings. This place was seductively safe, full of conventional comforts, somewhere for an English Rose to grow more fragrant and more lovely. The face in Calloway's consciousness could never fit here.

He made a search of the place, not entirely sure what he expected to find. The wardrobes and drawers were empty, the cupboards bare. There was no space beneath the divan bed, no sign of prescription drugs in the bathroom cabinet. There were no magazines in the rack nor books on the sleeves. No records beside the gramophone, no drinks on the trolley. The place had been emptied and scrupulously cleaned. It was waiting for the next Joyce Rose.

He locked up behind him and took the stairs this time. The manager was waiting for him in the lobby. There was a small and cheap-looking cardboard suitcase on the countertop in front of her, the kind travelling salesman take on overnight stays.

'I've been waiting for someone to collect this.' It sounded like an accusation. 'It was on top of the wardrobe,' she said, as if he should have known this. 'Pushed right to the back.'

'It belonged to Joyce Rose?' he said.

'It's not my business to say who it belonged to, but it came from flat 309. They should have taken it way.'

He wasn't sure who they were supposed to be but said, 'I'll take it off your hands.'

She looked suddenly reluctant to hand it over, but then said, 'I don't have much room, you see. Just a small office.'

Calloway looked over her shoulder into the hutch-like room. An electric heater glowed from its enamelled frame while an old tin kettle on a two-ring gas burner sent a small plume of steam from its spout as it started to boil.

'Did you know her well?' he said.

The manager wasn't expecting a question and paused before answering. 'Quite well,' she said. Quite meaning perfectly. 'Delightful girl, at least at first. She changed, you know.'

'Changed how?'

She thought for a moment, brushing the biscuit crumbs from her mouth. 'The joy went out of her.'

Hardly surprising, he thought. A diet of stimulants and barbiturates is no recipe for joy. He'd seen it during the war, seen men become dependent on the little helpers the medics gave out when sleep wasn't an option, then watched them counter the effects with drink when it was. Some became erratic, unreliable and reckless. They were the dangerous ones. Others became morose, a liability, a drag on morale.

'When did this start?' he said.

'When she started getting visitors,' the manger replied.

'What kind of visitors?'

'The wrong kind, if you ask me.'

'Wrong how?'

'Well,' she said, folding her arms in front of her. The sleeves of her cardigan had picked up more cat hairs since he'd been upstairs. 'Twice her age, by the look of them. Rough mannered too, although they tried to hide it with airs and graces. They couldn't fool me,' she said, tapping the side of her nose. 'Too smartly dressed for my liking. One wore correspondent shoes.'

'These visitors,' he said, 'did they come alone?'

She nodded. 'Their drivers would wait outside. Big expensive cars they had.'

'How long did they stay?'

'Sometimes an hour or two. Sometimes they were in and out very quickly, especially towards the end. That's when the trouble started.'

'What kind of trouble?'

'I heard one of them call her names as he left. Names I won't repeat. On another occasion she was in tears for hours.'

'How do you know she was in tears?'

'I don't listen at doors,' she said.

He hadn't suggested she did.

'I was taking a parcel up to 307 and happened to hear her from the corridor.'

'Were these men her only visitors?'

'Not at first. When she first moved in, friends would call on her. I would call them the kind of people she should be mixing with. Nice young girls.'

'Any male friends?'

'Some,' she said. 'They always left at a respectable hour.'

'Anyone in particular?'

'Yes,' said. 'I'm not one to talk about these things, but seeing as she's...' she hesitated before saying the word.

'No longer a resident,' Calloway said.

'Indeed.'

She looked down as an over-fed tabby cat brushed past her legs and walked into the office. She brushed the cat hairs from her sleeves, tutting as if she'd just noticed them.

'There was this one young man. A nice boy. She seemed happy enough when she was around him.'

'Can you describe him?'

'A bit skinny for my liking.'

He wondered what her liking was.

'Intelligent looking. Tweed jacket and cravat. Very high forehead.'

Tony from casting.

'He stopped visiting after...'

She hesitated.

'Did something happen?' said Calloway.

'The young boy was there when one of those rogues came visiting. There was an argument. The man's driver, well I didn't see, I only heard. A physical exchange.'

'A fight?'

She shook her head. 'I don't think the boy was the fighting sort.'

'He was attacked? By the man's driver?'

'I didn't see, I only heard. After that, the boy stopped visiting.'

The kettle on the gas ring started the whistle.

'I can't offer you tea,' she said, as if he'd been rude enough to ask for one. 'I don't have enough coupons for two.'

With this she walked back into the office and closed the door behind her. Calloway took the case from the countertop. It was light, perhaps half full. As he left Cypress Court, he took a last look up to the windows of flat 309. He tried to imagine the face that had fled the Producers Club dinner looking down at him, crying. Crying after being called names by rough men in correspondent shoes. But he couldn't. The face he'd seen that night wasn't a face that cried easily.

TWELVE

'Going on holiday?'

It was Bryant again. He was looking down at the suitcase in Calloway's hand. Calloway avoided the question by lobbing one back.

'Still hanging around then?'

Bryant was leaning against the unmarked Special Branch car that had been a permanent fixture in the studio's cobbled courtyard since the morning after the explosion.

'Like the proverbial bad smell,' he replied, and took a long drag on his cigarette.

Calloway held up the case for Bryant to see. 'I'm returning it to props. Someone left it on location.'

'You lead an exciting life,' the copper said.

You don't know the half of it, thought Calloway. 'You finished your interviews?' he said.

'For now' said Bryant.

'Learn anything?'

'Yeah. That half the people you work with are right up their own arses.'

'And that's news?'

'S'pose not. I don't know how you stomach it. All the pretension and the fancy talk. Bunch of fakes.'

'Of course they're fake. That's what we do here. Create fanciful imitations of life.'

'Not so fanciful when actors playing IRA thugs start planting bombs.'

'And you can prove that?'

'We've got to find the bugger first. And some help you're

being. You're dragging your feet I'd say. McCaffrey a friend of yours, is he?'

'Sure. The kind of friend I punch in the face and chuck through the main gates.'

'So you say.'

'Spelthorne was there. Ask him.'

Bryant flicked his cigarette onto the cobbles. 'I'm watching you, Calloway. You interest me.'

'Is that one of your little jokes again?'

'Might be.'

Bryant grinned an unfriendly grin, the kind you give a man when you're relishing the prospect of punching him one day. He climbed inside the car, started the powerful engine and drove out through the main gates.

Calloway crossed the courtyard towards the administration building. The two technicians he had spoken to in Studio B were unloading a new camera from the rear of a Morris van.

The technician in the store coat nodded at Calloway and rolled his eyes. 'We've had to hire in a replacement temporarily. Costing us an arm and a leg.'

His colleague in the tweed jacket frowned at him and said to Calloway, 'It's not the money. It's the lost time. That's the real trouble.'

'Got it,' said Calloway. He took the suitcase to his office and pushed it under his desk out of sight. One of his commissionaires appeared at the door, announcing himself by clearing his throat. 'A visitor to see you, Mr Calloway,' he said. 'A Mr Suskind. Shall I send him up?'

Calloway glanced down at the grazes on his knuckles. They had healed but were still a visible reminder of the fight in Ridley Road. He wasn't convinced he wanted an unplanned visit from his old pal Johnny. At the same time he was curious.

'Go ahead,' he said. 'Send him up.'

Suskind's big frame filled the doorway. He was wearing his demob suit, which had lost its shape through too much wear. But his shoes were polished brightly Calloway noticed. Old habits. He held a black trilby hat in his big hand.

‘I was passing so I thought I’d drop by.’

‘I don’t believe that for one minute, Johnny.’

The big ex-paratrooper grinned. He pulled out a pack of Woodbines and offered one to Calloway who lit up with a desk lighter he’d inherited from the previous occupant of the office. It was a present from Weston-super-Mare, apparently. Suskind looked around the office.

‘Not a bad little gaff you’ve got here, Reg.’

Calloway gestured to the chair opposite his desk. ‘Take a seat, Johnny, seeing as you’re here.’

Suskind sat awkwardly on the edge of the chair, as if getting comfortable would have been a bigger liberty than showing up uninvited.

‘I’ve looked at a couple of security jobs myself, as it happens,’ he said. ‘I’m working at Lipton’s at the moment, lugging tea chests around the Tea Building, but I reckon my talents are wasted there.’

He was right. Johnny had been a good soldier and a good NCO. A natural leader who had earned the respect of his men. But he wasn’t the only one. The war had created thousands of men like that and there weren’t the jobs for them now that they were back. Calloway had been lucky, twice. Centurion was his second job as head of security and he couldn’t complain. He just hoped he didn’t mess it up like the first one. Don’t get involved. That should have been his motto. Should have been.

‘Not at work today?’ Calloway said.

‘Half day,’ said Johnny. ‘I wanted to see you, actually. Thought it would be nice to have a chin wag. For old times’ sake.’

‘That’s very touching. But the old times weren’t pretty, were they, Johnny? You know damn well neither of us is the kind to reminisce.’

Calloway and Johnny had fought side by side in the final stages of the war. By that time the Germans were putting guns in the hands of children and old men. There was no glory in emptying the magazine of a Sten gun into an enemy like that, no matter what insignia they had on their uniforms.

Suskind held up his hands like he'd been tumbled. 'I can't fool you, can I, Reg?'

'Say your piece Johnny.'

'I've come to ask for your help.'

When Calloway helped, things had a habit of not ending well.

'Carry on,' he said.

'No rough stuff, I promise.' Johnny looked his old comrade up and down. 'Although I know you're good for it,' he said. 'Just a little shopping trip, that's all.'

'Shopping?'

'Something I need you to buy.'

Something for the group, Calloway thought. His mind raced forward several steps. Guns? No, Johnny's war was being fought with fists and boots. Guns weren't their style.

'I'm not one for shopping. There's nothing I want.'

'I get that. And it's nothing you'd want, believe me. I still need you to buy it though. It's something we can't buy ourselves.'

Calloway pulled a bottle of Black & White from his desk drawer and two cups filched from the canteen. He poured two generous measures and passed one to Suskind.

'Black & White, eh? Don't mind if I do. L'Chaim,' said Johnny, raising the cup.

Calloway presumed this was for effect. He remembered that Johnny's usual toast was 'to wives and girlfriends, may they never meet.'

'So spit it out, Johnny. What is this thing you want me to buy for you?'

As he heard the words tumble from his mouth, he was already wishing he hadn't asked. Johnny leant forward in the chair, lowered his voice and explained. It wasn't rough stuff, but it wasn't going to be an errand Calloway relished. There would be a risk in everything Johnny's group did. That was the nature of their operation. Dare to do what others seemed content to avoid. Calloway's reluctance to join in fought with his conscience, but his conscience fought harder. He and Johnny were too alike, their experiences too similar.

‘I suppose saying “just this once” would be a waste of time,’ Calloway said.

‘Probably, yeah,’ said Johnny. He downed the rest of his whisky. ‘You’re a good man, Reg. Marge will pick you up from your place Saturday and take you down there. She’ll brief you properly on the way.’

Another date with Marge. Joining in had at least some benefits, Calloway found himself thinking, then cursed himself inwardly. He was still being played.

***

Calloway rented a room on the top floor of a garment factory off the Kingsland Road. It was an attic space above three floors of workshops which by day were filled with machinists, making ladies fashions sold under the name Da Costa of London. Da Costa of Hackney didn’t have the same ring to it. He paid Mr Da Costa a reduced rent for his cold-water room, which had its own gas meter, a gas fire and an old stone sink. In return, he kept an eye on the factory at night. It was a good deal. The room was nothing to write home about, not that he ever wrote home, but it was dry, watertight and private. Calloway didn’t like neighbours. He’d never liked digs which meant sharing. Solitude suited him. At least that’s what he told himself.

Mr Da Costa was locking up the factory floors when Calloway arrived home that evening.

‘You have a suitcase Mr Calloway.’ He spoke as if Calloway didn’t know this. ‘I hope you’re not thinking of leaving.’

He prodded Calloway’s chest mischievously. ‘You are a very good watch dog.’

‘Not leaving, Mr Da Costa. Just bringing work home.’

Da Costa gave him a sympathetic look. ‘You work too hard. You look tired.’

‘So they keep telling me.’

‘You don’t sleep well,’ said Da Costa.

He didn’t. He hadn’t since the war. And having Belcher, Bryant, Spelthorne and Bernie on his case didn’t help him sleep any better.

'Work worries,' Calloway said, suddenly feeling he needed to explain.

Da Costa gave him a wry look. 'And no one to share them with, eh? No lady friend?'

'No,' said Calloway. 'Well...' He shrugged. 'Who knows?'

'Ah,' said Da Costa with a knowing look. 'So there is someone. That's good.'

'It's complicated.'

Da Costa gave a sage nod. 'Women are complicated, Mr Calloway. If they weren't, they would be very dull indeed.' He prodded Calloway's chest again. 'And who wants a dull wife, eh?'

Da Costa finished locking the big steel door to the factory floor and said, 'Get some rest. You'll be needing your strengths for that complicated woman.'

The old man laughed to himself as he walked down the dark stairway and out into the street.

Calloway's room was cold. The autumn temperature was dropping. He put a shilling in the meter and lit the gas. The small fire set into the wall spluttered into life. He watched the blue flame turn the ceramic plates to a comforting orange. He loosened his tie and took a bottle of gin from the shelf above the sink and poured a slug into his tooth mug. The gin tasted faintly of cloves from the tooth powder he used. It wasn't unpleasant. He kicked off his shoes, plumped his pillow and sat up on the iron-framed bed that doubled as a studio couch, the only place in the room to sit, apart from a hard kitchen chair. He dragged the small suitcase onto his lap and clicked the clasps. They were unlocked and popped easily.

There were papers, books and photographs inside. Mementoes. Colourful scraps of a girl's former life. Joyce, when she was Celeste. Small things, not in themselves remarkable, but significant enough to keep. Family photos. A handsome-looking couple in hotel uniform. Her parents, he assumed. Celeste as a child playing on a beach somewhere in England. Ice creams and donkey rides. Family holidays in France, a sun-tanned Celeste in a sundress and a big straw hat, legs dangling over the edge of a café chair. A school report from 1935. A pleasant and popular girl...must learn to concentrate in class...a chatterbox...could achieve higher marks if she set her mind to it...her Mary in this year's nativity play was a revelation. Two photos of Celeste in her teens, posing like a movie star with a boy that looked very much like Tony from casting. There was also an Oxo tin, the kind people kept cotton reels and sewing kit in. This tin was heavy. Inside was a small 8mm cine camera and two reels of film. The handwritten labels on the film reels read Film star diary 1/3 and Film star diary 2/3. He examined the camera. It was loaded and the film supply indicator showed that film had been taken. Calloway replaced the reels and the camera inside the tin and set it to one side. He rifled through the remaining contents of the suitcase. There were half a dozen postcards from Paris with recent post marks. He turned the postcards over and read them. Pleasantries from a young woman abroad, the signature Yvonne written with a creative flourish. The most recent card sent six months before the actress's death. And a copy of an earnest-looking magazine called London Poetry Review. He leafed through the pages. The editor's introduction was provocative. He was turning the world of poetry on its head. Challenging the poetry establishment. The editor signed himself Mephisto. Next to his signature, a satirical illustration of the devil reading William Blake. Then thirty-two pages of poetry by poets whose names meant nothing to Calloway.

Except for one.

THIRTEEN

Saturday. Marge was leaning against a borrowed Ford Pilot she'd parked opposite Da Costa's factory. She wore the same tatty trench coat she had worn on the night of the Union Movement rally. The tortoise shell cigarette holder was clamped between her teeth.

'Well, you certainly look the part,' she said, as Calloway emerged from the building.

He wore his old army boots, trousers from a suit that was now too shabby to wear, a dark roll neck jumper and a brown leather blouson jacket.

'I feel like a B-movie thug,' he said.

'I may have a part for you, love. Come and see me on Monday.'

She leaned forward and kissed him on the cheek.

'Now let's go shopping,' she said.

They drove south down Bishopsgate, then west onto Lombard Street. The roads were empty, the city deserted at the weekend, the directors, managers and clerks of its financial institutions enjoying their Saturday in the suburbs. Marge drove fast, although they were in no hurry. She clunked through the gears of the small car, changing up to get more power from the tentative engine. Then she fished for something in the pocket of her trench coat.

'Put this on,' she said.

She passed him a small enamelled pin with the Union Movement symbol on it. Calloway did as she asked. He felt slightly grubby all of a sudden. Marge looked at him and smiled.

'It completes the look, darling,' she said. 'Johnny told you the plan?'

Calloway nodded and recited the instructions he had been given.

'I go into the bookshop, browse for five minutes, then ask the man behind the counter whether he has any patriotic literature. He will ask me what kind of thing I'm looking for and I will say "books like My Answer". He will recognise this reference to Oswald Mosley's new book as a coded request to buy fascist literature and will then fetch a selection from a locked storeroom. I will note the place he keeps the key, the location of the storeroom and any other useful intelligence that can be used when your group returns to the premises at night to remove the aforementioned literature for destruction. I will purchase a selection of literature and leave the shop. I will report all intelligence gathered back to you.'

'Clever boy,' she said, taking a hand off the wheel and pinching his cheek. As much as he was enjoying Marge's company, the lapdog treatment irritated him.

They drove past St Paul's Cathedral, standing proud among the ruins that surrounded it. Some said the Luftwaffe spared it because they used it as a landmark for navigation. Others said it was divine intervention. Calloway reckoned it just got lucky. Ninety percent of war was about luck, in his experience.

He said to Marge, 'What do you know about the London Poetry Review?'

She laughed. 'Has that Stevie Smith quotation been playing on your mind?'

It had, but that wasn't his reason for asking the question. He figured anyone that could quote a modern poet might know the magazine he found among Joyce Rose's mementoes.

'I've read it once or twice,' she said. 'It's published by this bohemian sort who hangs around North Soho. He has a coterie of admirers who follow him around. They drink in the Fitzroy Tavern on Charlotte Street. Why on earth do you ask? Are you looking to broaden your mind, Reg?'

'Would that be so odd?' he said.

'You don't strike me as the type,' she said.

He didn't often take offence, but he was close to it this time. 'So what type am I?'

She thought for a moment, as if assembling everything she had learned about him in these last few days into a coherent character. She frowned and said, 'You're full of contradictions.'

'I'm straightforward enough,' he said, doubting himself as he spoke.

She shook her head. 'You're the type that puts on an accent that's not his own but stays loyal to his kind. You're the haunted type that wants to forget yet keeps their memories alive.' She glanced at him for a second. 'Especially the bad ones. And you're definitely the type whose instinct gets the better of his judgement.'

'A trait you're quite happy to exploit,' he said.

'In the face of very little resistance,' she said, crunching through the gears and accelerating down the Strand. 'Oh,' she said as an afterthought, 'and you're the type that doesn't like jazz.'

She turned up her nose and shook her head with disapproval. 'How can you not like jazz?'

'Easily,' he said. 'Especially the saxophone. It's like wind from the devil's backside.'

She laughed and muttered 'philistine' before fishing in the bag beside her and pulling out a packet of Park Drive.

'Light us both one up, darling,' she said.

His hand glanced across hers as he took the packet. He felt less offended.

They drove around Piccadilly Circus, its neon signage alight again after years of blackout. Guinness was good for you, Wrigley's gave you vim and vigour and Bile Beans kept you heathy, bright eyed and slim. With stout, gum and laxatives, you could conquer the world.

'Tell me more about this bookshop,' he said.

'It's owned by a fascist called Victor Dodds. He was a leading light in the BUF in the thirties and is now a pivotal figure in the Union Movement. He's not your typical Mosleyite thug. Educated, intellectual you might say, and very influential among the myriad fascist groups that have sprung up around the country in the last few years. A good speech writer and a frequent contributor to far-right magazines. The shop itself is unremarkable. A normal second-hand bookshop that earns Dodds a modest living.'

'Will Dodds be behind the counter?'

She shook her head. 'He doesn't work there on Saturdays. We've been tailing him for some time so we know his movements. He spends his weekends in the Union Movement offices on Arundel Gardens. There'll be a slack-jawed Saturday boy in the shop today. Should make your job easier.'

Easier than what, he thought. He couldn't see anything difficult in buying a few magazines and keeping his eyes open.

Dodd's bookshop was in a side street off Hammersmith Broadway, between a painter and decorator and a tobacconist. Marge parked a few yards farther down the street. She killed the engine and reached into her handbag.

'Now you'll also need this.'

She put a small tobacco tin into Calloway's hand. One side of it had been cut away. He opened the tin. It was filled with a smooth layer of plasticine.

'It's likely that wherever Dodds keeps the key to the locked storeroom, he will also keep other keys,' said Marge. 'We're hoping one of them will be the key to the front door of the shop. There might even be a duplicate of the storeroom key. Most locksmiths provide a spare key when they fit a lock. When the boy disappears into the storeroom to get the literature you've requested, we want you to take impressions of as many keys as you can by pressing them into the plasticine. You will need to take an impression of both sides. We've done a trial run and reckon you should be able to do half a dozen keys inside a minute.'

Calloway didn't like the sound of it.

'Johnny said I'd be observing and reporting back. He said nothing about taking impressions of keys.'

Marge faked innocent in a way that told him he'd been duped. 'Poor Johnny,' she said. 'He's so forgetful.'

A big part of him wanted to slap the tobacco tin back into her hand and walk away. Buying a few pamphlets was one thing. Risking arrest, or even a beating by Victor Dodds' bully boys, was something else. The trouble was, Marge was right. He was the type whose instinct got the better of his judgement, and his instinct told him to take impressions of those bloody keys so that Johnny and his 43 Group commandos could put a match to the filth that Dodds and Hamm and Mosley and every other tin-pot little fascist were spurting to a nation still hurting from a six-year fight against people like them.

He leaned across to Marge, took her face in his big hands and kissed her full on the lips.

'Wish me luck,' he said, pocketing the tobacco tin and easing his big frame out of the small car.

The bell above the door rang as he entered the bookshop. The place smelled musky, like a tom cat had sprayed the walls. There was a chemical tang in the air from the paraffin heater that burned beside the counter. It was too hot inside. At least Calloway felt hot, conscious of the tiny beads of sweat forming under his hairline. He shouldn't have worn the roll neck jumper. The boy Marge had described sat behind the counter reading PG Wodehouse. Ironic, thought Calloway, who knew through his old intelligence circles that the gullible fop author had agreed to make propaganda broadcasts to America for the Nazis after he was interned in France during the war. He wasn't a fascist, MI5's investigation established that. He'd just suffered a dim-witted aberration that anyone with an ounce of political savvy would have avoided.

The shop was empty apart from the boy, much to Calloway's relief. And the boy wasn't a thug. He was stick thin and white as a sheet. If things went sour, Calloway could snap him in half. The bookshelves were arranged in rows, making a series of darkened cul-de-sacs. Calloway rummaged among them, trying to look like people who browse bookshops look. He'd explored all three cul-de-sacs and seen no sign of a door to a storeroom. In fact, the place appeared to be a lock-up shop with only the street door for access. He was beginning to think he'd been given duff intelligence.

The five minutes Johnny had told him to spend browsing took an age. He flicked through books he'd no interest in, all the time checking his watch. The boy tore himself away from Jeeves & Wooster and peered at Calloway through the gloom. Calloway took this as his cue. He stepped over to the counter and gave the boy the agreed spiel. The boy took it in his stride, which suggested this type of routine was a regular occurrence. He noticed Calloway's lapel pin and looked reassured. He stood up and said, 'You'll have to wait a mo,' then opened what looked like a cash drawer under the counter. The drawer opened with a ding of a small bell inside it. Calloway cursed inside. In his mind he'd pictured a key on a hook on the wall, not inside a cash drawer with a bell. The boy pulled out a key from one of the drawer's compartments. There were other keys in there too. Johnny and Marge's hunch had been right. The boy pushed the drawer shut. There was another ding from the bell.

'I won't be a minute,' the boy said.

Take all the minutes you want, pal, thought Calloway, flicking away a small bead of sweat running down the side of his face to join more sweat under his collar. The boy walked into the third of the three cul-de-sacs and fumble with the key, pushing it through a gap in the row of hardbacks on the third shelf from the bottom. There was a click and the bookcase swung back on concealed hinges, opening onto a room lined with stacks of cardboard boxes. The boy stepped into the room and closed the concealed door behind him.

Calloway stepped behind the counter. The cash drawer was the size and shape of a shoebox, with a semicircular brass pull handle on the front. Calloway thought hard. He recalled that there had been a momentary delay between the boy opening the drawer and the bell ringing. Calloway eased the drawer open a fraction, slid his fingers into the gap and felt along the underside of the lid. His fingers felt the cool metal of the bell's circular dome and the small bell hammer beside it. The hammer was pulled back on a taught spring. Holding his breath, he slid his forefinger between the bell and the hammer and gently eased the drawer out with his free hand. The drawer opened silently. He breathed again. Beads of sweat dropped off his forehead onto the countertop and he wiped them with the sleeve of his jacket. He listened hard and heard the muffled sound of the boy rummaging through cardboard boxes behind the bookshelf. There were three keys in the drawer. A large mortise, which could have been the front door, a smaller key that looked like the one the boy had taken, and a tiny key, the kind you use to open a desk drawer. The boy wouldn't be long. The boxes looked easily accessible. Calloway made a snap decision to take impressions of the two larger keys and leave the small key. Desk drawers could be opened easily with a jemmy. Pulling the tobacco tin from his pocket, he took the first impression. A figure darkened the glass-fronted shop door. The bell rang as the door opened. Calloway jumped and dropped the first key. He bent down by reflex and retrieved it. When he straightened up, he was looking up at a stout, bald man in a suit that had long since become too small for him.

The man said, 'Got anything on ham radio?'

Calloway tried to recall the sections he'd browsed through on the shelves. He heard muffled rummaging again from behind the hidden door. It seemed more decisive this time, like boxes being closed and put back in their place. He waved a hand in no particular direction and said, 'Under hobbies and interests.'

The stout man tried to follow the direction Calloway was pointing in. He frowned and was about to ask again. Calloway said, 'Third row along, two shelves down, next to artistic photography.'

This piqued the stout man's interest. He looked the type, thought Calloway. This time he followed the directions. A furtive look had come over his pink, pudgy face. While his back was turned, Calloway took an impression of the second key, replaced both in the compartment of the drawer and eased his fingers under the lid again. In his haste, he fumbled and the hammer snapped on its taught spring. In a split second he muffled the bell with his hand. It made an audible thud, but not a shrill ring not loud enough to penetrate the books that lined the hidden door. The radio ham heard the thud and turned. Calloway repeated, 'Next to the artistic photography,' and gestured to a random shelf. The boy appeared with a sheaf of pamphlets and magazines just as Calloway was returning to the front of the counter.

'I think you'll find these of interest, sir,' he said, looking around to see if there were other customers in the shop. The stout man looked over, trying to see what the boy was showing Calloway. The boy nodded to Calloway to follow him into one of the cul-de-sacs, out of view. He showed him copies of Britain Defiant, London Attack, Gothic Ripple and Unity. Calloway pointed to two of the titles at random and said, 'I'll take those.' A bead of sweat dripped onto Gothic Ripple making a dark spot on the newsprint. The boy appeared not to notice. He gave an uninterested nod and returned to the counter. He slid the chosen magazines into a brown paper bag and took the money Calloway handed him. The stout man gave Calloway a perplexed look as he left the shop with the bag under his arm.

Calloway crossed the street and climbed into the passenger seat of the Ford Pilot. Marge already had the engine running.

'Well?' she said.

Calloway tossed the magazines onto her lap and laid the tobacco tin on top of them.

'I need a drink,' he said.

FOURTEEN

He borrowed a projector from the cutting room. They had an old 8mm Bell & Howell in their store. He returned to his office and threaded the flimsy film he'd found in the suitcase into the projector and ran it until he felt the cogs start pulling at the perforations in the celluloid. He pulled down the blind on his office window and focused the two-foot-square beam on his office wall.

There was Joyce Rose. She gave a coquettish nod and beckoned him to follow her. She wore a summer dress that was respectably revealing. There was enough of the English rose on show to turn heads but not enough to shock. The young actress was among a crowd at a public event. The opening of a cinema. Commissionaires held open the chrome-and-glass doors and Joyce cut the ribbon. Then there were photos, the cinema manager's arm firmly around the starlet's waist, his fish-lips pressed against her cheek for a posed kiss. Ivor Cole was there. He orchestrated the proceedings. Joyce beamed and waved. She was good at this.

The projector clack-clacked. He smelled the burning dust on the valves. Illuminated dust specks floating in the beam. The film cut to an interior. Studio A at Centurion. Joyce on set, taking direction from Bobbie Brand, the lone female director among the studio's all-male roster. Joyce looked nervous. She stood awkwardly. She fussed over the script in her hand. She snuck a look into the lens of the cine camera and bit on her knuckles mugging comic anxiety.

Cut to an evening event, a reception in an over-decorated ballroom. Glimpses of films stars more famous than Joyce would live to be. Joyce excited, however much she was overshadowed. Meeting and greeting studio luminaries with a deferential smile. This is the big time, her eyes said.

Drinks on set. A wrap party with co-stars. Horseplay. Joyce joining in. Then a word from Bobbie Brand, a glass in her hand. Applause and well done all round. A handshake for Joyce from a sheepish crew member. A peck on the cheek from the leading man. A hug from his co-star. Encouraging words from Bobbie, just for Joyce.

A young woman's first steps towards the career of her dreams.

The film ended. The screen turned brilliant white, the full reel spun a celluloid tail like a Catherine wheel. Calloway rethreaded it and rewound it at double speed. He replaced it in the Oxo tin and cued up Film star's diary 2/3.

The projector clack-clacked once more. Joyce winking to the camera in the make-up room mirror. A more confident Joyce this time. The film showed her in a sequence of similar settings as the first, but her demeanour suggested she was in the ascendant. And Spelthorne featured this time. Joyce on his arm and a proprietary look on his face. The studio boss showing off his latest asset.

Calloway replaced the second reel into the tin and let the blind up. He lit a Navy Cut, took a long drag on the hot tobacco and sat back in the chair behind his desk. He closed his eyes and recalled the night of the explosion. It played like a cine film in his mind, silently, the clack-clack of his mental projector the only sound that accompanied it. He saw the face of the woman. Blonde not brunette, older than the Joyce in the home movies, more world-weary. And tougher. The fear Calloway had seen on her face that night was a pragmatic, not vulnerable fear. She didn't want to be seen there, nor seen by him. And it wasn't the face of Joyce Rose. Of course it wasn't. Joyce had been dead for a year or more. Yet the resemblance was too close to be insignificant.

He picked up the small cine camera and left his office, locking the door behind him, then stepped out into the courtyard. A damp mist hung in the air giving the old brewery yard the look of a period melodrama, the kind Centurion made in its early days. He called the commissionaire over as he passed out of the main gates.

'Take this down to the lab when you get a moment. Ask them to bring the developed film up to my office. I'll be back this afternoon.'

'Righto, sir,' the commissionaire said, taking the small box from him.

Calloway jumped a trolley bus and found a seat. He pulled a list from his jacket pocket. It was the list of cleaners that worked weekends with names and addresses. One name and address in particular interested him. He didn't know that neighbourhood, but it wasn't far. He'd checked the AtoZ before leaving his office. The nearest trolley bus stop was a quarter of a mile from the street he was looking for. The neighbourhood had suffered heavy bomb damage. He walked past building sites where new blocks of flats were going up. Homes fit for heroes was the promise. He wasn't convinced. Time would tell. In between the building sites were the remains of Victorian terraces, substantial homes now divided up for multiple occupation. Washing hung out of the widows on makeshift lines. The smell of unappetising cooking billowed from the windows. Kids sat on the steps, scratching their names in the blackened brickwork or seeing how many steps they could jump down without falling onto their dirty hands. Some of the houses still had visible street numbers. Others Calloway had to guess at. He was looking for twenty-seven. The remaining houses were the odd numbers. He found twenty-one, he guessed the next was twenty-three, which it must have been because twenty-five came next. There was no twenty-seven. There had been, once. All that remained was a scattering of brick rubble next to the bare flank wall of the adjacent house. He pulled the list from his pocket and checked just to be sure. He was in the right place. He looked around for any remaining houses but there were none. The rest of the street had been flattened and cleared. A gathering mist billowed over the cratered rubble landscape.

A husky, high-pitched voice said, 'Who are you looking for?'

Two had crept up on him. Both around ten, he reckoned. He gave them a name.

'What's it worth?' one boy said.

Calloway took a shilling from his trouser pocket and flicked it, letting it spin long enough for the boys to see the glint of silver. He snapped it back into his fist.

'A bob,' he said.

'Each?' said the boy, figuring he was onto something.

'Between you,' said Calloway.

The boys conferred.

'Alright,' one said, and held out his grubby hand. Calloway withheld the coin and said, 'So do you know them?'

The boy who'd negotiated the deal grinned at his pal and said, 'Nah, mate. They don't live around here.'

His pal said, 'We'd know. We know everyone.'

Calloway didn't doubt it. They were the type who didn't miss a trick.

'Now give us our fuckin' shilling.'

'Does your dad know you talk like that?' said Calloway.

'My dad's dead. Rommel killed him. I've got his medal,' the foul-mouthed boy said proudly.

'North Africa Star?' said Calloway.

'Yeah,' said the boy. 'D'you want to buy it?'

'Clear off, the pair of you,' said Calloway, handing over the shilling and miming a cuff round the head. The boys sniggered then scarpered.

Calloway checked his watch. It would be opening time in twenty minutes. He jumped a bus to Tottenham Court Road. Smog hung heavy in the air. Visibility was poor. The busses and taxis had their lights on even at this early hour. They lit up the streets like glow worms. Calloway jumped off the bus and headed into North Soho on foot.

The Fitzroy Tavern was a bohemian zoo. A watering hole for charlatans, misfits and flakes. The pub was already filling up ten minutes after opening. A motley collection of drinkers with nowhere else to go. A place to sit, to keep warm, to pass endless time for want of a proper job to go to or a conventional life to live. Others used the libraries, but this place served booze. He ordered a half of Courage and propped up the bar. Spinster twins in their sixties sat immobile at a corner table in a matching ensemble that resembled mourning dress. They looked like they'd been there since Armistice Day. A rakish bachelor, long since past the age it was acceptable to be such, sat on a bar stool in a faded blazer, stained flannels and brown suede brogues that were scuffed to a shine. He sipped at a gin and something like he was making it last till closing time. Three rouged-up good-time girls cackled over port and lemons. They seemed happy to be themselves, without male company to entertain. That would come later. A couple of bums, at least that's what the new slang term for them seemed to be, read matching copies of Being and Nothingness in complete silence, as if oblivious to each other's presence. She had eyes painted black as anthracite and hair that shone like raven feathers. She wore a man's tweed overcoat cinched tight with a worn leather belt. He wore corduroys and a college scarf. He hadn't combed his hair since his last school photograph. Calloway nursed the half pint and watched the place fill up with more human oddities. As he was ordering the other half, the doors flew open. A man entered wearing a Bud Flanagan fur coat and a Nehru hat on his shaved head. The coat was moulting and the hat was askew. He wore old cricket whites and suede chukka boots with thick crepe soles. His eyes were rimmed with a fine line of kohl, although he was in no way feminine. His skin was dark, his race indeterminate, and he was built like a tighthead prop. Half a dozen acolytes followed in his wake. Most were puny and pale. He dispatched one of them to the bar while he commandeered two tables by the window. His booming voice drowned out the muted chatter of the pub and the acolytes hung on every word. He talked poetry and publishing.

Mephisto.

Calloway watched them from the bar. Mephisto held court while the acolytes proffered opinions on TS Eliot, Stephen

Spender and Cyril Connolly. He berated them or endorsed them depending on whether their views conformed to his own. They seemed happy with his judgement. He was their intellectual compass.

Calloway took the copy of the poetry review he'd found in Joyce Rose's suitcase from his pocket and walked over to their table.

'Mind if I join you?' he said.

The man in the fur coat glanced up at Calloway as if he couldn't care one way or the other. Then a look which said you could be interesting came over his face. He told an acolyte to budge up and gestured to a chair. Calloway sat. He put the poetry review on the table in front of them.

'I'm taking a guess that you're Mephisto?' he said, pointing a finger at the magazine.

'And you are Dr Faustus,' Mephisto said.

'I'm Calloway. I work at Centurion Studios.'

The acolytes exchanged glances. Mephisto's eyes lit up. 'A film mogul. Will you give me your soul in return for the best story never told?'

'I've heard all the stories,' said Calloway.

He looked Calloway up and down, as if judging him by a set of diabolical criteria. 'I doubt that.'

'I'm not a film mogul. That's a man called Spelthorne. I look after security.'

Mephisto suddenly looked bored. He glanced at the acolytes and rolled his eyes, as if to say why is this inconsequential man wasting my precious time? They gave him knowing looks in return, without really knowing at all.

'I wanted to talk to you about one of the poets you publish. Eve Clark.'

Mephisto thought a moment.

'Evie?' he said, as if recalling a dim memory. The acolytes tried to recall dim memories too. 'And why would you be interested in Evie?'

'I like her poetry.'

Mephisto looked him up and down again and shook his

head.

'No, you don't,' he said.

First Marge, now this. What was it about him that looked so lacking in intellect?

'Alright, I don't. She's a cleaner at the studio and she hasn't shown up for work. We've had some trouble lately.'

Grit in the cameras and water in the lights, found on Mondays after a cleaner called Eve Clark had worked the weekend shift.

'I'm head of security. I'd like to speak to her.'

Mephisto let out a laugh that made heads turn on the bar. 'So Evie Clark's a char lady? How terribly fucking proletarian.'

A voice said, 'How do you think she affords to buy you all those drinks, Phisto? You haven't bought a round since VJ Day.'

He was tall and distinguished, with big bushy hair and strong, chiselled features. He wore a belted tweed jacket and buff twills, with a pair of old brogues that looked like family heirlooms. Mephisto's manner changed. This man didn't defer to him like the acolytes did. In fact Mephisto seemed a little scared of him. The tall man pulled up a chair and put his pint down on the table.

'You're a new face,' he said to Calloway. 'I'm Julian.'

He held out his hand and Calloway shook it.

'Reg,' said Calloway. 'Are you a poet too?'

The tall man shook his head. 'A writer,' he said. 'Novelist.'

'Published?' said Calloway, expecting the answer to be no.

'Some short stories. I'm punting a novel around the houses.'

'Any luck?'

Julian took a sip of the pint. 'A few sniffs. Nothing definite. A bit too soon after the war for what I write.'

'How so?' said Calloway.

'I've based it on my experiences in the army. There's not much glory in it.'

'You're telling me,' said Calloway,

'What were you?' Julian said.

'Intelligence Corps.'

'Ah, a rampant pansy resting on its laurels.'

It sounded like poetry but Calloway knew it wasn't. It was army slang for the Intelligence Corps cap badge, with its red rose and two laurel branches.

'I was light infantry.'

'An Arfur,' said Calloway. The light infantry had 'alf a cap badge', because it lacked the usual crown and laurels

Julian nodded. He said, 'Does your studio normally send its head of security when a cleaner goes AWOL?'

'We've had a couple of incidents. Damaged equipment discovered after Eve Clark's shift. She's not the only one we want to talk to. There were others on the shift.'

But Eve was the only one published in a poetry magazine that Joyce Rose had kept as a memento.

'Does she drink in here?'

Julian nodded. 'Sometimes. Quite often, actually. And she normally stands Phisto a round or two. He's a total scrounger. Completely shameless. I don't think he's eaten a meal or drunk a pint in his life that someone else hasn't paid for. That's how he lives.'

Mephisto had turned his back to the two big men and was playing to his crowd at the other end of the table. He dispatched two of them to the bar. They rifled through their pockets trying to piece together the price of a round from loose change.

'Why don't you call on Evie at her place?'

'I did,' said Calloway. 'Her place has been a hole in the ground since the Blitz.'

Julian looked confused and shook his head. 'Eve has a flat off Goodge Street. Well, just a room really, with a how's-yer-father on the landing shared by the rest of the inmates. Horrible place, but a good spot.'

'Do you know the address?'

Julian looked hesitant. 'I don't want to get the old girl in trouble.'

'Are you friends?'

'Barely, but she's a good sort. She started coming here a year or so ago. She'd been living in France, writing. She fell in with this crowd of charlatans,' he waved a large dismissive hand towards Mephisto and his acolytes, 'but I don't think she completely likes them. She's certainly not in the thrall of him, like the others. I think she saw them as a route to being published. His poetry review is one of the few outlets for this new generation.'

'I just want to talk to her,' said Calloway.

Julian thought it over. 'Alright,' he said. 'Just so you can eliminate her from your enquiries, as they say.'

'You read detective fiction?'

'I do. Not the chintzy country house rubbish. The new American stuff. It's raw. It's honest.' He glanced over at the man in the fur coat and Nehru hat with a hint of disdain. 'Of course, snobs like Phisto dismiss it out of hand.'

Julian pulled a fountain pen from the inside pocket of his tweed jacket and wrote an address on a beer mat.

'I'd be very surprised if she's got anything to do with this trouble your investigating,' he said. 'Like I say, she's a good sort.'

A good sort who gave a false address when she took the cleaning job.

Calloway pocketed the beer mat.

He nodded towards Julian's empty glass. 'Buy you another?'

Julian shook his head. 'Don't bother. I can't buy you one back and I don't have Phisto's lack of scruples.'

Mephisto was berating an acolyte loud enough for the whole pub to hear him. It was something he seemed to enjoy.

FIFTEEN

The address Julian had given him was a corner building with a pawn shop on the ground floor and three pairs of filthy windows above. Next to the pawn shop window, with its wedding rings and wristwatches, was a side door whose peeling brown paint and cracked panels left no doubt as to the state of the rooms above. Calloway pressed the bell. An angry buzz sounded from behind the door, followed by stumbling footsteps on bare wooden stairs. The door opened and a sleepy-looking youth with unkept hair and a dressing gown over his jumper and corduroys said, 'Yes?'

He sounded vague, still half asleep. 'Who do you want?' he said in the accent of someone not born to these shabby surroundings. He sounded like one of Mephisto's acolytes. A well-bred brat that was slumming it. He looked at his wrist for a watch that wasn't there.

'Do you have the time?' he asked.

'Almost two. Sorry to wake you. I'm looking for Eve Clark.'

'Eve?' the youth said, yawning. 'Wait there a moment.'

He climbed the stairs. Calloway heard knocking on a first-floor door and Eve's name called several times. There was no reply. The boy descended the stairs.

'Evie's out I'm afraid. Can I take a message?'

'Do you know where she is?'

He shrugged and said, 'At work, I suppose.'

Calloway knew she wasn't. It wasn't her shift.

'Tell her Reg Calloway from the studio wants to speak to her. Tell her I'll call again this evening. Can you remember that?'

The boy ran a skinny hand through the mop of blonde hair

above his fine-boned face and nodded.

Calloway returned to the studio. Giordano, Spelthorne's personal security goon, was leaning against the big iron gates, a cigarette between his thumb and forefinger. His suit was as sharp as his boss's, but with more muscle inside it. He narrowed his eyes as Calloway approached and flicked the butt into the gutter.

'Where've you been?' he said.

'Looking for McCaffrey,' Calloway lied.

'So did you find him?'

'If I did I'd be handing him over to your boss right now.'

'Sounds like you should look harder.'

'Why don't you try looking for him?'

'Not my job.'

'That's right. Because your boss told me you don't have the brains for it.'

'Don't push your luck.'

'Then don't waste my time.'

'We fucking own your time.'

'In that case, get out of my way. I've got work to do.'

Giordano put a palm like a side of beef on Calloway's chest and said, 'You need to wait here. Boss wants a word.'

Calloway heard tyres rumbling over the cobbles of the studio courtyard. The snout of a Bentley poked round the gates. A newer model than the car the bomb destroyed with a new number plate: CP2. The Bentley pulled up alongside Calloway and the window wound down. Spelthorne looked up at him from inside and said, 'Come for a little ride'.

It was an instruction not an invitation. Calloway opened the passenger door and climbed in beside Spelthorne. Giordano took the passenger seat. Franco was driving. He had big hands too.

Spelthorne wound up the window and stroked the lacquered walnut trim of the Bentley's door, as if stroking the face of a new girlfriend.

'New car, Mr Spelthorne?' said Calloway.

Spelthorne smiled. It wasn't friendly

'Yeah, funnily enough,' he said. 'Someone put a bomb under the last one when my head of security was tucked up in his fucking bed. You felt that big Mick's collar yet?'

Calloway shook his head. 'He's gone to ground. He's not daft. He'll know the police will want to talk to him and if he does have the connections they say he has, they're the last people he'll want to run into. He'll be across the Irish Sea by now. Or halfway to Boston.'

Spelthorne tutted and shook his head.

'Sounds like you'll be looking for a new job then, son,' he said.

'With respect, sir, I can't find a man that's done a bunk abroad. Unless you want to pay my passage across the Atlantic.'

Spelthorne gazed out of the window, weighing up whether the return would justify the investment. Calloway needed to buy time. If he lost his job now, there would be no way he could stay at the studio long enough to find a bone to throw Special Branch. A bone that would get Bernie and her friends with guns off his back. He took a chance and played the Eve Clark card.

'I'm following another lead,' he said.

Spelthorne looked confused. 'What other lead?'

'Something that connects a studio employee to the damaged equipment.'

This piqued Spelthorne's interest. 'Which studio employee?'

'If I tell you there's a risk they'll do a runner too, and then we'll be no further forward.'

'And you think the damaged equipment is connected to the bomb under my car?'

'I don't know. But I want to look into things further. See if the pieces connect.'

Calloway gathered the evidence in his mind, as if to convince himself that what he'd just told Spelthorne might possibly hold water. There was the woman fleeing the dinner after the explosion, so keen to avoid Calloway, the head of studio security. A woman that bore a striking resemblance to the dead actress Joyce Rose, who kept a copy of a poetry magazine featuring a poet who was also a cleaner at the studio. A cleaner that worked shifts on the weekends before damage to expensive studio equipment was discovered the following Monday.

'Alright,' said Spelthorne. 'You carry on for now, but if you don't bring me something...' he grappled for a word, '...something meaningful, then our deal still stands.'

Before Calloway could enjoy a tiny moment of relief, Spelthorne added, 'Giordano and Franco will be keeping an eye on you for me. You don't mind, do you?'

Another question that wasn't a question at all. Spelthorne wasn't the type that sought approval.

'As you wish, sir,' said Calloway. The 'sir' hurt. 'Actually, I've been meaning to ask something. A security question, if you will. Why do you feel the need for...'

This time Calloway grappled for a word. A word that wasn't goon or gorilla.

'Private security,' he said, nodding at the two knuckle heads that were filling the front of the far from small car. 'What are you afraid of?'

There was a silence, a big hostile silence. Calloway half expected to be turfed out of the car there and then. Possibly without it stopping first. Spelthorne sighed. He turned to Calloway and smiled a tolerant smile, like it was costing more than he wanted to spend on it.

'Not all of us inherited our father's industrial empire like J Arthur Rank,' he said. 'I was raised six to a bed in a hovel off Saffron Hill. My family were Maltese immigrants. Do you know Saffron Hill, Reg?' Calloway shook his head. He'd lived in London less than a year, only three months of that north of the river. 'It's a shit hole. And a lot of the boys from that shit hole have ended up on the wrong side of the law. You must have read the papers.' Calloway nodded. 'That bloke Azzopardi that's just been put away? I grew up with him. And you know what? I reckon he deserves all he gets.' He pointed at Franco and Giordano. 'You want to know why I keep those two dogs close at heel? I'll tell you. I've made a lot of money, Reg. The kind of money boys like Azzopardi and the rest of them would love to get their hands on. Giordano and Franco are there to make sure they don't. You asked what I was afraid of? Try extortion, perhaps even kidnapping. I wouldn't put anything past them.'

He turned away and looked out of the window. They were passing through a bombed-out area to the east of the city. Two tramps with smoke-blackened faces were burning a brazier in the knee-high remains of what could have once been a townhouse. It wasn't especially cold. They just needed a reason to be somewhere that wasn't an alley or a doorway. Some place they could call theirs, in that moment of time.

'I've got where I am the hard way,' said Spelthorne. 'I didn't even have an education, not like that Jewboy Balcon over at Ealing. At least he had some schooling.' He laughed to himself. 'I started out as a stand-up comedian in third-rate variety halls.' He looked at Calloway. 'You can't imagine that, can you?'

Calloway couldn't. Spelthorne didn't strike him as a barrel of laughs. Especially when he was holding the threat of, at best, unemployment and, at worst, a difficult conversation with Giordano and Franco.

'I was the warm-up man for the foot jugglers and the female impersonators. I wasn't the best on the circuit, I have to admit. And I realised it was a mug's game. The club owners were the ones making the money. So I quit. I borrowed a few quid and opened my first club. We had blue comedians and fan dancers. Very pretty girls they were. The punters loved 'em. Soldiers, sailors, travelling salesmen. All sorts. Just wanting a bit of harmless fun. After a while I noticed the boys would hang around the stage door after the show had finished, asking the girls for autographs. Autographs, yeah. Like they were Hollywood stars. Well, I thought, there's an angle here. So I started a sideline selling photographs of the girls. Very artistic they were,' he said, as if hearing Calloway's thoughts out loud. 'We started making as much money from the photographs as we did on the door. I ended up selling the club and building up the pin-up business. I bought a little studio off Dean Street and went out looking for the prettiest girls in Soho. I paid 'em a proper fee,' he said, sensing Calloway's unvoiced thoughts again. He was in his stride now. He shifted on the leather seat to face Calloway. 'Now I'm ambitious. Well you can see that, can't you?' he said, waving a hand around the brand-new Bentley. 'So I expanded into films. Little 8mm reels of fan dancers. Nothing tasteless, just a bit of tease. I did pretty well, what with the films and the photo sets. That's when I started feeling the heat. You start selling films and sooner or later the vice boys at West End Central start taking an interest. Now I wasn't crossing the line, hand on heart. But I still got grief I could have done without. Then,' he said, 'in nineteen twenty-seven, I had a stroke of luck. The Cinematograph Films Act.' He spoke the words in proper RP. 'It required cinemas to show a quota of British films. The yanks had too much hold on the market and the act was supposed to prop up the British film industry. The films didn't even have to be any good. They just had to be made over here. I thought if I can sell fan dancers I can sell something with a few more clothes on. Especially in a market where the supply and demand equation was in my favour. And it would certainly keep the vice boys off my back. So I traded up the studio to something bigger, moved from 8mm to 35mm, got some old frocks from Angels & Bermans and started making historical romances. I already had a stable of pretty girls and some of 'em could act.' He reflected a moment. 'Well, they could at least deliver a few lines while looking the part. I advertised for writers, and there's no shortage of those needing a hot meal. Then someone introduced me to Roberta.' Bobbie Brand, the director in Joyce's home movies. 'She'd been making silent films, but since the talkies came in, she couldn't get the work. Not for love nor money. The studios didn't want women directors once the stakes were raised. Didn't trust 'em to be good enough. But I didn't have any choice. I was a nobody. So I offered her a job and she bit my hand off. She directed my first production.'

Spelthorne gazed out of the car window, remembering, with a satisfied look on his face. He turned to Calloway and pointed at him, as if accusing him of an unspoken criticism.

'Now others will tell you that the quickie was the lowest form of the film maker's art. Turned out as a necessity with no care or attention. The yanks would fund them just so they could get their Hollywood stuff in British cinemas. Some of them were so bad they didn't bother advertising. They used to screen 'em at breakfast time until the magistrates put the block on that. People in this business will say no one made a penny out of quickies. Not true.' He prodded his chest. 'I did. Yeah, I did alright. How? I took 'em seriously. Granted, the first few weren't so good. I was still using show girls as leading ladies. They couldn't act for shit, if I'm honest. But then I started getting some decent actors. Like Neville Wilde. You know him?'

Calloway did. Since taking the job, he'd dispatched a succession of women home in cabs who'd found themselves abandoned in Wilde's dressing room in a state of post-coital ambiguity.

'That boy Wilde was on his uppers when I spotted him. I knew the club scene, you see, and I knew he was selling himself at dance halls to middle-aged women whose husbands had long since lost interest in them. But Bobbie told me he was good. She remembered him from the theatre in the twenties. So I got him on contract. He still put it about with the old birds now and again, mind you. I guess he'd just got a taste for it.' Giordano sniggered. His big shoulders moved in time with his laughter. 'I got some good writers too. You can always get them cheap but you need to get the good ones. Terence Rattigan, Eric Ambler, Noël Coward? They've all written for Centurion. And I'd got Bobbie. Now she may be a girl, but she's a real asset. Knows her craft. She can make a better picture for ten grand than other studios can make for fifty. The other studios? They were spending three times what I was on quickies and not making a penny. I was making real money. I knew where to get the talent cheap and...' He paused for a moment and looked Calloway in the eye. 'Now this is really important. I knew the audience. They don't want to go out and watch high art. They want escape. In fact half of 'em just want three hours in a heated room with velvet seats.' He tapped his chest again. 'I know poverty, you see. I've lived it. I know what it means to seek respite from the squalor. Warmth, velvet seats and something just engaging enough to take their minds off the drudgery of life. That's what I sell, Calloway. Not dreams, or whimsies. I offer them escape.'

He pulled a cigar from his breast pocket and passed it to Giordano. The big goon unclasped a knife, the kind that's far too big for sharpening pencils, and cut the nub off before passing it back to his boss. Spelthorne lit up and sank back into the soft upholstery, in a cloud of his own smoke.

'A stroke of luck, a lot of hard graft and here I am,' he said.

He drew on the cigar and rolled the smoke around his puffy cheeks.

'And no fucker, Maltese, Irish or otherwise, is going to take it off me.'

SIXTEEN

The Bentley rumbled over cobbles in a narrow side street somewhere near Tooley Street. They drove alongside the high warehouse walls which cast long shadows across the road in the fading light. Franco turned off the road towards a set of dock gates. A Port of London policeman recognised the car and waved them through. Franco steered the Bentley between wharfside buildings towards the quay.

The Pool of London. The black heart of London docks through which flowed the flotsam and jetsam of six continents. Seamen from Marseille to Macao. Transient and rootless. At home in any port, yet strangers where they dock. All nations, all races. Liberians, Lascars and Latvians. Saint Lucians, Swedes and Senegalese. Hardened by the sea, loosened by drink, quick with their fists. And the dockers. Local men with a strict code. A law unto themselves. The pulsating arteries of the black market.

The Bentley looked incongruous. Franco parked and the four men climbed out. Spelthorne slipped a ten-bob note to a docker to mind the car. He looked up at the big dock crane that loomed over them.

'Don't go dropping any bales on it,' he said.

Calloway followed the three men along the quayside. Lights shone ahead of them. Then he saw the cameras. Cast and crew on location. Shooting at night. Bobbie Brand was wearing a sheepskin coat over heavy tweed trousers, with warm wool socks tucked into hacking boots. She conferred with the camera operator, peered through the range finder, consulted with the continuity girl. Calloway recognised the girl. Her name was Liz Francis. He knew her from his last job. She'd helped him, and in return he'd handed her a decent sum of money that she was owed. She'd used it to start a new life. She deserved one. She'd had more than her share of knocks. This life looked good for her. She looked up and saw him. She smiled and waved. Bobbie Brand dismissed her and returned to the set. Liz walked over to Calloway, beaming.

'Hello you,' she said.

'Hello you too,' he said.

She gave him a polite peck on the cheek.

'So how's the job going?' she said.

Liz had tipped him off that Centurion needed a new security boss. That was a few months back. Calloway was more than grateful. Liz said she owed him that at least. He'd not seen her since though.

'It's three months in and I'm still here,' he said. But for how much longer, he thought. 'Is this The Rebel Gun?'

He gestured towards the cluster of bodies under the harsh lighting.

She nodded. 'The continuity girl went sick so I got the job. I'd been pestering Bobbie long enough. She asked me if I'd fill in.'

'Going well?'

'I'm a bag of nerves,' she said.

'You look like you know what you're doing.'

She laughed. 'Well that's a start, eh?'

She fished in the pocket of her coat and pulled out a pack of Craven A. She offered Calloway one and lit up for the pair of them.

'So what brings you here?' she said. 'I see you got a ride in Sidney's car.'

'The perks of the job,' he said.

Perks that came at a price, he thought. He glanced over at his boss. Spelthorne was conferring with Bobbie Brand. They perched side by side on canvas chairs marked Director and Producer. Spelthorne had a cigar in one hand and a hip flask in the other. He took a nip without offering one to Bobbie.

Bright lights shone on the freighter moored along the quayside in front of them. One of the stars of The Rebel Gun stood on the gang plank with a kit bag on his shoulder. He was dressed in a reefer jacket and watch cap. He was skinny and fey. He made an unconvincing seaman. Bobbie Brand was discussing the composition of the scene, gesticulating and shouting instruction to the cameraman. The assistant director scurried back and forth between Bobbie and the engineers in the sound van. Another man was measuring the distance between the actors and the camera's lens with a tape measure. Bobbie returned to her chair. The microphone on its boom swung into place over the lot. The clapper boy positioned himself between the camera and the actor. Bobbie shouted, 'Roll 'em!' The clapper boy called out the scene number and snapped the clapper shut. The fey-looking actor stumbled on the gang plank, dropped his kitbag and swore. Bobbie shouted, 'Cut!'

'I reckon you're better off on this side of the camera,' Calloway said.

'Well I was never going to get anywhere on the other side, let's face it.'

When Calloway first met Liz, she'd just dropped out of the Centurion charm school. To him, the continuity job sounded preferable to a life spent parading around Ivor Cole's publicity pageants.

'Did you know Joyce Rose at the charm school?' he said.

'Joyce?' she said. His question seemed incongruous and she frowned. 'Why d'you want to know about Joyce?'

'She's connected to something I'm looking into. A problem at the studio. I'm not sure how she fits in exactly, but there are some coincidences I need explanations for.' He took a long draw on the cigarette. The tobacco tingled his nerves. He exhaled and said, 'It's not like she's around to ask.'

'No she isn't, poor cow. Whatever possessed her to do what she did?'

'From what I've read in the press reports, she was in quite a state in the months leading to her death. Living off pills and hard liquor. So did you know her?'

She looked concerned. 'You're not getting involved again, are you?'

She knew enough about his last job to know that he was the type that got in deeper than was good for him.

'It's fine,' he said, not at all sure that it was. 'Just studio business.'

'If you say so, Reggie,' she said, looking dubious.

She took a last drag on the cigarette and threw the butt into the dock. 'Joyce and I crossed over at the charm school for a couple of months. She was getting ready to leave when I joined. She'd just got her first role.' She laughed. 'She was one of the few girls that actually appeared in a film.'

She pulled her coat collar tight. It was dark now and the damp air was cold. She took his arm and they walked along the dock edge.

'She was Spelthorne's favourite,' she said.

'He seems to like a starlet on his arm.'

Liz shook her head. 'Joyce was different. She was his special one. He took her everywhere. Premiers, gala dinners, parties. He had the cigars, he had the car, he had the whole studio. Joyce completed the look.'

'Were they lovers?'

Liz thought for a moment. 'You know, I was never really sure. I suppose I just assumed so, at least at first. Especially given his fondness for having pretty girls on his arm, as you so delicately put it.'

Calloway felt a twinge of awkwardness as they walked arm in arm. She sensed this and looked up at him.

'This is different. We're pals,' she said and gave him a friendly nudge. 'Thinking about it, I'm not sure anything was going on. Joyce didn't seem the type. She was always slightly aloof. Focused on the job, you know. Especially when she got her break on her first film. Some of the girls just go along with it. Like it's expected of them. Especially the needy ones. The ones whose insecurities get the better of their judgement.'

She read his thoughts.

'Yeah. The ones like me,' she said.

He gave her arm a squeeze. 'We've all got pasts Liz. Now you've got a future, if you play your cards right. I reckon Bobbie likes you.'

She held up crossed fingers. 'Here's hoping.'

They walked for a moment in silence. It was dark now and they were in a quiet part of the docks. A steam whistle sounded in the distance. Liz shivered with the cold and leant into him.

'Did Joyce have any family, apart from the parents she lost in the war?' he said.

Liz thought about this for a moment. 'She mentioned once that she had a sister. She lived in France, I think.'

'A sister called Yvonne?'

The name on the postcards from Paris.

'That rings a bell.'

A sister in Paris. Where Eve Clark lived until eighteen months ago. Another coincidence that brought him no closer to an explanation.

'Did you ever meet the sister?'

'No. I hardly knew Joyce to be honest.'

'Ever see her later, when she was going off the rails?'

She shook her head. 'I'd quit the charm school by then. All I know is what was in the papers.'

They'd done a circuit of the wharfside and were now walking back towards the cast and crew. The cameras were running. Bobbie Brand sat in the director's chair, her eyes fixed on the action. Two actors were playing out their scene on the quay while their tall shadows danced on the rust-streaked hulk of the freighter. Calloway noticed that Spelthorne's Bentley was gone. He swore under his breath.

'Looks like you're making your own way back,' said Liz.

Bobbie Brand shot Liz a look which said get yourself over here. Liz gave her a quick, apologetic nod.

'I've got to go,' she said.

Calloway looked at his watch. There was just time to get back to the studio to check whether the cine film from Joyce Rose's camera had been processed before he returned to North Soho.

'It's been good to see you, Liz. I'm glad to see things starting to work out for you.'

She squeezed his arm. 'It's all thanks to you Reg. Without that money you passed me I'd still be holed up in that tenement on the Old Kent Road. Now I've got my own bedsit north of the river. Who knows, I might even make a go of all this,' she said, nodding towards Bobbie and the crew before giving him another peck on the cheek.

He walked out of the dockyard, down Tooley Street and over Tower Bridge towards Wapping Wall. The sky was black and the meagre street lighting ineffective against the darkness. He entered Wapping station and descended the dark, spiralling staircase, with its dripping brick walls lit by flashes of electricity from the electrified rails of the East London Line below. If Centurion ever made a horror movie, they should film it here, he thought. He rode the line until it terminated at Shoreditch, then walked through the chill to the studio. The main gates were locked. He let himself in the small side entrance that the big stars used to avoid the crowds out front. The cobbled yard of the old brewery was empty, the cars of the more senior staff gone for the evening. Studios A and B were dark, filming stopped for the day or, in the case of The Rebel Gun, on location down at the docks. The only sound was the eternal hum of the six diesel generators in the powerhouse.

His footsteps echoed along the corridor of the now empty administration building. There was a light on behind the door of his office. There shouldn't have been. He'd left the studio in daylight. He listened at the door. A faint scratching sound came from inside. He clasped his hand around the door handle slowly, swearing under his breath as the lock clicked loudly in the silence. The scratching behind the door stopped. He heard light footsteps. He braced himself, then gave the door a shove and stepped inside. A hand grabbed his wrist and twisted his arm until he felt his elbow joint was about to snap. He doubled over with the pain and felt a sharp chop to his forearm and again to his upper arm. He cried out in anticipation of his bones snapping. He took a harder blow to the back of the neck and another to his kidneys. The pain was intense, like his nerves were being stripped from inside him. He couldn't think. He hadn't the strength in that moment to respond. He slumped to the ground and lay on his side, doubled with pain. Then he took a boot in his guts which made the bile rise in his throat until he choked. He forced his eyes open to see his assailant, but they were gone, their swift footsteps echoing down the empty corridor. He tried to raise himself from the floor, but he couldn't summon the strength. He lay back, limp, and let the black cloak of unconsciousness engulf him.

***

He lifted his arm as best he could and checked his watch. He'd been out cold for half an hour. He checked the arm for a break. It was in still in one piece. He raised himself onto his hands and knees and cried out as a searing pain shot through his kidneys and neck simultaneously. Whoever had clobbered him knew what they were doing. Once on his feet he limped over to his desk. The drawer was still locked. A pair of lock-picking tools lay on the floor beneath it. Whoever he'd interrupted had not had the chance to get the drawer open. He pulled out his keys. Pain shot up his arm and he winced. He unlocked the drawer, gritting his teeth. The purse the fleeing woman had dropped on the night of the explosion was still there. So were the cine films and the bottle of Black & White. He pulled out the stopper and drank from the bottle. The warm liquor soothed him. He sat back in his chair. The hard wooden chair back pressed into his kidneys. He let out a squeal. Damn them. Whoever the hell they were, they were fucking experts. He swallowed down more of the scotch, trying to make sense of things.

What had the intruder wanted? The films? They were innocuous enough. The purse? There was nothing in that you wouldn't expect. He pulled the purse from the drawer and emptied its contents. Everything was there, just as before. Lipstick, compact, mirror, handkerchief, a little cash and the tortoise shell pencil. He ran his fingers around the lining of the purse, thinking there may have been a compartment or opening of some kind. But there was nothing. He scooped everything back into the drawer and locked it. Twisting the key hurt his wrist. Lifting the whisky bottle hurt his forearm. Leaning back in the chair hurt his kidneys and his neck felt like someone had yanked out both his collar bones and tied them in a knot. It was a miracle, or at least a testament to his thick hide, that nothing was broken.

He swallowed down more of the scotch. He didn't hurt any less, but he felt better. He eased himself out of the chair, switched off the desk lamp and left the office, locking the door behind him. There was no point making a search of the studio. Whoever had floored him would be long gone. He abandoned the idea of returning to Eve Clark's North Soho digs and took a bus home. The bus rumbled over cobbles and jolted at potholes, its every movement hurting Calloway somewhere. He alighted at Kingsland Road and walked to Da Costa's factory. Climbing the three flights of bare concrete steps to his attic room was an endeavour. If they ever conquered Everest, the last hundred feet couldn't feel worse than this, he thought.

Once inside the room he lit the gas fire, poured a hefty measure of gin into the tooth mug and collapsed onto the iron bed. The springs creaked under his weight. The sound they made was how his bones and muscles felt. Through the pain he tried again to make sense of events over the last few days.

Bernie and her republican friends weren't the bombers. He had figured that much, even if Special Branch hadn't. He couldn't shake the thought that the woman who'd dropped the purse was the key to everything. The dead actress, the postcards from France, the poet-turned-cleaner and the damaged studio equipment. Instinct told him they were all connected.

Sleep tugged at his eyelids. The air was warm and dry, the gas fire sucking the oxygen from the room. He tried to rearrange the pieces into a pattern that made more sense, but the gin he'd gulped from the tooth mug conspired with fatigue from the beating to drag him into an uncomfortable sleep.

SEVENTEEN

They stood at the southern end of Kingsland High Street. Calloway, Marge, Johnny and around thirty members of the 43 Group. A real tough-looking mob. Two ex-commandos, three paras, a burly chief petty officer and a platoon's worth of ex-soldiers, sailors and airmen. Johnny introduced Calloway to some of his comrades. There was Reg Morris, an ex-guardsman who was so good looking he worked as a stand-in for Stewart Granger. There were the Goldberg brothers, a tough and intimidating pair who were veterans of pre-war battles against the Mosleyites. And there was a neat and keen-eyed youth who worked as an apprentice hairdresser called Vidal Sassoon.

'You want to watch Sassoon,' Johnny said to Calloway. 'Always carries a pair of scissors.'

The lad patted his breast pocket and winked at Calloway.

Two dozen locals had also turned out in support, including a formidable-looking man known only as Big Arthur. The East End was the fascists' stomping ground but there were plenty there who'd sooner see the back of them.

Calloway still hurt from the beating. A street fight was the last thing he needed. But something compelled him to be there. It wasn't Marge this time. She hadn't needed to persuade him. When she told him about the next fascist meeting, he'd said he would be there without a second thought. Whether it was memories of the camp stirred up by that article, or the ease at which Spelthorne made Jewboy comments about his competitors, he couldn't tell. He felt it was right to be there, plain and simple. But no, he thought, it was more than that. He was feeling the pressure, from Bryant, Bernie, Franco and

Giordano. The pressure needed an outlet. He knew himself well enough to know it was only a matter of time before the pressure turned to anger and anger turned to violence. That's how he was. It wasn't good to be around him when it happened. He hated himself for it, but he knew no way to avoid it. If the violence broke through at the wrong time or with the wrong person, he'd be in deeper trouble than he was already. Tonight seemed as good an opportunity as any to get it out of his system.

He'd met Johnny and a few of the group members in Lyons Corner House. That's where they always did their planning so that they looked innocuous. A handful of pals meeting for coffee. Johnny suggested tactics. The others had agreed. This time Calloway would lead the first wedge. First in, he thought. Johnny's wedge would follow up once the podium was upturned.

Jeffrey Hamm was on the stage, a repeat performance of his last speech in full flow, only this time he was upping the ante. Instead of euphemisms for the targets of his hate, he was coming straight out with it, showing true colours as he stood between the union jacks that flanked the stage. He spoke of the Great Jewish Plot, the Jewish terrorists killing 'our boys' in Palestine and the need to break the hold of the Jews running Britain.

A fascist in the crowd shouted, 'Let's finish what Hitler started.'

Johnny turned to Calloway. 'Can you fucking believe this?' he said. 'It's like we fought six years for nothing.'

'It wasn't for nothing,' said Calloway. 'But it looks like we didn't finish the job.'

Johnny clapped him on the back. Calloway should have winced. The bruising from the beating had come up badly overnight, but adrenalin must have been surprising the pain.

'Ready?' said Johnny.

Calloway nodded. He looked into the eyes of every man in his wedge. There were thumbs-up all round.

They went in hard, shoving Hamm's supporters over like a

wrecking ball through a bomb-site wall and thumping them as they toppled. Hamm hesitated as the wave of fascists parted and Calloway's wedge advanced. But he resumed his rant, whether through bravado or stupidity Calloway couldn't tell. There was only one way this was going to end, he thought, and Hamm would wish he'd jumped from the platform sooner. Why was he standing there shouting and looking smug? Then Calloway heard a scream. The kind of scream he'd not heard since the war. He looked to his left and saw one of his wedge, the burly chief petty officer, clutching his bleeding face. Another scream, this time to his right. One of the ex-commandos had stopped on his tracks. Blood gushed from a three-inch gash on his face. He was looking round, eager to get his hands on a fascist with a blade, but there was none to be seen. This time Calloway felt it. A sharp nick to the side of his head, an inch or so from his eye. Moments before he'd seen something scudding towards him from the direction of the stage. Now he saw the attackers. Behind the platform big men in sharp suits were hurling potatoes with razor blades stuck in them. Dirty bastards. Calloway's wedge and Johnny's behind them were taking heavy casualties. There was blood everywhere and it wasn't fascist blood. Hamm's supporters had thinned out, as if the whole operation was orchestrated. He heard Johnny shout, 'Get the fuck out of here.' He was about to turn and run when he saw two faces he recognised.

Giordano and Franco.

Spelthorne's two goons were part of the mob throwing blades. Calloway froze. It didn't make sense. Two worlds had collided. Spelthorne's and Hamm's. Why should they connect? He heard Johnny shout, 'Cab. Get your wedge out of here.'

The two wedges ran down Ridley Road away from their attackers. Some of the fascists pursued them, but not many. The rest seemed happy to let the men with the blades do the dirty work. Two Black Marias appeared ahead of them. Their doors flew open and two dozen police ran towards them, whistles blowing and truncheons raised.

'Double back and head down Dalston Lane,' Johnny

shouted. This took them headlong into the half dozen fascists pursuing them. The two wedges set about them hard. Their blood was up. So was Calloway's. The switch had flicked. He grabbed one by the lapels and butted him so hard the sound of his nose breaking echoed off the walls. He smacked the fascist's chin up with the flat of his hand and planted his knee in his groin, just like he'd been trained. The fascist slumped to the pavement clutching his balls. Calloway kicked him hard in the kidneys. The fascist bellowed in pain. Then he summoned courage. From the ground where he lay he shouted up at Calloway, defiant.

'Wir kommen wieder!'

We will be back.

The accent was guttural Bavarian. Calloway had interrogated enough enemy prisoners to know. For a second he was confused. His past enveloped him. He was at war again. He raised his boot and stamped hard on the German's face.

'Reg,' shouted Johnny. 'Transport. Let's go.'

Three taxi cabs were heading towards them down Dalston Lane. Marge stood on the running board of one of them, clinging to the cab with one hand and beckoning Calloway, Johnny and their boys with the other. They piled into the three cabs, which each turned on a sixpence and headed east towards Dalston Junction. When they were clear of the action, he heard Marge shout, 'Pull over, Solly.' The cab driver obeyed the instruction and Marge climbed in the back of the taxi.

'Room for a little one?' she said.

She squeezed into the back seat next to Calloway.

'What the fuck was that all about?' said Johnny.

'Ted just got word from our man,' said Marge.

Ted Nathan, one of the group's intelligence officers. He'd been at the briefing in Lyons Corner House. 'Our man' was one of the group's agents.

'The boys with the blades were from a Maltese gang,' she said. 'Hired muscle.'

A Maltese gang. The very people Spelthorne employed Giordano and Franco to protect him from.

'Maltese?' said Johnny. 'Are they Hamm's supporters?'

'Ted reckons not,' said Marge. 'He says the Italian fascists supported the pro-Italians in Malta before the war, but there's no evidence of London's Maltese having fascist affiliations. They were just guns for hire.'

'Spuds for hire more like,' said one of the wedge, holding a handkerchief to his face to stem the flow of blood. Everyone laughed. It broke the tension.

Calloway said, 'One of the fascists was German.'

The others showed little surprise. Marge said, 'He'll be a POW from the camp in Victoria Park, most likely. The fascists sometimes set up on the corner of Gore Road to tap up the inmates when they're let out in the evenings.'

'Some of them were Waffen SS,' said Johnny. 'There's supposed to be a de-Nazification programme in the camp.' In the darkness of the taxi Calloway saw Johnny roll his eyes. 'Yeah,' he said. 'Like that's gonna work. The fascists are recruiting them. They've been turning up to the meetings for a few months now.'

Calloway shook his head. It was too much. British fascists and German Nazis, in London, side by side. Swastikas daubed on local walls, Nazi stickers on shop windows. Beatings and fire bombings. Six years of fucking war and now this, in his adopted neighbourhood. He shifted in his seat and winced. He remembered that he hurt all over. And now he had a gash on the side of his head.

Marge read his pain.

'Let's have a look,' she said, taking the hand he was using to press a handkerchief to the wound and pulling it away gently. She peered at the wound. 'You'll live,' she said. 'But you need to get that cleaned up. Then I'll find you a part as a Prussian officer and we can pretend it's a duelling scar.'

'You'd make a good Prussian, I reckon,' said Johnny. 'All straight backed and strait laced.'

'Someone's got to be,' said Calloway. 'This world's more rotten than ever.'

'You can say that again,' said Johnny.

The cab turned off Dalston Lane into Kingsland Road.

'Do you have any iodine?' said Marge, looking at Calloway.

'I think so,' he said.

He had what was left of a first aid kit somewhere.

She tapped on the glass behind the driver. 'Drop us here, Solly,' she shouted. 'I'm going to help patch up Reg.'

'Alright for some,' said one of the group, from the darkness on the cab.

Marge took his arm as they walked into the narrow cobbled lane. There were no lights on in Da Costa's factory ahead of them. The machinists had clocked off for the night. She nuzzled into him as they walked through the gloom of the lone street lamp.

'I'm sorry I got you onto all this,' she said.

'You didn't,' he said. 'I got myself into it. And don't be sorry. What you and your group are doing needs to be done. I know. I've seen where this leads if it's not stopped. Like Johnny said, never again.'

'The Maltese gang is a new twist,' she said.

'Hamm and his boys are rattled. It means what you're doing is working.'

'What we're doing,' she said, correcting him.

They stood in front of Da Costa's door.

'This is your place, isn't it?'

'I'm three floors up and there's not much to look forward to when you get there,' he said. 'I've got a bottle of gin and a tooth mug. The tooth mug tastes of cloves.'

'I adore cloves,' she said.

'I'm quite keen on gin. Especially after a night like tonight.'

Their footsteps echoed off the bare brick walls as they climbed the darkened stairway. Marge held his arm tightly. He unlocked the door to his attic room and flicked on the light. For the first time he saw the room through another's eyes. It was dismal. A single bare bulb hung from the ceiling casting a dingy glow over old utility furniture. His two suits and best overcoat hung on hooks in an alcove. There were no pictures on the walls, no ornaments, no personal touches. Even a barrack room had pin-ups. Calloway's attic had nothing. It wasn't damp, being so high up, but the cold air smelled faintly of gas from the fire and coal tar soap from the bar he washed with over the old stone sink. The only sign of any pride in his surroundings was the presence of a pair of worn but highly polished leather shoes that stood beside his bed. He felt Marge shudder.

'I'll light the fire,' he said. 'There's a bottle of Beefeater on the shelf. Perhaps you could pour us a couple of large ones.'

She found two mugs, poured the gin and passed one to him. He knocked it back in a single gulp and she did the same. She refilled the mugs and they drank the gin straight down again. His adrenalin subsided and the alcohol took its place. It calmed him. It heightened his senses. He smelled her scent and felt her warmth. Being close felt good. It was what he needed. He wanted to hold her. No, to be held by her. In that moment he felt a vulnerability that only she could soothe. It frightened him. He craved closeness but he feared himself too. His volatility. He drew away.

'I'll get that iodine,' he said.

She laughed. 'Don't bother. The cut's just a scratch.'

'But...'

'A ruse, darling. Remember that poem?'

'I remember.'

'You look tired, luvvie,' she said.

She nodded towards the bed. 'Go and lie down.'

He gave in. He was tired. He wanted to lie down. With her. The fear could go to hell.

She switched off the overhead light, crossed the room and started to undress in the orange glow of the gas fire. He lay on the bed watching her.

'Lucky for you I'm not shy, isn't it, darling,' she said, holding his gaze.

'I figured that out some time ago,' he said.

He unbuttoned his shirt and threw it into the corner, then pulled his vest over his head, trying to ignore the pain from the bruising. Marge noticed the dark patches on his flesh where the blows had struck him. She must have assumed he'd picked them up during the fracas in Ridley Road.

'Poor Reg. Look at you. I still can't help thinking this is my fault.'

He would maintain the pretence that he'd been hurt scrapping with the fascists. Telling her about the beating in his office, and the threats from Bernie, and the threats from Spelthorne and the obsession with the woman that fled the explosion, was all going to be far too complicated to explain.

'I told you,' he said. 'I know what I'm doing.'

She climbed onto the bed next to him. He felt her warmth against his hurting body. She kissed him full on the lips, hungrily, intrusively, leaving no doubt that she knew what she was doing too.

'Am I still being played?' he said.

She pressed her lips against his ear and whispered, 'Yes, darling. But this time it's a different game altogether.'

EIGHTEEN

There was a queue around the block. It was always the same when Centurion advertised for extras. Two hundred men and women, shabby and in need of a free meal, lined up along the old brewery walls waiting to be checked in by the commissionaires. The wardrobe department had set up trestle tables in the studio's courtyard. Each table held a different item of clothing. Coats, jackets, trousers, skirts, hats. Wardrobe girls handed out the appropriate items as the extras filed past the tables towards the dressing rooms. Kitchen staff from the cafeteria handed out cardboard lunch boxes from a large metal trolley. A pork pie, bread and cheese, tart and bicarbonate of soda for indigestion. Calloway saw the looks of relief on the hungry faces as they took the boxes in their hands. The sight of it disturbed him. The scene had echoes of his war. Prisoners, refugees, the wounded. They were all made to queue.

He left the courtyard and climbed the stairs to his office. It was still tainted by the lingering smell of Belcher's pipe. He opened a window and lit a cigarette. There was a package on his desk. The processed film from the laboratory. He still had the projector. He wound the film onto the spool and ran it through the machine, then closed the blind to shut out what passed for daylight on the overcast and misty autumn day. The film flickered into life.

Joyce looked older. Heavily made up, masking a tired face that had lost the sparkle of the previous two reels. Forced smiles. Hum-drum openings and graceless exchanges. Glad-handing dignitaries. A flash bulb. Recoiling slightly. Not on form. Cut to a party. A small event. An apartment or hotel room. Half a dozen starlets. A handful of men, middle-aged, suited, flash. One wearing correspondent shoes. Arms around the girls. Girls sitting on the men's knees. Squeezing girls. Pawing girls. Girls with tolerant smiles. Professional smiles. Joyce among them. Staggering. Drunk or pilled. The man in the correspondent shoes grabs her. Squeezes her. Calloway reads his lips. Have a drink. Don't be a kill-joy. Let your hair down. It's a party. How about a dance? They dance. Joyce is clumsy. Flaccid. Dazed. The man's annoyed. He turns full face to the camera and rolls his eyes.

Calloway's arm shot towards the projector. He flicked the switch. The frame froze. Joyce stared out at him, her face set with a pained smile. The man she danced with stared out too. Hair slicked back from a widow's peak. Neatly trimmed sideburns framing a long, mean face. The eyes of a reptile with a bird in its sights. Calloway recognised him from the newspapers.

Alfredo Azzopardi. Vice ring boss. Jailed for eight years.

He snapped up the blind and lit another cigarette. He waited for the nicotine to soothe him so he could think. First Spelthorne tells him he lives in fear of criminals from the London Maltese community he grew up with. Then Franco and Giordano show up at the fascist meeting, part of a Maltese gang hired as muscle. Now a convicted Maltese gang boss is dancing with Joyce Rose, Spelthorne's favourite starlet, in the final reel of the dead actress's cine film diary. For a man claiming to fear such people, Spelthorne seemed uncomfortably close to them. Calloway's brown-job copper's nose told him things didn't smell right. He rifled through his wastepaper basket and pulled out the newspaper. There was Azzopardi's face. A mug shot, cold and detached, but undoubtedly the same face as the man in the film. He rolled up the paper and pushed it into his jacket pocket, pulled the plug on the projector and left the office.

Tony from casting was organising the extras in the courtyard.

'Spare me a moment?' said Calloway.

The young man gave an apologetic wince, as if he was too

busy to speak.

'I need to get this lot into Studio A. They're tucking into their lunch boxes already and we've not even started.'

Calloway gripped his arm and moved him away from the crowd. Tony looked nervous. Calloway walked him towards the power house where the hum of the generators would shield their conversation from passers-by.

Tony said, 'Look here Mr Calloway, I really don't have time for whatever this is.'

Calloway gripped his arm tighter. 'Humour me,' he said.

He felt like the school bully, intimidating this weak little man. But he needed some answers.

'I visited Joyce Rose's old flat,' he said. 'The manager told me that you once got yourself roughed up by the driver of one of her visitors.'

This gave Tony start. 'Why the hell are you bringing that up?'

'Studio business. There's a few things I need to make sense of. Let's call them irregularities. I need to know about your late friend Joyce and her trouble with ugly men in fancy shoes.'

The description of the men struck a chord with Tony. He side-stepped it. 'Why drag up Joyce's past? Good god, man, she's been dead for over a year. Can't you let her rest in peace?'

Calloway ignored him.

'Tell me about the men that called at Joyce's flat. Tell me why you confronted one of them and why it earned you a beating.'

Tony looked uncomfortable. He tried to pull away. Calloway squeezed his arm harder.

'That's none of your business,' he said with unconvincing bravura. Calloway leaned in towards him and pressed his mouth to the young man's ear.

'Everything's my business, son,' he said.

The humming from the power house was relentless. It rumbled like nearing thunder, ominous and unsettling. Calloway raised his voice above it.

'I need to know how Joyce was connected to those men.'

He pulled the newspaper from his pocket and held up

Azzopardi's picture for Tony to see. 'This man in particular.'

Calloway loosened his grip on the young man's arm. 'Now be a good lad and tell me what happened.'

Tony looked as if he was about to run. His eyes darted towards the crowd of extras, as if they might offer him some sanctuary from Calloway's questions. Then he sighed and looked defeated. Calloway felt the puny arm muscles relax beneath his grip.

'Alright,' Tony said. 'But not here.'

'Where then?'

Tony thought for a moment. 'Do you know the S&F Grill on Denman Street?'

'I can find it.'

'Meet me there at five o'clock. I'll be finished here by then.'

The S&F Grill was a coffee shop in a side street off Piccadilly Circus, a few yards from the Windmill Theatre. It was light and airy and sold good coffee, for which Calloway was grateful. He had arrived early and nursed a cupful until Tony showed. As he waited, a gaggle of bright young things took up their regular tables. They were noisy and animated. The place attracted a film and theatre crowd, Calloway had heard, and these types looked the part. He recognised some of the faces, although he couldn't name them. A handsome jack-the-lad with black hair piled high on his head was hamming up a crafty cockney routine a little too obviously. A platinum blonde held court among a table of admirers, one of whom held her arm possessively, her boyfriend, Calloway assumed. Another boy, athletic looking with a long face and overly large chin, complained about losing a much-needed part in a new comedy to a worn-out has-been twice his age.

When Tony arrived just after five, he noticed the young film types immediately. They recognised him, waved and said hi, beckoning him to join them. He smiled back but looked uncomfortable. He squeezed past their tables towards Calloway.

'We can't talk here. I know these people. We'll have to go somewhere else.'

Calloway nodded. 'Alright,' he said, pulling two shillings from his pocket and leaving them on the table. 'Any suggestion where?'

Soho was unfamiliar to him. He didn't socialise. He didn't go to clubs or theatres or the girly shows. Since living in London, he'd never had much call to frequent the capital's seedy playground.

'I know a place,' said Tony. 'A few minutes from here.'

He nodded at the young actors. 'Somewhere this crowd doesn't go.'

They left the grill and walked east through the busy Soho streets. The light was fading and the neon signs glowed through the gloom like beacons. They lured expectant punters with the promise of excitement that would, in Calloway's experience of such places around the world from his army days, turn out to be an expensive disappointment.

The two men turned left off Old Compton Street and walked a few yards until Tony pointed to an anonymous-looking doorway set back from the pavement behind two dustbins overfilled with beer bottles.

'Up here,' he said, leading Calloway up a darkened staircase whose meagre lighting failed to illuminate its dirty, peeling walls. Calloway caught the smell of damp, mingled with cigarette smoke and a hint of cheap cologne. They reached a door. Behind it there was noise. Tony led Calloway inside. The decor was fake colonial, with bamboo screens, high stools and tropical houseplants spilling over the mirror-backed shelves of a tiny cocktail bar that ran along the wall towards two tall windows. A stern-faced diva who was perched on the nearest bar stool glared at them between deep drags on the cigarette she held high between long, slender fingers. She was masculine and feminine all at once, part Googie Withers, part Robert Helpmann. Tony gestured towards Calloway and said, 'This is Reg. He's my guest.'

The diva looked Calloway up and down, weighing up whether to admit him to her club.

'And Reg is...?' she said.

Calloway answered. 'I run security at the studios where Tony works.'

She raised her plucked and pencilled eyebrows. She could have been sceptical, impressed or bored. Calloway couldn't tell. He wasn't used to these types. He looked around the club. Rakes, rogues and reprobates the lot of them. He doubted any of them were holding down steady work. Artists, writers, actors, that sort. Cadgers and scroungers, who compensated for their financial embarrassments with flamboyant dress and camp exuberance. Homosexuals, men in suede shoes, women in berets with cigarette holders. A black pianist clunking thorough jazz standards that no one seemed to be listening to. A Liverpudlian seamen talking jazz and telling filthy stories. And all of this at five-thirty in the afternoon.

'Head of security, eh?' said the diva. 'We could do with someone like you. Keep the wrong sort out.'

Calloway glanced around the room. 'And what do you consider the wrong sort?'

The diva frowned at him. 'The police of course, cunty.'

Tony winced and felt the need to interject. 'That's her term of endearment, by the way,' he said, looking apologetic.

'I'd hate to hear her term of abuse,' said Calloway.

'They're much the same, actually,' said Tony laughing too hard.

The diva nodded and blew smoke at Calloway. 'In you go,' she said and turned away, as if utterly bored by their brief exchange.

Tony bought two bottled beers and gestured to an empty table by the window which offered a degree of privacy. The background hubbub would be loud enough to drown their conversation.

'So you're a member here?' Calloway said.

Tony nodded. 'For a few months now. It's not been open long. I used to drink at the White Room until the Rank crowd took it over. That lot back at the S&F,' he said, to clarify who he meant. 'Too full of themselves. Not really my type. I like it better here. The members are a rum lot but it's easy enough to fit in once you've had a few.'

'Not very pukka though, is it?' said Calloway. 'I thought you were the more the country club type.'

'Don't let the tweeds and cravat fool you, Mr Calloway. I'm just another film business flake that acts above his station. My parents were strictly below-stairs folk. In service all their working lives. Mother's too old for domestic work now. Since father died we've been sharing a basement flat at the back of Euston station.'

'Not the marrying kind then?' Calloway said, using a euphemism he'd heard around the studio.

Tony looked embarrassed, then laughed. 'Actually I'm very much the marrying kind. I've just not had much luck. Living with mother doesn't help, but it's a financial necessity.'

'I'm sure it is, at these prices,' said Calloway, nodding towards the bar.

Tony laughed to himself. 'I'm surrounded by beautiful girls all day long. It's ironic isn't it?' He took a sip of the beer. 'I just can't get one to notice me.'

Calloway thought of the file he'd taken from the casting office, the file on Joyce Rose that read like the scrapbook of an obsessive fan.

'Too hung up on a dead actress, eh?'

Tony sighed and gazed out of the window into the neon glow. 'You might be right,' he said. 'Joyce was wonderful. She was beautiful, talented, ambitious. I suppose I'd been in love with her since we were children.' He thought a moment. 'If not in love, then certainly in awe. She was the most wonderful person to be around. Her joie de vivre was infectious. Spelthorne saw that. He recognised that she was different. Not like the glorified swimwear models that the charm school churns out. She was Centurion's English rose. A breath of fragrant air that this damp and dusty country was so desperately in need of. God, I sound like Ivor Cole. Spelthorne took her everywhere. Showed her off wherever it would bring him some advantage. She was always on his arm, in his car, at his table.'

'In his bed?' said Calloway.

Tony looked hurt. He shook his head. 'It was a business relationship. For both of them. Joyce wasn't daft. Like I say, she was ambitious. She knew that being the young queen to Spelthorne's king was good for her career. They weren't lovers. She wasn't Spelthorne's type.'

'What is his type?'

'Have you met Miss Hope?'

Calloway nodded. The blonde secretary, bursting the seams, who could take a memo without a pencil or a pad.

'He's not one for subtle beauty,' said Tony, with a nervous laugh, as if Spelthorne might be listening. 'The problem wasn't that Spelthorne was interested in Joyce, well not in that sense. It was that someone else was.'

'Who?'

'The man in the newspaper.'

'Alfredo Azzopardi?'

Tony nodded. 'He'd seen Joyce in the press and in her film roles and asked to be introduced to her.'

'Who did he ask?'

'Mr Spiteri, one of Spelthorne's fixers.'

Calloway had not heard the name. He looked quizzical.

'Giordano Spiteri,' said Tony. 'He told Joyce she should host a party at her flat. She had no clue as the reason.'

'But she agreed?'

Tony sipped his drink and nodded. 'She assumed this was something that Centurion wanted. She thought it might help her career.'

'What happened at the party?'

'Nothing much, apparently. She was the perfect hostess. Everything was perfectly proper. The party wasn't the problem. The trouble started when Azzopardi started calling.'

'At the flat?"

Tony nodded.

'It didn't take long for Joyce to realise his intentions. He didn't waste time. She refused of course. Giordano got to hear about it and told her she should be nice. That's what they call it in this business, isn't it?'

'Giordano put pressure on Joyce to sleep with this man?'

'He did. At first he was subtle, making out that he was matchmaking. When that didn't work he was more direct. He let her know that unless she agreed to sleep with Azzopardi, she wouldn't have much of a career.'

'What did she do?'

He seemed affronted by the question, as if it was improper. 'She said no, naturally.'

'And then what?'

'The studio dropped her.' He clicked his fingers. 'Just like that. Giordano called on me one morning and said that Joyce's popularity was waning and that we weren't to consider her for any more roles. It was nonsense. She was a star in the ascendant. Her press was getting better all the time. She was photographed wherever she went. Even the critics seemed to be warming to her.'

'And you agreed on Giordano's say-so? You didn't put any more roles her way?'

He looked shameful and nodded. 'He's the sort of chap you don't argue with,' as if this might absolve him.

'What did Marjorie think of this?' said Calloway.

Tony seemed reluctant to answer. Calloway pressed him. He needed to know.

'Did Marge agree to dropping Joyce?'

Tony picked at his fingernails, considering his answer. When he responded he sounded reluctant.

'Marge didn't know,' he said. 'Giordano told me to see to it personally. He told me under no circumstances was I to involve Marge. He knew he'd get a different response if she got to hear about it. Marge is one of the few around here that's not afraid of him.'

Calloway could believe it. Somewhere inside he felt a bristle of pride.

'After that, Joyce's work was strictly charm school. Public appearances, openings, fucking swimming galas. Ivor Cole even leaked a story she was engaged to one of Centurion's actors and made sure she was seen with him in public. She had to go everywhere with him. Even spent the night at his flat once, just so the gossip columnists would find out.'

Calloway looked confused.

'It was a cover, you see? In reality he was what they call a confirmed bachelor. Not the marrying kind, to borrow your phrase.'

'And it was around that time that she started going off the rails? Drinking and taking pills?'

'She was a different person after that,' said Tony. 'Bitter. Nasty sometimes. She'd lost her confidence. She used the booze and the pills to compensate, but she wasn't the same. And Azzopardi kept calling.'

'And she kept turning him away?'

'If she could, yes, but sometimes she ran out of excuses. She'd let him in the flat for a drink. Sometimes he'd bring his friends. Sometimes Spelthorne sent other charm school girls around too, to make up a party. I don't know what went on. She said he just showed her off. Made out there was something between them.'

'Do you believe her?'

'I've no idea either way. She wasn't the Joyce I knew. Not the girl I grew up with.'

Calloway remembered the school report. A pleasant and popular girl...her Mary in this year's nativity play was a revelation.

'I'm not sure I'd have trusted what she told me. It would have been the drink and drugs talking.'

'And how did the fight start?' said Calloway.

Tony laughed, incredulous. 'Fight?' he said. 'Look at me. You think I can fight? I can't fight my way out of a paper bag.'

'But they did rough you up.'

Tony nodded. 'I'd called on Joyce one evening. I was worried about her. Azzopardi arrived and I told him to leave. I'd had a couple of drinks and I suppose it was Dutch courage. He just laughed. I lost my rag. There was pushing and shoving and the next thing I know his driver was dragging me down the stairs of the apartment block, using his fists along the way.'

Tony picked up his glass and drained the last of his beer.

'A fortnight later Joyce was dead,' he said. He looked across to the bar. A moustachioed rake was edging himself closer to a tired-looking woman whose glaze of inebriation gave no clue to her interest in his advances. 'She was a fucking commodity. That's all she meant. A tradable asset.'

'Aren't they all commodities, the charm school girls?' said Calloway.

Tony shrugged. 'I suppose so. But usually there's a line that isn't crossed. You can look, you can touch within limits, but you don't get to have. With Joyce they crossed the line. Offered her to Azzopardi like a tribute. It killed her.'

'Yes, it killed her,' said Calloway. 'Well, that and someone ending her film career because he didn't have the guts to say no to Giordano.' Calloway fixed Tony's stare. 'That couldn't have helped, could it, Tony?' he said.

The skinny man was on the verge of tears, but he held them back. Calloway was grateful. He wasn't good with emotions. Especially men's. He went to the bar and bought another round. A young man, shabbily dressed with a face crumpled beyond his years, slipped off his bar stool and swore loudly.

'That fucker can't paint for shit, but he gets an exhibition on Cork Street...' He held up his beer glass like Hamlet with the skull. 'While I'm raiding the gas meter for the price of a drink.'

His drinking partner frowned, grappling for words of consolation.

'The art world is as corrupt as its favoured artists are inept,' he said.

The artist seemed not to hear.

'Perhaps I should sell my arse,' he said, to no one in particular.

Calloway paid for the drinks. He was glad he had Spelthorne's cash to cover them. A woman in a beret touched his arm. When he turned to face her, she seemed to wake from a trance and said, 'I'd like to paint you naked.'

'What colour?' he said.

She gave a disinterested shrug, shifted on her stool and

stared into the mirrored glass behind the bar. Calloway returned to the table and set the drinks down. Tony had composed himself now, but he drank the beer eagerly.

'Joyce had a sister,' Calloway said. 'Did you ever meet her?'

Tony hesitated before answering. He gulped his drink like it was a condemned man's last request. Calloway must have frightened him as much a Giordano.

'Yvonne?' he said quietly. 'Of course. But I haven't seen her since we were children. She lives in France, I think.'

Yvonne. The name on the postcards from Paris.

'Did she go to the funeral?'

Tony shook his head. 'If she did, I didn't see her. Not sure I'd recognise her. It's been a long while.'

'Did she resemble Joyce in appearance?'

'A little, at least when they were young. Look, what's all this about? What's this got to do with studio security?'

'Best you don't know. And keep this chat to yourself.'

Calloway's tone left no room for doubting these instructions. Tony nodded like he'd got the message.

They finished their drinks and rose to leave. As they approached the door, the artist was on his knees begging for credit and the diva was responding with language Calloway hadn't heard since leaving the army.

NINETEEN

He took a bus to Aldwych, then the 569 trolleybus eastwards. He jumped off at Broad Street station and walked towards Shoreditch. As he turned into his street, he noticed a black Austin parked outside his building, its engine running. The door opened as he passed.

'Get in, Calloway.'

It was Bernie. She sat in the back, the raglan coat pulled tight around her neck. Curly sat at the wheel. Blue eyes was in the passenger seat. He was pointing the muzzle of the Colt automatic in Calloway's direction. Calloway eased himself into the back seat beside Bernie.

'You can put that down,' he said to Blue Eyes.

'I'd rather he didn't,' said Bernie.

She nodded to Curley, who took the gear stick in his big mitt and pushed the car into gear. He drove slowly westwards, the same route they'd taken when they'd bundled Calloway into the car.

'Are you taking me dancing again?' he said.

Bernie shook her head. 'We're going to a little place I know. I want to show you something.'

Somewhere off the Kilburn High Road they pulled up at a crossroads. Curly cut the engine. There was a wide street opposite them running south to north which Calloway didn't recognise. He wasn't a Londoner. There were huge swathes of the capital he'd never visited. The road was lined with the usual collection of shops you found in the city's Victorian suburbs. A greengrocers, a drapers, a Home and Colonial store. The shops were closed - it was past seven - and their windows reflected the glow of the street lamps. On the corner opposite was a pub. He couldn't read the pub sign. Place looked full and cheery. It was Friday night. End of the working week for most.

'Do you hear that?' said Bernie.

He heard singing.

'That's 'The Mountains of Mourne'. A lament for a country they left behind. Lured by the NHS and London Transport with the promise of a pay packet and a better life. Plucked from the poverty of De Valera's isolationism by your desperate and opportunistic government. They're the mailboat generation, Calloway. They came here via Fishguard and Holyhead to build your roads, drive your busses and nurse your sick. Those homes for heroes they keep telling you about. You know what they're made of? London bricks and the sweat of the Irish.'

'And I'm sure we're very grateful.'

'Are you now? Have you seen those signs outside the boarding houses?'

He had. No blacks, no dogs, no Irish. A good old British welcome.

'What's your point, Bernie?'

Something distracted her. She held up a finger to silence him.

Curly said, 'They're coming, Bernie.'

He gestured to the far end of the street. A Black Maria and two police cars were turning the corner, their bells silent but their engines roaring. They sped past the row of shops and pulled up outside the pub. Their doors flew open. Police dismounted. Uniformed and plain clothes. Grim faced. Meaning business. They piled into the pub, slamming its double doors back like a blue tornado. The singing stopped. There was shouting and screaming. The smashing of glass. The crash of furniture. Half a dozen drinkers were pushed back out of the doors and dragged into the van. Roughed up. Some were bloodied.

'We had a tip off,' she said. 'A sympathetic lad on the force.'

'And this is what you brought me here to see?'

'I don't expect your support, Calloway. We're old adversaries. You served the army of occupation. But I do credit you with enough common sense to know that we can all do without this.'

'I'm working on it,' he said.

It was true. He needed to find the real car bomber for the sake of his own neck.

'Then work harder,' she said, sliding the Webley out of her coat pocket just far enough for him to see.

Blue Eyes tensed suddenly. He sat bolt upright in the passenger seat looking through the windscreen at three men in trench coats heading up the street towards them.

'Christ Bernie. It's the Branch.'

Curley started the engine and slammed the car into gear. He accelerated hard towards the three detectives. One drew a pistol but leapt sideways out of the car's path before he'd had a chance to aim. As the big Austin neared the junction of the main street, a police Wolseley pulled up blocking the way ahead. Curly stamped hard on the brakes. The four of them lunged forward inside the car. Curly's forehead slammed into the steering wheel with an audible crack. His body slumped, lifeless. Bernie flung the door open and rolled onto the damp bitumen of the road. She scrambled to her feet and ran. Blue Eyes followed, swivelling his body as he ran and loosing off three rounds in the direction of the detectives. One detective took cover. Another kneeled and took aim at Blue Eyes. He fired two rounds. Both went wide. Calloway piled out of the nearside door of the Austin and crouched on the pavement, shielded from view. He figured all eyes would be on the sound of the gunfire. He lifted his head and peered through the Austin's windows to the opposite side of the street. The three plain clothes men were on their feet now, pursuing Bernie and Blue Eyes up the street. Two uniformed officers had dismounted the Wolseley and were following them. Calloway looked back towards the police car. The way ahead was clear, for now. There was no one between the abandoned police car and the commotion outside the pub on the far side of the junction. He stood upright and double-timed towards the Wolseley, adopting the manner of a concerned passer-by keen to get away from the shooting. No one challenged him. He turned left and continued past the parade of shops. On the opposite side of the road, uniformed officers bundled the last of the pub goers they had rounded up into the Black Maria and slammed the doors shut. A metallic clang echoed down the street over the hubbub of aggrieved voices coming from the gaggle of angry punters that had spilled onto the pavement outside the pub. Calloway stayed close to the shopfronts. He tried his best to stay in the shadows. He was thankful this wasn't the kind of neighbourhood where shopkeepers kept their lights on. He glanced back down the street towards the pub. The police were leaving, cars and vans heading in the opposite direction. He sighed, relieved to be clear of them. As he turned back again there was a figure blocking his path.

'And where the fuck do you think you're going?'

Before he could answer, DS Bryant jabbed him in the guts with a truncheon.

TWENTY

Calloway's eyes adjusted to the gloom. This wasn't a police station.

He judged from the old bed frame, the basin in the corner and the set of dog-eared fire instructions pinned to the door, it was a disused room in a guest house. A cheap and shoddy one. The walls were stained with damp and the carpet was as threadbare as a mongrel with mange. There was a strong smell of dead rodent coming up from the floorboards.

They'd sat him in an old metal chair. Bryant stood behind him, casting a shadow across the room from the bare and inadequate bulb in the ceiling above him. Belcher sat in front cowboy style, the chair reversed and his arms draped over the back rest.

I like a good western as it happens.

No sign of the pipe. It would have masked the putrid smell that clung to Calloway's nostrils.

'So no chance of a phone call then?' said Calloway.

'We thought we'd keep this informal,' said Belcher.

Calloway swore he heard Bryant crack his knuckles behind him. No, that would have been too melodramatic, even for Bryant. He felt in his pocket for his cigarette case.

'Mind if I smoke?'

'Be my guest.'

Belcher looked up at Bryant. 'Give mister Calloway a light, will you? He must be gasping.'

Bryant flicked open a lighter. As Calloway leaned towards the flame he smelled cologne. He'd not noticed it before. Something soapy with a sailing ship on the bottle. Perhaps

Bryant was on a promise.

'So, Calloway,' said Belcher. 'Here's how it is. There's us lads from the Branch and our uniformed pals, out to feel some collars in a well-known Irish pub. Round up a few of the boyos and see what they know about this car bomb business. Then all of a sudden, you pop up like an oversized leprechaun. What's that all about, eh?'

Give them something close to the truth, Calloway thought. And stick to it.

'I was looking for McCaffrey.'

'Were you now. And why would you be doing that?'

Calloway glanced back at Bryant, who was stubbing a cigarette out in the basin.

'Because your DS told me to.'

'Don't give me that,' said Bryant, flicking the butt in Calloway's direction. 'I asked for his known haunts, not for you to go stomping all over Kilburn in your old army boots.'

Calloway shrugged. 'I like to go the extra mile.'

Belcher raised an eyebrow. 'It seems you do,' he said. 'And along that extra mile you met one Bernadette Doyle and her big Mick boyfriends.'

'Never heard of her.'

'You were sitting in her car.'

Calloway took a long drag on the cigarette. 'If you say so,' he said, exhaling.

It looked bad, he knew that, but there was no law against it as far as he was aware. Then again, he wasn't in a police station. This was big boys' rules. A different kind of law.

'Bernadette Doyle is known to us. She's believed to have been part of an IRA active service unit operating on the British mainland during the war.'

The time of the S-Plan

'That's news to me. Like I say, I was looking for McCaffrey. I didn't get to choose who I ran into along the way.'

Bryant cuffed Calloway across the back of his head. 'Stop fucking us about, son. You've been seen with Doyle twice in the past fortnight.'

Calloway swivelled in the chair. 'Keep your bloody hands off me,' he spat at Bryant.

'I mean it doesn't look good, does it?' said Belcher, taking out his pipe and filling it from a small leather pouch.

'I don't care how it looks. I was looking for McCaffrey. Same as you. He's a potential threat to the studio. I want him caught and quickly. I was making my own enquiries.'

'And did you find anything?'

Calloway shook his head. 'Nothing yet. My money's on him skipping across the Irish Sea, or even to America.'

'Let's say we believe you,' said Belcher. 'We could just give you a slap on the wrists and leave it at that.'

The sentence hung in the air. There was a but coming.

'The trouble is you're a complicated sort, Calloway.' He nodded to his colleague. 'Show him, Bryant.'

The DS picked a brown foolscap envelope off the old bed frame and passed it to Calloway. Inside were photos. The surveillance kind. Taken at the fascist meeting at Ridley Road. There was Calloway, fists raised, piling into Hamm's cordon of semi-uniformed stewards.

'You didn't strike me as the political sort.'

'I'm full of surprises.'

'Do you consider yourself,' he thought for a moment, 'an anti-fascist?'

'Don't you?'

Christ, thought Calloway, we'd been at war with the bastards for six years. Belcher ignored the question.

'We keep an eye on the likes of Mosley and Jeffrey Hamm.' He gave Calloway a sympathetic look. 'I mean we can't have that sort of thing, can we?'

'You said it.'

'But these anti-fascists are a rum lot too. There's the Jews of course. Well you can't blame them, can you? But we can't have them fighting in the streets. What we're more concerned about is the communists. They seem to be mobilising against these fascists too and frankly, that worries us. I mean, they're the real enemy now.'

'So why don't you drag them off the street and sit them in this chair?'

Belcher dropped the chummy act. 'Don't be smart with me, son. You're in no position.'

Stand your ground, he thought. Don't be cowed. He has nothing on you. You've done nothing wrong.

'So what position am I in? What the hell has this got to do with me?'

Belcher took a long drag on the pipe. 'I'm one of those coppers that doesn't believe in coincidence. Everything's connected in some way or another.'

'Get to the point.'

'We've been looking into your story Calloway. You have an interesting background. Raised by a family of socialists. Your father was a trade union activist.'

'Like every other coal miner. That doesn't make him a communist.'

Belcher smiled. 'Well in his case, it does. He was a member of the Communist Party between 1933 and 1946. Don't tell me you didn't know.'

Calloway didn't know, but it didn't surprise him. 'The last time I saw my father I was sixteen.'

'Yes, you left home to join the army. Military Police. Posted to Belfast in 1935. Tense times, I imagine. Plenty of time for a someone with communist sympathies to make new friends, especially if he was sympathetic.'

'I wasn't sympathetic.'

Belcher frowned. 'Is that so?' He puffed on the pipe. The sickly smell was marginally better than the dead rat under the floorboards. 'Do you remember a Private Alfred Tallis?'

'Vaguely,' said Calloway.

Alfie Tallis. He knew him alright. A nasty piece of work.

'Only vaguely? I'm surprised. I'd say you knew him better than that. You reported him to your commanding officer in Belfast, claiming he'd used undue force on a Fenian during a house search.'

'You're wrong about that,' said Calloway.

But he was only half wrong. It was the height of the rioting. Things kicked off during the Orange parades and quickly escalated. Beatings, shootings, looting. From the start, the Catholic neighbourhoods bore the brunt of it. Catholics were sacked from their jobs, turned out of their homes and attacked by the mob. But intelligence reports suggested more than thirty IRA men were on their way back to Belfast from their training camp in Dundalk. The RUC feared reprisals.

Tallis and Calloway were sent to a house in Sailortown. The police planned to raid it. They had information that a man called Redmond was hiding a cache of arms on the premises. The two soldiers were there to back up the police but the police failed to show. They'd been caught up in rioting near the Customs House.

Calloway told Tallis they should wait. Tallis ignored him and banged on the door. Redmond wasn't there, but his wife and ten-year-old son were. His wife was uncooperative, although not any more so than was usual in that neighbourhood at the time. She stood in the doorway refusing them entry. Tallis pushed her to the floor. The ten-year-old went to the defence of his mother in the way that ten-year-olds do. He kicked Tallis in the shins with dirty unshod feet and started beating on the soldier's legs with his small fists. Tallis smashed the child in the face with his rifle butt. The child fell backwards onto the bare floorboards screaming. His urchin face gushed blood. Tallis shouted at the child to shut up. The mother was on her feet now and shrieking at them. By this time neighbours had rushed into street and were closing in behind the two soldiers. Calloway grabbed Tallis and dragged him backwards through the crowd. Tallis was swearing. Baying for blood. Calloway told him to shut up, but Tallis kept taunting the crowd. The neighbours were grabbing at them, shouting and screaming. Calloway made a run for it and Tallis followed.

They made it to the end of the street. A Rolls Royce armoured car was passing on a routine patrol. A mean-looking beast, all rivets and plating. Its turret swivelled, training its Vickers gun on the mob. It fired a burst of .303 rounds into the crowd. The mob stopped in their tracks. Two of them lay dead on the ground. Then they kept coming. Calloway and Tallis scrambled onto the rear of the vehicle. The driver accelerated hard along York Street as the two soldiers clung on to the turret. Calloway shouted to Tallis that he was bang out of order. Tallis told him the family were Fenian scum and deserved what they got.

They got in a fight back at the barracks. Tallis wouldn't let it go. He told Calloway he was soft. He hadn't got what it takes. A crowd of squaddies had formed around them, egging them on. Tallis played to the crowd. He kept digging at Calloway. All the old jibes. Calloway snapped. He fought like a beast. He beat seven shades of shit out of Tallis before two NCOs pulled them apart. The next day they were called before their commanding officer. Calloway broke an unwritten rule. He ratted on Tallis. He didn't care.

'Tallis was a liability,' Calloway said to Belcher. 'He was the type that get you killed.'

He took a last drag on the cigarette and ground the butt into the leg of the chair. 'I'm not a Fenian sympathiser. I never have been.'

'That's not how it looks.'

'So how does it look, Inspector? You tell me?'

Belcher answered as if reading a report. 'Reginald Calloway, raised by a communist, sympathetic to nationalist Catholics, fighting fascists in the street shoulder-to-shoulder with communists, fraternising with republican terrorists. And his boss's car blows up after he sacked an angry paddy from a film about the IRA. It paints quite a picture, doesn't it?'

Calloway shrugged. He opened his cigarette case and put another Navy Cut in his parched mouth, gesturing to Bryant for a light. Bryant gave an indignant snort and pulled out his lighter. Belcher changed tack.

'How do you know Bernie Doyle?'

'I don't know Bernie Doyle.'

'You were in her car.'

'I mistook it for a taxi.'

'Don't play the fool.'

'Then don't treat me like one.'

'I'll treat you how I damn well please.'

'I've done nothing wrong. Why don't you let me go?'

'Why were you at the pub tonight?'

'I was looking for McCaffrey. I already told you.'

'Why that pub?'

Calloway glanced at Bryant. 'It's one of his known haunts.'

'Who did you meet there?'

'No one. You lot turned up and spoiled everyone's evening.'

Belcher kept up the questioning and Calloway kept batting them back. They couldn't touch him and they knew it. They wanted information, not him. If they had anything on him, he would be in a police cell by now. Nothing they got from this informal interview would be admissible. He guessed they used the guest house for grilling sources, not sweating suspects.

'Did your anti-fascist friends introduce you to Doyle?'

'No. Why would they?'

'They're all communists, after a fashion.'

'Now you're clutching at straws.' Calloway took a deep drag on the cigarette. 'Anyway, I don't follow politics.'

'You were seen smashing up a political rally.'

'A man needs a hobby.'

'You're not a Jew, are you?'

'Would it matter if I was?'

'Does it matter to your lady friend?' said Bryant.

'I don't have a lady friend.'

'Come off it. You're knocking off that old bint in Casting.'

'And what's that to you?'

'Nothing, mate.' Bryant sniggered loud enough to ensure Calloway heard him. 'I wouldn't touch her with...'

Calloway was on his feet before Bryant finished the sentence. He grabbed the detective by the lapels and head butted him hard. The noise of the impact filled the room. Bryant clutched his face. Calloway kicked his legs from under him. The copper fell. Calloway was about to aim a kick at the copper's head when he heard a click. The cocking of pistol. He felt its cold metal barrel against his temple.

'If you move so much as an inch, I'll blow your fucking brains from between your two jug-ears.'

Special Branch was one of the few branches of the police which carried guns routinely. But putting one to Calloway's head was a dumb tactic on Belcher's part. At that distance Calloway could have batted the gun away in a single move before the detective could squeeze the trigger. But he did as he was told. These were coppers and wrestling a gun from a copper could end very badly.

Belcher spoke calmly. 'Now sit down and don't budge. We haven't finished.'

Calloway complied. Belcher pulled his chair closer and sat. He leaned in close.

'You've done it now, mate,' he said. 'Assaulting a police officer. I doubt you'll get another security job. Not to mention the prospect of a few years inside.'

He was right. Calloway had messed up. Up to that point he'd being playing them at their own game and winning. He could have kept that up all night. They would've let him go eventually. But when Bryant mentioned Marge, the switch had flicked.

'There's a very big question mark over you, Calloway,' said Belcher.

'So ask the fucking question and let me out of here.'

Belcher rose from his chair. He tapped his pipe out on the chair back, pocketed it and stood in front of Calloway.

The blow hit him hard in the jaw before his eyes could tell his brain it was coming. Christ, Belcher was fast. Calloway tasted the ferric tang of his own blood. Belcher leant forward and shouted in his ear.

'Stop lying to me boy and tell me everything you know about the explosion.'

Calloway spat blood onto the bare boards. He turned his head sideways until he was nose to nose with the copper.

'What I know is that it wasn't me. I'm almost certain it wasn't McCaffrey and I doubt very much it was Bernadette

Doyle.'

He stopped himself there. He wasn't telling them about the woman that had fled the gala dinner, or the damaged studio equipment, or what the connection might be between Spelthorne and his Maltese gangster minders. He was keeping quiet about all of that. In Calloway's experience it never paid to play an incomplete hand. There was still more he needed to find out. To do that he needed to be out of this rat-infested room and away from Belcher and Bryant.

'Pass me a pencil and paper,' Calloway said.

Belcher exchanged looks with Bryant. This time Bryant's knuckles cracked for real. Belcher looked at the DS and shook his head. He took a police note book from his inside pocket and ripped a page out. He passed it to Calloway and handed him a pencil. Calloway wrote down a name and number. He passed the paper back to Belcher.

'Call him. He'll vouch for me.'

It was a gamble. A big one. He was calling in a favour that arguably wasn't owed to him. He was relying on old loyalties. Belcher stared at the paper. He sucked on his empty pipe while he thought it over. Then both men left the room. Calloway heard a bolt sliding into place on the outer side of the door. He looked over at the dirty windows. He looked through the moth-eaten net curtains and saw that the windows were barred. He'd not noticed before. He wondered what happened at the other informal chats Belcher and Bryant had here.

TWENTY-ONE

'You better have a damn good excuse for this, Cab.'

Only Sammy Mackay called him by his old army nickname. Cab Calloway, after his Jumpin' Jive namesake. In fact Sammy had coined it during the war when they were both in army intelligence, part of 316 Field Security Section, attached to the 6th Airborne Division. Sammy had been his commanding officer from Normandy to the Balkans, then onto Palestine in forty-five. They'd seen each other once since then. That reunion hadn't ended well.

'I figured you owe me a favour,' said Calloway.

'I owe you a favour? For God's sake man, last time I had anything to do with you I spared you from the hangman's noose. You owe me a debt you'll never repay.'

'That's all in a day's work in your world.'

Sammy was a civil servant now. The kind that spied on our enemies and occasionally removed them. Last time Calloway met Sammy he'd stumbled into some bad business. The kind of business where people get killed. Sammy had got him clear of the law in return for some very deniable freelance work. It was a moot point who owed who the favour.

They drove west through the night. Sammy gripped the wheel of the car, a brand-new MG roadster - in racing green, naturally. Its engine growled like a puma about to pounce. The car suited Sammy. It would have suited any ex-army major with the same camel coat, cavalry twills and ridiculous moustache.

'Where are we going?' said Calloway.

'Chelsea. My place. We need to talk.'

Sammy lived in a mansion block off Sloane Square. One of

those places where single gentlemen share a man servant who enters each morning via the back stairs and wakes them with breakfast. Sammy would like that, Calloway thought.

Sammy parked the MG outside his block and pulled the tonneau cover over the cockpit. It was quiet on the street. Getting late. Calloway had lost track of time. Nine o'clock perhaps. A cool autumn breeze found its way up from the river between the ornate blocks of blackened terracotta. Calloway took a big lungful.

Sammy's flat was small but well furnished. Paintings in gilt frames hung from the picture rails above deep green walls. Oils and watercolours, traditional styles and safe subjects like horses, ships and landscapes. The landscapes looked Scottish. The furniture was old but expensive. There were antique pieces polished to the point of obsession and books of a kind no one read. Leather-bound editions of Scott and Thackeray. The carpet was Persian and suitably worn. It looked like an heirloom. A generous sofa covered with an Arabic throw nestled between the full-height windows with their Juliet balconies. Beside it, a sagging armchair with a side table just large enough to take a tumbler of scotch and an ashtray. Sammy's chair he guessed. The fireplace was ornate, with art nouveau tiling. There was an ormolu clock ticking on the mantlepiece, flanked by a pair of foot-high Greek statues, a male and female nude.

Sammy poured two whiskies from a bottle of single malt and passed one to Calloway.

'How the hell did you end up in a Special Branch safe house?' he said.

It hadn't felt all that safe to Calloway. As he started to reply, the phone rang. Sammy cursed and picked up the receiver. Calloway heard squawking down the line.

Sammy said, 'No, not tonight. I can't.'

More squawking. The caller wasn't taking no for an answer. Sammy looked uncomfortable. He glanced over at Calloway, then turned his back to him. He pressed the receiver closer to his mouth and said quietly, 'I have a visitor. Unexpected.'

Calloway could make out the caller's quizzical tone.

Sammy replied, 'It doesn't matter who. We will have to rearrange. No,' he said emphatically, 'don't come over.'

The caller sounded irate.

'Look, it's work, alright? I can't explain right now but...'

The caller cut him off.

Sammy said, 'Damn,' and slammed the phone down. He took a big gulp of the whisky and gestured for Calloway to sit.

'What have you got yourself into, Cab?' Mackay said.

'Not what Special Branch thinks.'

Sammy tutted and shook his head. His frustration showed.

'Alright, so tell me what they think, then tell me what you think.'

'They think I'm mixed up with an IRA cell in London. They think that cell's behind a bombing at the film studio I'm working for. They're wrong.'

Sammy let this sink in. 'Why so sure?'

'Because the IRA cell dragged me off the street, stuck a Webley service revolver in my guts and told me to find the real bomber.'

'Presumably there was an "or else" at the end of it.'

Calloway nodded. 'They want the Branch off their case as quickly as possible. They're using me to make that happen.'

'It doesn't mean they're not involved. They could just as easily be using you to find a scapegoat. To cover their tracks.'

'The IRA's got nothing to do with it. The Branch believes the bombing was revenge for my boss sacking an Irish actor for his republican links. That's ridiculous. They wouldn't mount such a high-risk operation for such a trivial reason. There's no strategic or tactical benefit.'

'The Branch can't ignore it though. It's too much of a coincidence.'

'Yes, but that's all it is. And unless I find the real bomber, the police will have a murder to investigate. Mine.'

Sammy calmed down. His earlier frustration ebbed.

'I know people who can help with that, Cab.' he said.

Calloway shook his head. 'I'll deal with it.'

Sammy shrugged as if to say Calloway was a fool for refusing the quick fix he was offering. He topped up Calloway's glass.

'You know I had to pull strings with the Irish desk at Curzon Street to get Special Branch off your back. They'll want to know what's going on.'

'Tell them to get lost.'

Sammy glared. 'It may be some great personal adventure for you, Cab, but this is my job. My contacts and connections are hard earned and I don't want to foul them up over some wild goose chase you've taken on as your next noble cause.'

'Nothing noble about it. It's just where I've found myself. And telling you more than you need to know isn't going to help me any. Tell your friends at MI5 to whistle. You used to be good at that.'

Sammy was not averse to cavalier behaviour when Calloway knew him. Arrogance and swagger carried him a long way. And when it didn't, Calloway was there with the muscle to fix things.

Sammy shook his head. 'I can't do that. I've got to throw them a bone. You can't interfere with a police investigation without consequences, Cab. The old boy network does have its limits, you know. It's bad enough having to deal with Special Branch at the best of times. I never did like policemen. Rude mechanicals in mackintoshes. But pulling favours from MI5 to lean on the Branch to let you go is well beyond what passes for friendship between us. I need to know what the hell you're up to. You can't keep secrets from me.'

The doorbell rang.

Sammy said, 'Oh, Christ'.

He sat for a moment as if weighing up whether to answer the door. The bell rang again, twice this time. Two long, insistent rings. Sammy rose and crossed the room towards the hallway. He looked afraid of what might happen next.

Calloway heard Sammy open the door. He started to speak.

He said, 'You can't...'

A voice interrupted. 'Fix me a drink love, my throat's dry as a witch's tit. They were such a rowdy lot tonight. I really had to belt out the closing number. I'm all husky.'

The visitor laughed. 'But then you quite like that, don't you luvvie?'

Calloway heard Sammy say, 'Look, I told you, you can't be here tonight, it's not...'

The visitor carried on, oblivious to Sammy's pleading. 'I had to get a taxi here like this. There was no room to change. The dressing room was full of dwarves. Dwarves! That show gets cheaper by the week. I said to Ronaldo, this is not a fucking circus and I'm not a fucking clown. He never listens. It'll be performing chimps next week. I must sit down, these heels are killing me.'

Sammy said, 'Look you can't go in there...'

He was too late. The visitor appeared in the room.

Framed in the doorway was a vision worthy of a screen goddess. Eyes, lips, hair, curves, legs, and an evening gown with sequins that shimmered like liquid gold. Calloway didn't know much about this kind of thing, but he had to admit, for a man, this young chap made a very beautiful woman.

'Oh, hello,' the vision said, raising a perfectly painted eyebrow. He looked Calloway up and down then turned to Sammy and said, 'Who's your handsome friend, Samuel?'

Calloway rose and said, 'It's a pleasure to meet you, Miss...?'

Sammy's visitor gave him a mischievous smile, then cackled like a fish wife. He held out his hand.

'Margot Montmartre,' he said. His voice dropped an octave, 'But you can call me Barry.'

'The pleasure's all mine,' said Calloway.

Barry gave him a wink.

'Cut it out, Cab,' said Sammy. 'This is awkward enough.'

There was a cold silence. Sammy was seldom lost for words. This was the exception. His face tensed and he stared into the mirror above the fireplace as if hoping to see the reflection of a very different scene playing out in the living room of his bachelor flat. Barry seemed oblivious. He pulled off his wig, kicked off his heels, crossed the room in his stockinged feet and helped himself to a drink.

Calloway leaned in to Sammy and whispered in his ear.

'Don't worry, Sammy,' he said. 'We all have our secrets. You keep mine...' He looked Barry up and down. 'And I'll keep yours. But I need a favour.'

Sammy scoffed. 'You've had more favours than a whore on payday.'

Calloway ignored him. 'I need to know about a man called Giordano Spiteri. If he has a criminal record, who his known associates are. He may be connected with organised crime.'

'That's not my bailiwick and you know it.'

Barry cut in, 'Sammy, what's this all about?'

He'd dropped his female act and sat ungainly in Sammy's chair, rubbing his feet, a cigarette dangling from his painted lower lip. With his pale powdered face and tight black hair net, he looked like Pagliacci.

'Shut up, will you,' Sammy shouted.

Barry scowled. He looked Sammy in the face and pointed a perfectly manicured finger at him. 'Don't you talk to me like that, Samuel. You know what happened last time.'

He took a swig of scotch and continued rubbing his feet.

Calloway said, 'You've got clearance to access Scotland Yard records. Use it, will you. Just this once.'

Sammy rolled his eyes. 'You don't know the meaning of "just this once". I'm not lifting a finger until you tell me what's going on.'

Calloway looked over at the young man in the chair. Consorting with female impersonators wasn't high on the list of qualities the secret service considered desirable in an operative.

'Like I said, Sammy. You keep my secrets and I'll keep yours.'

***

Calloway didn't give a damn who Sammy chose to share his evenings with. He was surprised, of course, but since the war he'd learned to divide life into things that mattered and things that didn't. Life and death mattered. Love and sex didn't, at least they weren't reasons to judge people. He'd seen the worst the world could do when judgement was let loose. Everything else was trivial now. But he needed a reason for Sammy to back off and he'd used the beautiful night-time caller to shut him up. Until Calloway had made sense of the past week's events, he wasn't letting anyone in on his investigation.

He slept badly that night. He was bruised from Bryant's truncheon blow and Belcher's fist. He still ached from the beating he'd received in his office. A professional beating hurt for longer. And he couldn't purge the woman's face from his mind. The scene of her fleeing the gala replayed over and over as he fought for sleep. He was convinced she was the key to everything. The IRA angle was irrelevant. He was satisfied of that, even if others weren't. It was the fear on the woman's face. Different to the others. The dinner guests were fleeing danger, the woman was fleeing the scene. The difference was subtle but significant. His brown-job copper's instinct told him so.

When he slept he dreamed again. The same dream, but with scenes from the present merging with the film loop of his past. And an incessant soundtrack of insinuating voices.

Twenty thousand bodies in a heap, just lying in the sun like wax.

A family thrown into the street while their possessions burned on the fire.

Wir kommen wieder!

TWENTY-TWO

Giordano was sitting at Calloway's desk when he arrived at work the following morning. His bulk almost fit into the chair. He was leaning back, smoking, his big feet in his big Italian-looking shoes up on Calloway's desk.

'Make yourself at home,' Calloway said, hanging up his mackintosh.

'Boss wants to see you,' Giordano said.

He stood up and gestured to the door. Calloway shrugged. As he turned to leave, the phone on his desk rang.

'Leave it,' said Giordano.

Calloway ignored him. He lifted the receiver. It was Sammy.

'You're early, Sammy.'

'Well it's not the sort of loose end I want hanging, Cab. I have what you want. Luckily for you, the duty liaison officer at Scotland Yard knows me. I caught him at the end of his night shift. He read the file over to me. Can you take this down?'

Calloway wedged the phone between his head and shoulder and wrote in his notebook. He shielded his notes from Giordano's view with his free hand. When Sammy had finished, Calloway pocketed the book and said, 'Thanks Sammy. I'd say we're square now.'

'And I'd say you're the worst kind of shit, Calloway.'

The phone went dead.

Calloway and Giordano walked in silence down the empty corridors. Outside, stage hands were dressing the flank wall of Studio B with fake foliage. Ivy leaves cut from cloth which even at a distance failed to look convincing. One of the hands was nailing a pub sign onto the jamb of the doorway, while another rolled empty barrels into position. A painter was doing his best to daub a thick coat of brown paint onto the metal-framed windows in an attempt to make them rustic. None of it worked. Calloway thought the whole scene looked as fake as everything else in this tawdry dream factory.

Spelthorne's selection of secretaries was as fragrant as usual. Two were typing. They looked up when Giordano entered the office. Calloway felt them tense, only slightly, but enough for him to notice. It told him a lot about Giordano. The third secretary, who he now knew as Miss Hope, was leafing through a film magazine. She looked bored. She didn't react as the two men passed.

Spelthorne was at his desk reading paperwork. Giordano pointed to a chair opposite. Calloway sat. Giordano remained standing. Looming. That's what he did, Calloway had noticed. Giordano loomed.

'I've just had the bills for the equipment we had to replace,' said Spelthorne.

He tapped the papers with his thick fingers.

'Arm and a bleedin' leg it's costing me.'

He stretched so that the sinews stood proud through the layer of well-fed flesh on his neck. 'So what have you got for me?' he said.

It was too early for an offer of a drink. Calloway could have done with a cigarette though, but the silver cigarette box on the desk stayed shut.

'I need to speak to you in private,' said Calloway.

Spelthorne looked like he didn't understand. 'We are in fuckin' private.'

He looked down at the foot well under the desk.

'You think someone's hiding down here?'

It was entirely possible, had Miss Hope not been sitting in the next-door room.

'I need to speak to you personally. Just you.'

Calloway nodded at Giordano. The big goon bristled. He looked at Spelthorne for a steer on what to do. Spelthorne waved his hand at Calloway dismissively.

'We're all friends,' he said.

Calloway rose to leave. 'I'm not sure we are.'

He felt Giordano's beefy hand on his shoulder, pushing him back into the chair. Spelthorne shook his head. Giordano released his grip. Spelthorne gave an irritated sigh and signalled for Giordano to leave. Giordano shot him an aggrieved look then left. When he was gone Calloway said, 'How long have you known him?'

'Giordano? Long enough. We grew up together. Both Saffron Hill boys.'

'And you trust him?'

'I wouldn't have him around if I didn't. Get to the point.'

'You told me you had your own security because you believed that you were at risk personally from organised criminals.'

'I did. So?'

'Criminals from London's Maltese community.'

Spelthorne pulled a cigarette from the box and lit it with a desk lighter. He didn't offer one to Calloway. 'That's what I said. What's that to you?'

'I told you I'd investigate the damage to equipment at the studio. In the course of my enquiries I learned two things that might trouble you. I feel it's my duty to report them.'

He had Spelthorne's full attention now. The studio boss took a long drag on the cigarette and pushed the cigarette box towards Calloway, who helped himself.

'Go on,' said Spelthorne.

'About a year ago Giordano Spiteri was leaning on the actress Joyce Rose to sleep with an associate of his. When she refused, he ensured she was no longer offered roles by Centurion.'

Spelthorne shook his head, incredulous.

'What the hell are you digging around in Joyce's past for? The poor girl's dead and gone. Nothing anyone can do about that.'

Calloway ignored the question.

'The associate Spiteri wanted Joyce to sleep with was Alfredo

Azzopardi. You know, the gangster jailed last week for running a vice ring. I've reason to believe Spiteri and Azzopardi were both members of a Maltese gang.'

Spelthorne frowned. Irritation showed on his face. 'I'm really not following this, son,' he said.

'It means the man you've entrusted to protect you and your money from Maltese gangs is actually part of one.'

Spelthorne sat back on the chair. He closed his eyes as if to let this sink in. When he opened them he was looking daggers at Calloway.

'I know that boy better than you know your Saturday night finger. Someone I trust more than my own mother, God rest her soul. Are telling me I've been duped? Are you telling me I'm stupid?'

'I'm just telling you what I've found out. If you're worried about people being out to get you, then a gangster on your payroll is the first place I would be looking. Especially when someone just turned that nice car of yours into a shower of scrap.'

Spelthorne shook his head and smiled, as if Calloway was the stupid one.

'You've been misinformed, son.'

'How do you explain him matchmaking for the gangster? Although that's not what I'd call it.'

Spelthorne waved his fleshy hand, dismissing the question.

'Listen. We're in a business that attracts all sorts. And we deal in glamour. Yeah, girls. What do you think Ivor's charm school is for? We're not looking for the next Vivien Leigh. We're dressing the shop window. Pretty girls attract window shoppers. You throw a party. People gate-crash it.'

Calloway hadn't mentioned a party. He wondered why Spelthorne had.

'They want to get their hands on the merchandise. That's what Giordano's for. He doesn't just watch my back. He keeps an eye on the starlets.'

'Which would make him well placed to coerce them into being nice to his criminal friends.'

'I doubt he's got criminal friends.' He laughed. 'I don't think he's got any friends. Apart from Franco, but even they're not close.'

They were pretty close when they were standing side by side with the fascists cutting up Johnny's commandos, thought Calloway.

'If you expect me to take this seriously, you're gonna need to do better than that.'

Calloway took his notebook from his pocket. He flipped a page and read his notes aloud.

'Giordano Mario Spiteri, born Saffron Hill, London, 23rd September 1913. Served three years for grievous bodily harm in 1937. Laced up a whore he was pimping, apparently. Then a two-year stretch for grievous bodily harm in 1941. He'd beaten up a punter who'd racked up a big debt with the owner of an unlicensed spieler. The owner got his money. The punter never walked again. Then six months in March 1945 for living off immoral earnings. Known associates in the criminal underworld, Salvatore Vella, Emmanuel Camilleri...' He paused. 'And Alfredo Azzopardi.'

Calloway put the notebook back in his pocket. Spelthorne sat back in his chair. He was silent. A full minute passed. Then Spelthorne said: 'Giordano is no saint. He's got a past, like the rest of us.'

'We don't all have that kind of past.'

'He was a bad lad in his youth. He's different now.'

'Can you be sure?'

'Like I said, we go way back. I know that boy. I trust him.'

Calloway thought of the intelligence report from Ted Nathan. The Maltese gang hired as muscle by Hamm and his fascists. Giordano and Franco in the thick of it with them.

'I think your trust is misplaced. My sources suggest that Giordano and Franco are mixed up with a Maltese gang. It's possible they may have been involved in the bombing and the damage to the studio equipment.'

This last part was pure speculation on Calloway's part. He wanted to see how Spelthorne reacted. The studio boss's eyes narrowed. Behind them, he seemed to be weighing up whether Calloway could be right.

'Why would they do something like that? What would their motive be?'

'A show of strength as a prelude to extortion. Demonstrate what they're capable of, then squeeze you for money.'

Spelthorne shook his head. 'Ridiculous. Not Giordano. He doesn't have the brains and Franco's barely smart enough to read the road signs when he's driving.'

'They don't need to be smart. The gang bosses would be the ones with the brains. All your two goons need is muscle and menace. They've got both of those in spades.'

Spelthorne glanced at the ornate clock on the wall. It looked like something you'd give to a retiring employee you didn't rate much. It was not yet ten. Spelthorne shrugged and eased his bulk out of the seat. He gestured to the drinks trolley.

'Need something?'

'Too early,' said Calloway. It wasn't. His mouth was dry, and he could have easily downed a large one. But he wanted to remain sharp.

'Suit yourself,' said Spelthorne, pouring himself a generous measure of Johnny Walker. He knocked it back in one.

'Let's just say you're right, that they're naughty boys and their friends have got their eyes on some of what I've made. What then? I'm not going to the police with something like that. I can't have that kind of stink hanging over the studio. My investors would run a mile.'

'I could help,' said Calloway.

He wasn't yet sure how, or indeed whether he was barking up the right tree. The gang angle didn't tally with his hunch about the woman fleeing the gala. He had little actual evidence of her involvement, but his instinct was strong. She was significant somehow. The only reason he had for playing the gangland card was to buy time with Spelthorne.

'Let me speak to Giordano in private,' said Calloway.

'You mean brace him.'

'I mean speak to him.'

He meant brace him. Part of him looked forward to it.

Spelthorne poured himself another large measure of the scotch. He mulled Calloway's suggestion over.

'Why would you do that? I mean, what's it to you?'

'I'm your head of security.'

'You're just a night watchman with an office.'

At least he knew where he figured in Spelthorne's empire. It came as no surprise.

'I sort this out for you,' said Calloway. 'You let me keep my job. And the two hundred pounds.'

Spelthorne scoffed. 'Now who's squeezing me for money?'

'It's a fair trade. The police aren't going to sort this out for you. They're still obsessed with the Irish connection. There is no Irish connection.'

Spelthorne nodded. 'Seems a bit far-fetched. That McCaffrey's not got it in him.' He laughed to himself. 'Fucking pisshead with a gob on him, that's all he is.'

He set his glass down and looked Calloway in the eye. 'Alright, son,' he said. 'You've got yourself a deal. But do it quickly. I want this over with. I want Gio in the clear. That's the only reason I'm agreeing to this.'

'And I'm sure he will be,' said Calloway, not sure at all.

TWENTY-THREE

Water rushed from the pipe. The level rose around him, past his chest, his neck, then up over his head until he was fully submersed. He held his breath. Beneath the water the muffled sound of metal handles cranking and water pouring. He lay still and counted the seconds, then the minutes. He felt the tightness in his chest, his lungs aching as he held onto the single breath he'd gulped down before the water covered his mouth and nose. His counting reached two minutes. He struggled against the urge to breathe. His fists clenched by his sides. He counted to three minutes before bursting upwards through the surface of the steaming water, gasping. He let out a loud grunt, which echoed around the terrazzo tiling of the bath house cubicle.

It was Saturday morning. The public baths were part of his weekly routine. And right now he needed to cleanse himself of the filth that clung to him, the whole dirty business he'd fallen into. He scrubbed with carbolic until his flesh burned.

Mornings were better at the baths. Quieter. By Saturday afternoon the place was full of noisy young blades scrubbing up for their night at the Palais. Big bars of foul-smelling soap scrubbing away a week's worth of grime. Then preening with hair oil, crafting their hair into a poor imitation of the latest movie star's style. Kings for a night.

He'd treated himself to a first-class cubicle at the Gainsborough Road baths. It was a thirty-minute bus ride, but was newer and cleaner than the local alternative. A confident Art Deco building opened before the war, with separate wings for men and women, and a public laundry. The first-class baths had their own changing rooms and lavatories.

Calloway needed some time alone. He needed to soothe the bruises from the beating in his office and scars from the melee at Ridley Road. It gave him time to think. Time to plan. He needed a plan now. He'd played Spelthorne along with the gangland angle to buy time, but also to test him. He wanted to know how much his boss knew about the goons that followed him around. But he'd found him too hard to read. Spelthorne was a practised manipulator, at least that's how he seemed the closer Calloway got to him. He guessed you needed to be to succeed in films, as much as in any business. Spelthorne wasn't one of the big names. He wasn't a Rank or a Balcon. But he'd done alright, from humble beginnings. You didn't get that way by wearing your heart on your sleeve. People like that got taken advantage of. Calloway couldn't imagine anyone taking advantage of Spelthorne, with or without his goons in tow.

He needed to get Giordano on his own, away from Franco. That wouldn't be easy. Most of the time they were a double act. Like Flanagan and Allen without the songs and jokes. In the meantime he would try Eve Clark's place again. Catch her in this time. Find out why she'd gone AWOL from her shifts as cleaner and why Joyce Rose had a poetry magazine with her poems in it. It could have been a coincidence, but like his Special Branch friend Belcher, Calloway didn't believe in them. He was grateful to Sammy for getting those two off his back, however little choice Calloway had given him in doing so. It was one less complication.

He heard Mr Da Costa's voice in his head. 'Women are complicated, Mr Calloway. If they weren't, they would be very dull indeed.' He thought of Marge. Should he call her? Hell, he didn't even have her number. Each time they'd met she had reeled him in. A part of him felt like being reeled in again. It was the kind of complication that he was prepared to tolerate.

He dressed in the small changing room that came with the first-class cubicle. Then he rolled up his towel - you had to provide your own - and let himself out into the corridor. Sweat, soap and steam hung in the air like mist. The sound of bathers echoed down the tiled corridor. Some sang, some coughed and spat. He was glad he'd paid the extra to go first class.

He heard a familiar voice from behind.

'Nice bath? I can't get enough of them since the war. Trying to wash the stink of death off me, I guess.'

It was Johnny Suskind. His hair was wet-combed into a severe parting and he held a rolled up towel under his arm. His shirt was unbuttoned to his chest, under his old blouson jacket.

'Nice coincidence, meeting you here,' Suskind said.

'I don't believe in them, Johnny,' said Calloway.

Johnny gave an impish grin. 'You're a creature of habit, Reg. I figured you might be here.'

'You figured right then.'

Johnny was a pal, but it didn't stop Calloway being suspicious.

'I need a quick chat,' said Suskind. He nodded towards the end of the corridor. 'We can go to the caretaker's office. He's a good friend.'

'A member of your group?'

Johnny put a finger to his lips. 'Walls have ears, Reg, like the posters used to say.'

Calloway followed Johnny down the corridor towards a door marked Resident Engineer. He heard Liz Francis's voice saying, 'You're not getting involved again, are you, Reg?'

Johnny knocked on the door and a voice behind it told them to come in, as if he already knew who was knocking.

'Borrow your room for half a mo', Sid?' said Johnny.

Sid was five foot one and easily half has a wide. For a short man he had the musculature of a heavyweight. A proper mighty atom. His jaw was an anvil covered in leather. His nose was flattened like a pug's. He stubbed the last of a Woodbine out in an old tin ashtray and picked up a battered tool tray.

'One of the hydro-extractors in the wash-house is playing up,' he said. 'I need to go give it a whack. Take your time and help yourself to tea.'

He nodded towards the kettle on the gas ring in the corner of the small wood-panelled room. There was a calendar on the wall from a company that manufactured toilet cleaner. This month's photo was of a gleaming lavatory cubicle. Next to the calendar some postcards pinned to the panelling with drawing pins. Southend, Margate, Weston-super-Mare and somewhat incongruously, Jaffa. Sid left the room, shutting the door behind him. Johnny placed a big hand on the kettle and nodded, satisfied the water was still hot enough. He spooned tea into Sid's teapot and added the water, then stirred it around with vigour.

'Time for a brew,' he said to himself.

Johnny poured the tea into two tin mugs without waiting. He spooned in three sugars each without asking.

Calloway took one of the mugs from him and sipped the pale, lukewarm liquid.

'You never could make proper tea, Johnny.'

'I know,' the big man said. 'Too impatient.'

'Sid seems like a good sort,' said Calloway, giving Johnny time to work up to whatever he had brought Calloway into the small room to say.

Johnny nodded. 'He was a lightweight contender in his day. Fists like dumbbells. He once knocked out Jackie Berg.'

Suskind took a sip of the tea and winced. 'Yeah, I never could make tea,' he said.

'What's up Johnny?' said Calloway.

Suskind looked relieved at the opportunity to get to the point. 'We've got to step it up, Reg. That episode with the Maltese and the blades. The fascists have upped the ante. We need to as well.'

'Why are you telling me?'

Johnny looked around as if the panelled walls might have ears too. He lowered his voice. 'We're planning a raid. Catch 'em off guard. Hit 'em where it really hurts. Make a statement. Instil some fear.'

Calloway didn't like where this was going. Protest was one thing. A few fisticuffs and a few sore heads, maybe. Whatever Johnny had up his sleeve sounded like the group might be going a step too far. Something Belcher and Bryant's friends at

Scotland Yard might take more than a passing interest in.

'Tell me you're plan, Johnny.'

Suskind laid it out for him. It was a simple plan. It required audacity, brute force and very little else.

'We need you to front it, Reg. To go in first.'

Calloway didn't like the sound of this. It was crossing a line.

'Why me? You've got plenty of big lads who could do that kind of thing, not that I'm endorsing it.'

'We can't put Jews up front. The fascists would tumble to that straight away and we'd never get through the door. We've got one man who's put his hand up already. A Welshman. Methodist. Lives local. But it's a two-hander. You're the other man, Reg. We need you.'

'I'm not your man, Johnny. Not for this one. I'll fight on your front line at the rallies and I'm not afraid to crack a few heads in the heat of battle. But you're going to need someone else for this one.'

Suskind nodded. He was trying hard not to show his disappointment. Not disapproval. It was clear he respected Calloway's decision. But Calloway sensed that there wasn't a ready supply of non-Jewish group members with what it was going to take to front the operation Johnny had planned.

Johnny supped the last of his tea. 'Fair do's Reg,' he said. He put the mug down and crossed the small room to the door. He turned before leaving and looked Calloway in the eye.

'They daubed a swastika on mum's door last night,' he said.

The light was fading when Calloway crossed the Regent's Canal towards Ndungu's street. He was calling on the off chance, hoping that the young law student would be home. There were four bell buttons beside the door. He'd no idea which was Ndungu's flat. He pressed them all. He heard an inner door open and heavy footsteps descend a single flight of stairs. He also heard coughing and swearing. A balding middle-aged man opened the door. His stained vest and unbuttoned fly were clues to his temperament. He grunted at Calloway.

'Who are you?'

‘A friend of Paul Ndungu. Is he in?’

The man sneered as if he could suddenly smell an odour worse than his own.

‘See for yourself. Third floor,’ he said, pulling a grey, mucus-filled handkerchief from his trouser pocket and blowing something green into it. He showed no signs of stepping aside. Instead he stood for a moment examining whatever he’d produced from his red raw nostrils. Calloway flattened himself against the hallway wall and edged past, trying not to pick up anything slimy on his suit.

The hallway was damp, but no more so than usual for such a property. It had a familiar smell. Damp, gas and boiled veg. The odour of multiple occupancy. Calloway knew it well. He’d served his time in such places since leaving the army.

He knocked on the door of the third-floor flat.

A voice said, ‘Let yourself in, I’ve got my hands full.’

It was Ndungu. He was standing on a flimsy-looking stool reaching for the light fitting in the high ceiling, plugging in an electric iron which stood on a stained wooden ironing board beneath him. Calloway saw tiny blue-white sparks coming from the ceiling rose. They made Ndungu jump. The stool tottered ominously beneath his bare feet.

‘What’s that expression you mentioned?’ said Calloway. ‘Only scratch where you can reach?’

‘This bloody house should be condemned,’ said Ndungu.

Calloway looked around the room. It was shabby and cheerless, with dark wallpaper two decades old. But it was clean and tidy and Ndungu had done his best to make it his own. A new-looking gramophone stood on a plain wooden cabinet in the corner. Next to it, two long rows of records, Ndungu’s jazz collection, Calloway imagined. There was a modern desk and chair and above it more shelves, with books on law and business. A portion of the room was divided by a half partition to create a kitchenette, with a gas ring and stone sink. A pile of freshly washed breakfast dishes stood on the drainer. The bed doubled as a studio couch with brightly patterned cushions. Three suits and a sports jacket with flannels hung from a rail beside the bed, together with five crisp white shirts. Ndungu liked to iron, in spite of the risk of electrocution. Two un-ironed shirts lay on the ironing board waiting.

'I've lived in worse,' said Calloway.

'Did you meet my delightful landlord on the way in?'

'If he was part man, part mucus, then yes.'

'He's pretty unsavoury. But less selective than many round here, if you know what I mean.'

Calloway had seen the signs on neighbouring buildings. No coloureds.

'I get your drift,' he said.

Ndungu clicked the iron's Bakelite plug into the ceiling socket with a concerted shove. The socket stopped sparking. He climbed down from the creaking stool.

'I'll put on some music, but I know you hate jazz.'

'I like Mahler.'

Ndungu smiled. 'I have Mahler,' he said, looking pleased. He took a shellac disc from a plain sleeve and placed it on the turntable, laying the needle down with an expert hand. A soothing symphony filled the room. To Calloway, it brightened it. He'd lost most of his own record collection in a break-in at his last digs. He seldom listened to music now. He missed it. He missed the memories it evoked.

Ndungu made coffee from an Italian percolator and passed Calloway a cup. He tested the iron with a spit ball, which hissed back at him. Satisfied, Ndungu started ironing the first of the shirts.

'It's a pleasure to see you, Reg, but I suspect this call isn't social.'

'It's not. I've come to ask for your help. Something that might just clear your friend Terrence McCaffrey's name.'

'I'm not sure what I can do, but if it helps Terrence, then I'm willing to try. I've not known him long, but we've become good friends. His mouth runs away with him, but his heart's in the right place. I'll help, on the condition of course it's strictly legal. I have a career in law ahead of me. I can't risk blotting my copy book at this early stage.'

He put the iron down and took a sip of his coffee. 'What do you have in mind?'

'I need someone who knows their way around company accounts to look in to Centurion Pictures' business. You said you were studying company law.'

Ndungu nodded. 'What should I be looking for specifically?'

'Who its shareholders are and where the money comes from.'

Ndungu considered this for a moment. 'There are places I can look. Companies House for a start.'

'Good. Come straight to me with what you find.' Calloway took a pencil and paper from the desk and wrote down his number. 'Speak only to me about this. No one else. Especially no one from the studio.'

Ndungu looked apprehensive. 'I'd like to know more. Can I ask what the context is?'

'Best you don't. Leave that to me. If you can look at the names and numbers, I can do the rest.'

Calloway sipped the coffee. It was good. He missed good coffee too.

'You've got your career to think of.'

'I have. More to the point I have my father to think of.' He waved his hand at the law books on the shelf. 'He's paying for this education.'

'Is he a lawyer too?'

'A civil servant. And mother's a teacher.' He laughed. 'Terrence calls me bourgeois.'

'Terrence would. So would my father.'

'A communist?'

'Apparently so.'

'But you're not.'

'I'm not my father's son, put it that way.'

'I fear I am.'

He glanced over at the records. 'Apart from my love of jazz, of course. Father hates it. He suspects I spend all my money on records.'

Calloway looked along the two long rows of discs. 'I suspect he's right. Thanks for the coffee. And the music. Call me when you've got something to tell me.'

The two men shook hands and Calloway left. He heard the landlord hacking up phlegm as he closed the front door behind him.

TWENTY-FOUR

Saturday evening, after seven. He walked up Tottenham Court Road. It was already busy. Couples queueing outside the Dominion for a dance band. Women in their best coats, worn over their going-out frocks against the autumn chill. Higher heels and more made up than usual. Men with hair that glistened, combed flat against their heads in neat rows, ending abruptly just shy of the base of their skulls where the barber shop clippers had shorn them near to bald. The more dapper ones coiffured it up into a neat, cheeky quiff. Some had pencil moustaches, mere lines of darkened bum fluff hinting at their prowess.

It was the kind of Saturday night normality that Calloway avoided. A night of mandatory good humour, obligatory fun, accepted inebriation. People letting go. Calloway didn't let go. Not of his own volition. His episodes of abandon were beyond his control. They chose when they came. When they did, things generally ended badly. But there was something in the mood of the crowd that cheered him on this night. Just for a moment or two. He imagined Marge and him in the queue. Her arm through his. No talk of 'getting off', just warm and undemanding chatter. Like the other couples. A reassuring normality. Something he seldom enjoyed, not since the war, at least. He shook the thought off. It would do him no good.

He quickened his pace as he headed north to the junction with Goodge Street. He hoped to catch Eve Clark at her lodgings. He didn't see her as the dance hall type. He didn't imagine her kind headed out until well into the night.

He stood in front of the pawn shop and looked up at the

windows above. Eve's first-floor room was dark. The second-floor window above was lit. The well-bred poetry brat's room, he guessed. He rang the bell. Its electric rasp seemed angrier than last time. He heard the sound of feet thumping down the wooden stairs. Fast, with a sense of urgency.

The brat was fully dressed this time, after a fashion. The same corduroys, worn with a check shirt and brown flannel jacket a size too big for him. Shoes he may have owned since school, scuffed with fraying laces. He'd combed his hair too. Or at least shown it the comb.

'Oh, you again,' he said. 'I was expecting someone else.'

He frowned, like a child denied a second iced bun.

'Sorry to disappoint you,' said Calloway. 'I was hoping to catch Eve Clark.'

'She's out. Been out for an hour or so. I heard her leave.'

'Do you know where she went?'

He shrugged. 'The Fitzroy, probably. That's were her gang are usually found.'

'Buying drinks for Mephisto.'

The brat looked surprised. 'You know Mephisto?'

'He publishes my work,' Calloway lied.

The brat seemed about to laugh, then stifled it. Perhaps it was Calloway's big frame filling the doorway that stopped him.

'I'll check there,' said Calloway. 'But if she comes back in the meantime, tell her I called, will you?'

The brat sulked at the thought of such responsibility. 'Not much point. She'll be out for the rest of the night. They'll go to someone's place after the pub.'

He shuffled, showing some impatience at Calloway's presence. 'Anyway, I'm going out myself later.'

'What time?'

The boy gave a petulant shrug. 'I don't know. Just later. When I feel like it.'

This last line spoken as if to a nanny he no longer had to take instruction from. Calloway had had enough. He left the boy to his sulking and tried the Fitzroy Tavern. No joy. He walked back towards Tottenham Court Road. He'd give it an hour or two. He thought about a drink but he didn't relish the joviality of a pub. The neon lights of a cinema pierced the smoggy haze that hung over the street. Now showing: Dangerous Beat. A Centurion Pictures Production. The poster showed two young hoodlums fighting a uniformed policeman. The sell-line read: In the battle for the streets, the heroes wear blue. In the few months since taking the job, Calloway had not seen a Centurion picture, at least not all the way through.

There was no queue outside the cinema. He read the showing times on the board and checked his watch. He could catch the next showing, wait out a couple of hours and return to Eve Clark's lodgings.

A voice from behind him said: 'Get us in, will ya?'

There were two of them. One short, one lanky. Both skinny in their hand-me-down jumpers and shapeless flannels. Calloway reckoned they were eight or nine, ten at a push, if you allowed for a decade of poor nutrition. The lanky one stood with his hands in his pockets looking sheepish. The short one stuck his hand out, proffering a shilling, the price of two tickets.

Calloway glanced up at the film poster in the case beside the cinema doors.

'It's certificate A,' he said.

A for adult. Not U for Universal. Nor U for urchin, unkempt, untrustworthy.

'I'm eleven and he's twelve,' the small one said. 'We just don't look it, that's all. Can't help that, can we? The old cow in the box office won't sell us a ticket 'cause she doesn't believe we're old enough.'

Calloway raised an eyebrow. He didn't believe they were old enough either.

'It's true,' the lanky one said. 'And the commissionaire said he'd cuff us if we came back.'

'He's a right bastard,' the short one said.

'Does your mother know you talk like that?' said Calloway.

'Ain't got a mother. She ran off with a sailor. I live with me gran. And she swears like a trooper.'

'It's true,' the lanky one said, like it was his catch phrase.

Calloway looked around him. The commissionaire stood sentinel outside the two large chromium doors. He was at least sixty, with a sallow face that hung loosely from a bony skull. His uniform was a size too big for his wizened frame. The braid on his epaulettes was unravelling. He didn't seem too alert.

There was no queue at the box office window. Calloway told the boys to stay where they were then bought a ticket for the circle and two for the stalls.

'Here,' he said, handing the small boy the two cheaper tickets. 'I'll distract the old man, you slip in when his back's turned.'

The boy gave him a conspiratorial wink. Calloway walked up to the commissionaire, flipped open his cigarette case and asked for a light. The old boy rifled in the pockets of his sagging uniform trousers and pulled out a box of Bryant & Mays. Calloway leaned in for the light, his broad back shielding the boys from view. He heard the doors open behind him and the faint scuffle of small feet. The commissionaire seemed not to notice.

The circle was half full. He took a seat two rows back from the balcony. The seats smelled musty. Above him, the beam of the projector illuminated dust. There was a faint metallic whir of film reels turning in the projection room. They were still showing the short. Popeye was downing spinach and beating hell out of a villain three times his size. Calloway could see the two boys in the stalls below. They jiggled in their seats and cackled.

The main feature opened to a menacing score. Strings and brass. The titles appeared over the shadows of darkened backstreets. A lone constable pursued two figures in silhouette, their footsteps smacking the cobbles and echoing above the music. The names of the writers Cedric Dryden and Michael Balfour appeared on the screen. Then the title: Dangerous Beat. The silhouetted figures appeared in the street light. The copper blew his whistle, its shrill tone jarring with the music. Cut to a quayside, steamers moored alongside, their masts puncturing the skyline. A steam whistle blasted in the background. The young copper leapt over a parapet onto the foreshore, the river glistening like hot tar. His helmet fell onto the stones and rolled towards the water. The hoodlums were an arm's length away now. One turned. Light shone on the pistol in his hand. The copper stopped in his tracks, truncheon raised. He was young, fresh-faced and blonde, his jaw clenched, fighting down the fear. The hoodlum was younger still. His hair was piled high, his face scarred. The score reached a crescendo. The pistol filled the screen. There was a flash from the muzzle. A gunshot echoed. Cut to the face of the copper, shocked, his jaw tightening as he feels the creeping pain. Then he fell. His dead eyes filled the screen. The score tailed away. The screen went dark. Words appeared: Director, Bobbie Brand.

Calloway was no expert but he had to hand it to Centurion. They knew how to make a picture. He looked down at the boys. They were silent and still. Transfixed. Calloway smiled. He settled into his seat and stared at the screen. He followed the plot for the first hour before sleep tugged at his eyelids.

He woke with a start. The end credits were rolling. He looked at his watch. Enough time had passed.

There was still no light in Eve Clark's window. The window above was dark too. The brat poet had gone out. The whole place appeared empty. He looked up and down the street. Not a soul about. The doorway was dark, the nearest streetlight a good twenty yards away. The darkness covered him. He reached into the inside pocket of his jacket and withdrew the six-inch metal ruler he'd taken from his desk. He slid it between the door frame and the lock. The door was old and loose. The lock was a simple night latch. It popped with little effort. Calloway looked around him. The street was still empty. He pushed against the door and stepped into damp-smelling hallway. It was pitch dark. Calloway flipped open his lighter. The flame lit up a gloomy stairway, with a cheerless floral print on the wallpaper. The bannister was worn and chipped. He headed up the stairs to the first floor. He trod firmly, with the footsteps of someone that was meant to be there. There may have been another tenant still in the house. He didn't want anyone to hear him creeping. Creeping would sound suspicious. He passed a lavatory on the half landing. The shared 'how's-yer-father' that the writer Julian had described. It smelled of Zal Pine with a hint of something nastier. He reached what he assumed was Eve Clark's door on the first-floor landing. He flipped the lighter shut and leaned in close to listen in the darkness. There was no noise from the other side. No light under the door. He tried the knob. It yielded to his turn. The door was unlocked. He stood there still and listened for signs of life in the rest of the building. He heard nothing but the intermittent rumble of car tyres on cobbles outside and voices of Saturday night revellers leaving the pubs and cinemas. He eased the door ajar. Its hinges creaked. The boards under his feet rasped as he stepped into the darkened room. The curtains were still open and a distant street lamp cast enough glow for him to make out furniture. A bed doubling as a couch, with a bolster and patchwork throw. A small reading light above it with a shade that looked like parchment and a braided flex leading down to a plug socket on the skirting. Bookshelves stuffed with paperbacks and magazines. A small drop-leaf table with two chairs, and a single armchair, well worn, wisps of horse hair bursting from cracks in the leather upholstery. A typical rented room, if your budget was slim and your expectations low. He guessed there wasn't much money in poetry. Especially when Mephisto was your publisher. He probably took more in free drinks than he gave out in royalties.

Calloway felt for a light switch. He found one to the side of the door. He flicked it down but no light appeared. Maybe the bulb had blown. He tried the reading light above the bed. No joy either. He flicked his lighter open again and looked for a meter. It stood on a shelf on the other side of the door, like a stout, sleeping robot with its rivets, pipes and dials. Fumbling in his pocket, he pulled out a shilling, pushed it into the slot and cranked the key until the coin dropped and the two lights came on. The faint ticking of the meter's dial irritated the silence.

With the benefit of light, the room was cheerful enough, with coloured cushions strewn around the place and surfaces draped with floral scarfs and throws. The pictures on the walls were chosen well, cheapish bric-a-brac but bought by someone with a good eye. Foreign landscapes, still life and nudes. They looked European. There were wax-encrusted wine bottles with candles in. The wine was French and reasonable. The table was covered with back issues of bohemian magazines. The Studio and Mephisto's poetry reviews. There was an old iron fireplace on the chimney breast and a plain mantlepiece above, with framed photographs in mismatched frames. Calloway examined the photos.

There was Joyce Rose, a teenage Joyce, and beside her the woman who'd fled the dinner, but brunette and younger. The picture looked at least a decade old. Seen side by side, the similarity between them was unmistakable. So too was the setting. Paris. Montmartre, by the look of it. Calloway had been there on leave from the front in forty-four. Here was Joyce and the sister from Paris. Sister Yvonne. The name on the postcards. Yvonne Leclerc. Anglicised, Eve Clark, as near as dammit. The poet and the missing cleaner. And the woman dolled up to the nines who seemed so keen to avoid Calloway on the night of the explosion. All one and the same. Deep down, Calloway had suspected this all along. The photo confirmed it.

He examined the other photographs one by one. Yvonne with friends mostly. In France again. One friend in particular. A young man. Tall and good looking. A little rugged perhaps, but distinguished too. He looked like a special friend. And he appeared in the last photo on the mantle. Just him and Yvonne. A studio portrait. Both in uniform. British uniforms from the war. Calloway picked up the photo and held it under the reading light to see better. He was looking at the insignia. The cap badges and shoulder flashes. It's what you do when you've lived half your life in uniform. He recognised both their units.

Everything made sense now.

He heard the floorboards creak. There was a figure in the doorway. Then a flattened hand struck him hard across the neck. A searing pain shot upwards to his skull. A second strike made his knees buckle. He steadied himself against the bed frame. He felt a blow to the kidneys, like a bad bruise multiplied a thousand times. Then an upper cut slammed into his jaw so that his teeth crunched together, the sound of grinding bone reverberating through his skull. He felt faint from the pain. A blanket of dazzling white light started to envelop him until only a chink of vision remained. Through it he saw the face. Eve Clark. Yvonne Leclerc.

He knew that by the next blow he'd be unconscious. He sank to his knees and thrust out his arm to grab her ankle. He jerked hard and saw her topple. Reaching up he pulled the reading light from above the bed and smashed it hard into her face. He saw sparks as the bulb shattered. Yvonne screamed, but just for a second. She recovered and scrambled to her feet. Calloway was on his feet too, a surge of adrenalin giving him a strength he'd not had moments before. Yvonne could kill him. Right there and then. He knew she was more than capable. Instead she ran. She was smart, a quick thinker. Better to flee and survive than to attempt a kill and die in the process. And she wasn't a killer by nature. He knew that too.

He ran for the door and threw his big frame down the stairs, stumbling downwards two treads at a time. He saw Yvonne, silhouetted in the open doorway. He fell into the street and looked around. He saw her twenty yards ahead, heading towards Tottenham Court Road. She wore a pale raincoat and red beret. At least it made her easy to spot. But she was fast. Faster than him. He gulped air deep into his lungs and tried to summon strength. He pushed himself on, towards her, seeing her turn left, losing herself in the late evening bustle.

He reached the street corner, panting. He looked to the left. He didn't see her, not at first. Then he caught a glimpse of the raincoat and beret. She was still running, turning right into a side street, attracting curious looks from passers-by. Women didn't run. Not unless they were caught in the rain or trying to catch a bus. Then they only ran in neat little steps. Ladylike running. Yvonne was sprinting. Calloway darted through the traffic. Angry horns blasted at him. A cabbie leaned out of his window and swore. A bus conductor hung off the pole at the back of a passing bus and shouted, 'You trying to get yourself killed?'

The side street was dark. At least darker than the road he'd just crossed. No proper lampposts, just small white lights on brackets bolted to the buildings along the street. They cast circles of dim grey light between swathes of black. Yvonne appeared in the light for a second then disappeared. She appeared again, her red beret glowing like a beacon. Calloway followed, running through the light and shade, watching her appear and disappear. Then she disappeared for good. He'd expected to see her under the next streetlamp. By the time he reached it himself, she was gone. He looked around. No doorways, no pubs, nowhere to hide. Yet she was definitely gone. He stopped and steadied himself against the wall. He gasped and wheezed, all the pain of the beating flooding back in one big wave. He drew up a gobbet of phlegm and spat between his feet. He looked around again. Yvonne Leclerc had vanished into the night.

Calloway took a taxi to the studio. He sat back in the worn leather bench seat and stretched his aching limbs. The cabbie made conversation. Calloway blanked him until he got the message. He heard the cabbie tut. Too bad. He hurt. But his brain was racing. The photographs told him everything. Well, almost. The cab reached the studio and pulled up outside the main gates. Calloway paid him without thanks. He resented being tutted. He let himself into the studio courtyard. His muscles hurt as he eased the heavy iron gates apart and squeezed between them. He nodded to Arthur the night watchman, who was pulling a Saturday shift. Arthur stuck his head out of his booth and said, 'Everything alright, Mr Calloway?'

He sounded almost guilty, as if Calloway's visit was

somehow due to him and he was going to receive a reprimand. That's the type Arthur was.

Calloway said, 'All correct, Arthur. Just need something from my office.'

Arthur didn't look convinced but pulled his little frame back through the window.

Calloway unlocked the administration block and climbed the stairs. His legs ached with every step. He unlocked his office door, walked in and fell back into the chair behind his desk. He fumbled in his drawer for the last of the Black & White and swigged from the bottle. The liquor helped, just like before. He unlocked the opposite drawer with a small key on his key ring. He pulled out the clutch purse, Yvonne Leclerc's clutch purse, and emptied the contents. He ignored the make-up, the loose change and the handkerchief. He picked up the tortoise shell pencil and unscrewed it. He was deliberately gentle. He laid the two unscrewed sections of the pen's barrel on his desk and pulled them apart to reveal a slender metal tube inside. Part copper, part brass, with a small pin and striker at one end. He'd seen something like it during the war. It was a time pencil. A fuse to trigger explosives.

TWENTY-FIVE

Ndungu called him at the office on Monday. He had news. He suggested a place to meet. Calloway slipped out of the studio early. By the time he reached Soho, the evening was drawing in.

'This place has just opened. Isn't it great?' said Ndungu as they took their coffees and sat on high stools at a chest-high bar opposite the counter. It was an Italian coffee bar, the first Calloway had seen in London. The Italians were back in Soho and this place screamed the fact. Calloway had never been to Italy. The war hadn't taken him there. He'd no way of telling how authentic the place was. The accents of the men behind the counter seemed exaggerated. But he guessed the coffee was good. It ought to be, given the size of the chromium machine that spat it out, with a roar like a Bugatti banking the corners at Brooklands.

Calloway watched Ndungu pull a sheaf of paperwork from an envelope in the reflection of the mirrored wall above the Formica bar top.

'You asked me to look into Centurion Pictures,' said Ndungu. 'Who its shareholders were, where the money comes from, that kind of thing.'

Calloway nodded.

Ndungu continued. 'The company has two shareholders. Sidney G Spelthorne owns forty-five percent. The majority shareholder is a holding company called Primipilus Group.'

Calloway looked quizzical.

'In the army of imperial Rome, the Primus Pilus was the chief Centurion.' Ndungu smiled. 'They clearly saw themselves as empire builders.'

Calloway nodded. 'What's a holding company?' he said.

Business wasn't his strong point. You tended not to worry about such things when the army gave you three meals a day, a bed and a pay-packet. You worried about being late, getting killed or losing a part of you that you'd really rather hang on to.

'Essentially it's a company that owns other businesses.'

'So what kind of businesses does Primipilus Group own?'

'Aside from their majority shareholding in Centurion, they have three operating companies. One runs a couple of dance halls in north London. Another is a private car service. Neither of those make much. The largest of the three is a property company, Mayho Estates Limited. They own a portfolio of properties in Mayfair and Soho, hence the name. Good income-producing stock by the looks of the figures, very good in fact.'

'So what do they do with the money?'

'A large proportion of their capital appears to be funnelled into Centurion.'

'To fund pictures?'

Ndungu nodded. He stirred his coffee and took a sip, pausing for a moment as if to judge its quality. He smiled, seeming satisfied.

'So Primipilus Group is crucial to the whole studio set-up?'

Ndungu nodded and took another sip of the coffee. He smiled again. The coffee must have been that good.

'Who's behind Primipilus? Who's on the board?'

Ndungu rifled thought the papers and handed Calloway a page listing the directors. One of the names struck a chord. Charles Lewis, who resigned his directorship less than a year ago, according to the list. He'd seen the name before but couldn't think where. It nagged at him like an itch he needed to scratch.

'Do you recognise any of those names?' said Ndungu.

'Perhaps. I'm not sure,' said Calloway. 'What kind of properties does Mayho Estates own?'

Ndungu looked apologetic.

'It's hard to tell from the addresses. Sorry.'

‘You have the addresses?’ Calloway said, surprised.

‘Yes, well, some of them at least. After I’d finished at Companies House, I paid a visit to the Land Registry. I did some digging around and found these.’

He passed over the details of almost a dozen buildings owned by Mayho. Most were walking distance from where they sat.

‘Fancy a stroll?’ said Calloway.

Ndungu nodded. He seemed to enjoy playing detective. Calloway placed the papers in the envelope, folded it in two, and slipped it into the inside pocket of his suit jacket. They paid and left.

The properties were easy to find. Most were on Greek Street and Frith Street. Most had shops on the ground floor. A newsagent, a hairdresser, a hardware shop. All pretty nondescript. None of them looked like big payers when it came to rent. But all had one thing in common. A shabby-looking side entrance and windows above with lamps in them. Night was falling and the lamps were on. They were all red.

The two men heard a voice from behind. ‘Are you looking for a little entertainment, gentlemen?’

He was short and swarthy and dressed like he was going to sell you a stolen watch. He could have been a shady character in one of Spelthorne’s crime stories. The stripes on his suit were too loud, the jacket cut too long. His shirt contrasted with his tie in a way that could induce a migraine. He gave Calloway a cursory once-over before looking Ndungu up and down more carefully. Next to Calloway’s ancient demob suit, the African student was dressed sharply and well, in his brown worsted two-piece, crisp white shirt and hand-made shoes. The small man’s eyes twinkled.

‘Of course if you were looking for something a little more exclusive, we have an establishment in Mayfair. A private club, if you will.’

He passed Ndungu a card. It was thick and embossed. No name. Just an address. Ndungu looked at Calloway and raised an eyebrow. They recognised it as one of the properties owned by Mayho Estates.

Calloway took the card from Ndungu. 'I think this looks very suitable,' he said.

The small man gave a conspiratorial nod.

'Tell the doorman you're there at the recommendation of Mr Rossi. He'll take care of you.'

As they walked away, Ndungu said, 'Good grief. He couldn't be more obvious if he tried. How does he get away with being so blatant?'

'His bosses must have coppers on the payroll.'

Ndungu looked surprised. 'The police can't be that crooked, can they?' he said. 'I read in the papers that they've just sent down the boss of a major vice ring.'

Calloway stopped. He remembered the article in the paper. Alfredo Azzopardi, sentenced to eight years, who sometimes went by the less incongruous name Charles Lewis.

'I'll say goodbye, Paul,' said Calloway. He waved the card. 'I'm going to take a look at this place. You've been very helpful. No need for you to get involved any further.'

Ndungu looked relieved. 'Even if I did want to join you, I'm not sure my student budget could stretch to it. My father's right. I spend far too much money on jazz records.'

'A far better thing to spend your money on,' said Calloway. 'No matter how God awful that music is. Bloody saxophones.'

Ndungu laughed. 'It's a mercy they don't have a smell, as you might say.'

He clapped Calloway on the arm with genuine warmth. Calloway thanked him again.

'I don't pretend to understand what all of this is about,' Ndungu said, 'but if it helps my friend Terrence, then it was worth the effort.'

The two men parted and Calloway headed west towards Mayfair. He was glad Ndungu was gone. The man was too good to get any more involved in the business Calloway had found himself in.

You're not getting involved again, are you Reg?

No, he thought. Not much. Just up to the fucking eyeballs.

The property was a narrow, stucco-fronted town house on Curzon Street, four storeys high with a grand-looking balustrade on the roof. Two laurel trees stood in polished brass planters either side of the shiny black door, each manicured into perfect spheres. There were net curtains behind the tall windows. They were impermeable. No club interior visible through them and nothing to identify the building beyond the number on the door. No brass plate, no club name. The porcelain dome of the bell button said Push. He pushed and a grand sounding bell rang in the hallway behind the door. There was a pause and the sound of a heavy bolt being slid back. A large figure in a dark coat and striped trousers filled the frame of the open door, his chest at Calloway's eye level. His face was flat and featureless, his leathery skin stretched taught like rhino hide. His expression gave nothing away. He waited. Calloway mentioned the name Rossi and without speaking the doorman stood back to let him into the hallway.

He was greeted by a woman announcing herself as Madame Lacroix, in an accent that was too French to be credible. She looked about fifty, or forty if you accounted for the hard life she'd no doubt had. She was powdered too pale and rouged too pink. Her hair was high and brittle. She'd packed an ample body into too little dress. She led him to a high-ceilinged drawing room on the first floor and asked him to take seat. He eased his big frame onto a velvet love seat that left little room for a lover. Madam Lacroix managed to squeeze in beside him nevertheless. Her undersized dress tightened as she sat. One false move and she'd spill out all over him.

The room was dimly lit by table lamps with deep red shades. Pictures in ornate gilt frames hung on the sage green walls. Regency-style prints of bawdy scenes. Something to get the punters in the mood, as if they needed it. A gramophone played a sickly dance number. There was company in the room too. Three girls perched daintily on chairs set against the wall. They smoked and toyed with what looked like soft drinks. A fourth sat on a high stool at a small bar in the corner. They wore modest cocktail dresses, showing no cleavage and not much leg. The dresses appeared expensive. The girls looked at him and smiled well-practiced smiles. Lacroix offered him a drink on the house. He ordered a gin and lime. She clicked her fingers at the girl at the bar, who gave a tolerant nod before slipping off the barstool, straightening her skirt and reaching for a half-full bottle of Beefeater on the glass shelf behind the bar. She held the cigarette between her painted lips while she poured the gin and splashed in some cordial. No ice, he noticed. And not much gin.

The Madame explained the terms of the house. Calloway agreed. She invited him to choose a girl. There were two blondes, a brunette and a redhead. He looked at each in turn. None of them gave the impression they wanted to be chosen, not deep down. They kept smiling, inclining their heads and crossing their legs with tired coquettishness. Their dead eyes bore into his soul. It made him uncomfortable. He'd never liked these places, even in the army, where a visit to a brothel was almost compulsory. He'd make excuses, even cried off sick. His comrades saw through it, nicknaming him Reverend. The name stuck until he made sergeant.

He wanted a talkative one. Someone who'd open up, given some encouragement. He settled on the redhead. She looked less jaded than the rest. Perhaps twenty, twenty-two at most. A tinge of apprehension behind her emerald eyes. She took his hand and led him to an upstairs room. Her hand was cold. She told him her name was Claudette.

The room was fake boudoir style. Faux silks and satins and furniture with gold legs. He sat on the round, pastel-pink button-backed chair by the closed curtains and took out his wallet. It was bulging with Spelthorne's hundred, which he'd barely touched. The redhead noticed. She turned away and unfastened the hook on the back of the cocktail dress, then eased down the zip. Calloway saw scars across her freckled white flesh.

'You can stop there,' he said. 'I just want to talk.'

She turned to face him and raised an eyebrow. 'One of those, eh? It starts with talking, but they always want the rest.'

'Just talk. And not that kind.'

She shrugged with indifference. 'It's your tenner,' she said.

'How long do we get?'

'Madame Lacroix tells us to aim for ten minutes. Fifteen's alright. At twenty she knocks on the door. Any longer than that, Charlie comes up.'

'The giant downstairs?'

She nodded. 'They don't hang around once Charlie shows his face. Some of the drunk ones try it on with him. They don't come back.'

'I want to ask you some questions. About the owners of this place.'

'Who the hell are you?' she said, lighting a cigarette as if by nervous reflex. 'You're not with Vassallo, are you?'

'Who's he?'

She looked at him as if he ought to know. 'They say he's trying to muscle in, demanding protection from the street girls. If you're with Vassallo, I'm calling Charlie.'

She made for the door. He jumped up from the chair and grabbed her by the arm, trying not to hurt her. She seemed so delicate. He'd always imagined they were bigger girls, more robust. Blowsy and foul-mouthed. She looked like a doll, a brittle, china doll.

'Sit down,' he said. 'I've never heard of Vassallo.'

He let go of her and she sat down on the bed. She drew hard on the cigarette and exhaled through tense lips.

'How much do you make?' he said.

She didn't look sure that she should answer. 'A hundred a night some nights.'

A brittle, china doll taking in ten punters a night. He felt nauseous.

'How much do you get to keep?'

'Fifty quid a week,' she said, with a hint of defiance.

He opened the wallet and counted out ten fivers. 'Here's the ten, and another forty for yourself. Got somewhere you can hide it?'

She laughed. 'They don't go a bundle on privacy here.'

She tucked two of the notes under the lamp on the bedside table, before easing up her skirt and slipping the remaining eight inside her stocking top.

'And that's private?' he said.

She shot him a look. 'Just ask your fucking questions,' she said.

She stubbed the cigarette out in a tiny glass ashtray. He offered her another, which she took.

'Ever heard of a company called Mayho Estates?'

She shrugged. 'Who are they when they're at home?'

'How about Primipilus Group?

She rolled her eyes. 'We're whores not chartered accountants, in case you hadn't noticed.'

She used the word whore like it tasted sour on her tongue. Then she laughed. 'Not that we don't get the odd chartered accountant in here.'

Calloway checked his watch. Five minutes gone already.

'Ever met a man called Charles Lewis?'

She shook her head.

'How about Alfredo Azzopardi?'

The emerald green eyes bore into him. 'Of course. I do read the papers you know.'

Calloway waved a hand around the room. 'Is this one of his establishments?'

'Of course not. He's in jail.'

'But was it?'

She looked around as if someone might be listening. She lowered her voice. 'Him and the old girl go way back, they say.'

'Madame Lacroix?'

She scoffed. 'Madam Lacroix, my arse. You mean Edna. Edna Purves. She's as French as I am. Nothing special about Edna. Been on the game since she was fifteen, they reckon. Azzopardi's dad was her ponce.'

'You ever see a man called Spelthorne in here? Sidney Spelthorne?'

She thought for a moment. 'I don't think so. What's he look like?'

'Middle-aged, bald, stocky, wears smart suits.'

She snorted. 'That's most of 'em.'

Calloway looked at his watch again. He'd been there ten minutes.

'What about a man call Giordano Spiteri?'

The girl that called herself Claudette froze.

'Gio?' she said. Her tone was hostile. 'I don't want to talk about Gio.'

She stood up and said, 'You're time's up. Edna will be knocking on the door soon. You need to leave. And do me a favour.' She stuck out a hip. Her nostrils flared. 'Look happy on the way out.'

He put his hand on the door, preventing her from opening it.

'When do you finish tonight?'

She glared. 'Why?'

'I want you to tell me about Giordano Spiteri. Meet me later. There's another fifty in it for you.'

'We're not allowed to meet clients outside.'

'Another fifty,' he said.

She stared at him, silent, weighing up the risk and return.

She lowered her voice. 'I'm on a half shift today. I finish at nine. The rest of the girls will be on till at least two. Meet me in the Chez Cup Bar at the Regent Palace Hotel at nine fifteen.'

There was a knock at the door.

'He's just on his way, Madame,' Claudette shouted, patting her stocking top to ensure the money was secure before ushering Calloway out.

TWENTY-SIX

The Chez Cup Bar was in a circular room under the hotel's entrance rotunda. Its upholstered banquettes with their jazz-age fabrics formed concentric circles, rimmed by the broad horizontal stripes of the curved walls. The floor followed a similar pattern, with circles of geometric tiles radiating outwards from a bullseye. It felt like being inside a giant roulette wheel. Calloway could almost sense it spinning. The place was past its prime now, its thirties heyday as a luxury nightspot for the people long since gone. The wear and tear of a decade and a half was showing badly. And the big tills behind the bar lowered the tone. They looked like something you'd find in Woolworths. But it was full enough to be anonymous. Calloway had bagged a table and two chairs, whose covers were worn and chrome legs chipped and tarnished. He ordered a gimlet, which to him was an overpriced gin and lime. The illuminated clock above the bar said ten past nine. He waited five minutes before Claudette appeared. She was punctual but didn't seem pleased to see him. He guessed she'd be pleased to see the other fifty pounds. She ordered a drink called an 'aviation' with Tanqueray. The waiter said they only had Gordon's. She and Calloway made small talk, which was awkward. Calloway got to the point. He asked about Giordano.

'I'm going to need another one of these,' she said, gesturing to the waiter. She ordered another for both of them. 'I met Gio at the Trocadero. I was a dancer with Cochran's review. I remember that show well. The two Hermiones were top of the bill.'

Calloway sensed he was supposed to be impressed. Instead

he looked blank. Claudette rolled her eyes.

'Baddeley and Gingold,' she said. 'You don't get out much, do you?'

Calloway shook his head but said nothing.

'He was there with Franco and two girls. If you know Gio you'll know Franco. Inseparable they were.'

'Still are, pretty much.'

She nodded without asking how he knew. In fact she didn't ask him anything about why he wanted to know these things. He guessed money talked and that was the only talk that counted.

'The girls weren't up to much,' she said. 'Nothing to look at really. I suppose they'd scrub up alright. I didn't realise what was happening.'

'What was happening?'

'Gio and Franco were doing to them what Franco did to me.'

Calloway wasn't following. His face said as much. She continued regardless.

'I noticed Gio straight away. His table was right at the front, almost touching the stage. I'd seen him from the wings and when I was doing the routine, I made sure I caught his eye. He was big, rugged, handsome. You could see his muscles through his dinner jacket. That's the first thing I noticed. He was a strong man. I liked strong men in those days.'

She looked Calloway up and down. Her face said he didn't measure up.

'After the show I met Gio at the bar. He'd left the girls with Franco. Us dancers weren't supposed to go out front with the diners but I never took any notice of that. I loved the glamour. Gio bought me a drink. He asked all about me, like he was really interested. Where I was from, did I have family, how I started dancing, what my ambitions were. He said I was the best dancer in the chorus line, which I knew I wasn't but I took the compliment gladly. I loved the attention he was giving me. Like no one else in the world mattered. I said, "What about your girlfriend?" He glanced over his shoulder to the girls with Franco and said she was only a date for the night. He'd agreed to make a foursome because his friend Franco was keen on the other girl. I believed him. Course I did. I wanted it to be true.'

The cocktails arrived and she took a large sip. She looked around the room, lost in her thoughts.

'I loved his accent. He told me he was Italian. Said he was a cousin of the great Caruso. I believed that too.'

She toyed with the glass, distracted. Calloway pulled put his cigarette case and offered her one. She accepted and leaned in to share the light. He smelled face powder and MaGriffe.

'He took me to the Cafe Royal on our first date. The Cafe Royal,' she said, emphasising the point. 'We had champagne. I'd never had champagne before. By the end of the night I knew that's all I ever wanted to drink. Next time we met he took me to the American Bar at the Savoy. We drank martinis and listened to the pianist. Gio held my hand and hummed along to the songs. He has a sweet voice would you believe.'

Calloway believed it, but he didn't care. A gorilla with a good singing voice is still a gorilla.

'Then he started taking me shopping. Bought me an evening dress and shoes and took me dancing. One day we met for lunch and he passed me a beautiful box tied with ribbon. You know what was inside?'

Calloway shook his head. He hadn't come here to hear about Spiteri's shopping habits.

'A mink stole. For me. A big, strong, handsome man who said he was Italian bought me a mink stole.'

'Very nice,' said Calloway without enthusiasm, wondering where this was going.

'He took me everywhere. The best restaurants, the most fashionable bars, the hottest night clubs. He lavished gifts on me you wouldn't believe.'

She stopped there. Her face hardened. She downed the cocktail and drew hard on the cigarette.

'Everything came at a price,' she said. 'That's how they work, right?'

'Who's they?' said Calloway.

'Christ. Were you born yesterday? Ponces,' she said, spelling it out. 'Get you hooked on the good life then tell you you've got to pay for it. You know the bastard even proposed to me. On one fucking knee.'

'So Giordano ponces for the Curzon Street club?'

'Club's a polite word for it. Yes, he does. Franco does too but he's not as good. Doesn't have Gio's looks and charm. God I was naive.'

Calloway couldn't say he'd noticed Giordano's looks and charm. He ordered two more drinks.

'Why do you stay?' he said.

She shook her head and tutted. 'You don't understand the game. When they've got you, they've got you. You're dependant. You've nothing to go back to. You've nothing to look forward to. You're stuck. On your back a dozen times a night, with a dozen different men. Even the Piccadilly commandos don't notch up that many in a night.'

Those he'd heard of. The whores that took pissed-up soldiers down back the alleys off Piccadilly Circus for a quid a time. They left their knickers off to make it easier.

'Have you ever tried to leave?'

'Once,' she said. 'Gio has a way of dealing with girls that try to leave.'

She put a hand across her chest and touched the back of her shoulder. Calloway remembered the scars he'd seen when she'd started to undress.

'He uses an electric light flex,' she said.

He had nothing to say to that. All he could think was what he might do to Giordano next time he saw him.

'So Giordano and Franco work for Alfredo Azzopardi procuring girls for their brothels?'

Claudette nodded. 'I've heard they provide muscle as well,' she said. 'For a few of Alfredo's friends.'

'And you've never seen or heard of a friend called Sidney Spelthorne? Think hard.'

She gave him a petulant look. The drinks arrived and she took hers straight from the tray before the waiter had a chance to set it down.

‘He runs a film studio,’ Calloway prompted. ‘Centurion Pictures.’

She looked blank at first, stared at the table for a moment, then looked up at him. ‘There’s a man they call Carmelo,’ she said. ‘He’s in pictures, I think. He came to Curzon Street once. Edna and Alfredo seemed to know him.’

‘Does this man Carmelo have a second name?’

She frowned, thinking for a moment. The third aviation seemed to make it harder to remember. Then she snapped her fingers and said, ‘Portelli. Edna once said that if we were good, her friend Mr Portelli might get us in pictures. It was the kind of bullshit she and Alfredo would feed us to keep us keen.’

She sat back in her chair and looked around the room for a distraction. It was a signal that Calloway’s time was up. At least he’d had more than ten minutes, he thought, even if he was paying five times the going rate. He took her hand and pushed a wad of bank notes into it. Her hand still felt cold, in spite of the heat of the bar and the three aviations she’d downed. Instinctively she stuffed the money straight into her handbag.

‘Not enough to retire,’ she said. ‘But thanks all the same.’

Calloway slid his wallet back into his pocket. That was his hundred gone. But he was a step closer to understanding the whole sordid picture.

TWENTY-SEVEN

He left Claudette at the bar. She claimed to be meeting someone. He wondered how many aviations she could hold. He already felt light-headed from the three gimlets he'd downed in the space of an hour. At least the alcohol dulled the pain of the blows Yvonne Leclerc had so expertly administered. He needed to confront her. To establish that last, indisputable fact that would connect everything. He flagged a cab to North Soho.

There was no light from Yvonne's room. He rang the bell. There was no reply, but the room above Yvonne's was lit. He couldn't risk breaking in again, not with someone in the building. He banged on the door with his fist.

The boy poet answered. When he saw it was Calloway he summoned some authority, the type they bang into you at expensive schools, and said, 'Now look here, I'm getting pretty fed up with you turning up on the doorstep. What the hell do you want this time?'

He sounded like Wooster berating Jeeves.

'Same as the last two times. Eve Clark,' said Calloway.

The boy smiled a satisfied smile. 'Too late, chum. She's cleared out and I don't blame her.'

Calloway pushed past the boy, ignoring his protestations as he climbed the stairs. Yvonne's door was unlocked. Half her possessions were gone, the rest abandoned. The place was a mess, like she'd packed in a hurry. The boy stood in the doorway muttering something about private property.

'When did she leave?'

'Sunday,' the boy said. 'I went out for lunch, came back and she was gone.'

'Where's she gone?'

The boy shrugged. 'Search me, chum.'

Calloway turned on him. He grabbed the boy's lapels and dragged him out onto the landing.

'Call me chum again and I'll throw you down those bloody stairs.'

The confidence of breeding was suddenly gone. The boy looked terrified, as if wishing he could hide behind nanny's skirts. Calloway let him go.

Out on the street he retraced his steps on the night he'd pursued Yvonne. It was less busy tonight. A week night. He crossed Tottenham Court Road into the side street where Yvonne had vanished. He walked through the circles of street light into the intermittent darkness. There were no doorways or windows. Nothing to suggest a hiding place. He felt along the wall with his hands, letting his fingertips glance over the rough brickwork and damp bill posters. In a darkened part of the street he felt a smoother surface, partly concealed by posters. It was cold metal and from behind it he heard a faint humming. Some kind of ventilation intake. They were common enough. The kind that sucked air down into the tube network. He eased his fingers around the vented metal panel. One side was loose. He pulled at it. It moved easily, being hinged on the opposite edge. Behind it was darkness. Pitch black darkness, the humming louder. Calloway flipped his lighter open. On the other side of the panel was a narrow set of spiral stairs. Some kind of maintenance shaft, he assumed. The flame of his lighter flickered on the stream of air being sucked downwards. Calloway placed his foot on the first step to test it. It was solid. He squeezed himself fully into the void behind the panel and started to descend.

The walls were filthy with years of dust and soot, the darkness sucking in all the light so that the flame of Calloway's lighter was barely enough to see by. He stepped lightly but the sound of his feet on the metal stair treads still reverberated down the shaft in a series of regular clangs cutting through the hum, which grew louder as he descended. He lost count of the number of steps, but reckoned he must have descended a good fifty feet by now. Still there was no sign of the bottom. He paused and pulled a small coin that felt like a halfpenny from his pocket. He dropped it down the shaft, hearing it clatter as it fell. There was another fifty feet to go, he guessed, although he couldn't be sure. He found a second vented panel at the bottom, opening into a tunnel which must have been at least fifteen feet high. The tunnel housed a huge extractor fan, the height of man, its oversized blades rotating with the noise of an aero engine. Calloway squeezed past the casing of the fan, the noise and vibration hurting his eardrums. Behind was a bulkhead from floor to ceiling and within it a door. Calloway tried the door. It opened onto a far longer stretch of tunnel, which was divided horizontally into two floors, a stairway to his right leading to the upper floor. The lower floor was as dark as the ventilation shaft, but there was light coming from the upper floor. He climbed the stairway into the light.

'If you move another muscle, I'll shoot you dead.'

It was a woman's voice.

She stood between two rows of abandoned bunk beds under the dim light of the bulbs overhead. There was a pistol in her hand aimed at Calloway. A strange-looking weapon of simple construction. Just two tubes, one for the grip, another for the barrel. Calloway knew this weapon. A Welrod. A six-round silenced pistol. An ugly beast. It looked like something a plumber had made but was no less deadly for it. It fired 9mm parabellum rounds that could tear a man's guts apart or blow his brains from his skull. And it could do it without a soul hearing.

'I just want to talk, Yvonne,' he said.

The name he used surprised her. 'Where would talking get me?' she said.

'Somewhere better than you'd end up if you pulled that trigger.'

'Really? You think anyone would find you here?'

'You might have killed before Yvonne, but this is different. This is peacetime.'

'There's no peace for me,' she said.

'I know what happened to Celeste. I can guess why you're angry. But what you're doing needs to stop. The only one that'll end up hurt is you.'

She laughed. 'And why would you care? Why would Sidney Spelthorne's head of security care about someone he's never met. Someone he knows nothing about.'

'I know more about you than you think. I've pieced your story together, at least parts of it. I know enough about Celeste and enough about you to know you're not a bad person.'

She scoffed. 'There's bad in everyone, believe me.'

He knew that too. War brings out the best and worst in people, but usually the worst.

'I just want to talk, Yvonne. You can keep the gun on me if it makes you feel better.'

He wasn't sure it would make him feel better, but he was short on options. It wasn't as if he could run for it. They were a hundred feet underground.

Yvonne stood silently, the gun in her hand level with his guts. That would be a slow and painful death. He'd seen enough stomach wounds during the war to know. All blood, shit and screaming.

'Turn around,' she said.

Calloway did as he was told. He braced himself. If it was going to happen, it would happen now. She wouldn't want to look him in the eye. This wasn't personal. He was just an inconvenience. One that could put her in jail for a very long time. He didn't often pray. He didn't believe. He'd seen too much during the war to believe a higher power would allow such things. Lapsed chapel, Marjorie had called him. He was way beyond lapsed. The trauma of war had instilled him with a deep and lasting atheism. But right now he found himself praying for a head shot. Quick and deadly. He heard Yvonne take two paces forward. His stomach knotted and his bowels constricted. He felt faint. A blinding white light started to envelope him. Then he heard her voice.

'You see the office?'

He saw a room built against the curved wall of the tunnel.

There was a sign on the door that said Warden's Station.

'We can talk in there,' she said.

There was a light on inside. It lit up a room about twelve feet square, with official-looking posters on the walls. Air raid procedures, fire instructions, a list of telephone extensions. The posters were dog-eared and damp-stained. There was a bunk bed along the far wall like the ones in the tunnel dormitory, but this one had a makeshift mattress of bedding and cushions. He recognised the patchwork quilt from Yvonne's room.

She gestured with the pistol for him to sit on the bed. He complied. She pushed a stacking chair against the wall furthest from him and sat. There was a table beside her, strewn with a few possessions. The framed photos of Yvonne and Celeste in France, and of Yvonne and the officer in their uniforms. Some brushes, make-up and a small shaving mirror, the latter he assumed had been the warden's whenever this place was last used, probably during the war. She'd been cooking from tins on a Primus stove. There was also a bottle of wine. It was opened but still two-thirds full. She picked up a tin mug and poured a generous measure. She passed this to Calloway, the Welrod gripped firmly in her other hand. She gestured for him to drink then swigged from the bottle herself. She kept hold of the pistol but rested it on her knees.

'You wanted to talk,' she said. 'So talk.'

The authority had gone from her voice. She sounded resigned. And she looked tired. She was still beautiful, Calloway thought. As beautiful as her film star sister. But Yvonne's beauty was tarnished, turned ugly by bad experience and no doubt worse thoughts. Calloway had seen so many faces ravaged by war. Fresh-faced boys turned to tired old men. Handsome young bucks returning frail and bitter. All manner of beauty besmirched.

Calloway downed the wine in thirsty gulps. He held the tin mug in both hands and leant forward, his elbows resting on his knees.

'I saw you running from the gala dinner on the night of the bombing. I picked up the purse you dropped. You were dressed up like a charm school starlet but there was something different about you. You weren't the usual type of Centurion hopeful. And you knew me, knew I was security at least, and when you saw me, you ran. You looked afraid. But not of the explosion or the chaos that ensued. You looked afraid of getting caught. That made me curious. More than curious. I'll admit you became something of an obsession. Special Branch was chasing the IRA, but I was more interested in you. I checked the charm school files. I found a photo that I thought was you. It was your sister, although I didn't know it at the time. Then someone told me the actress in the file was dead. Killed herself with gin and pills. I looked into Joyce's story. Let's call her Joyce for now. The name the studio gave her. She was Spelthorne's favourite. I mean favourite like a racehorse is a favourite. Something you put money on. She was good too. She could act and she was starting to get the parts. The trouble was she got noticed. I don't mean by the folk that go to the pictures, although they certainly warmed to her. So did the critics. She got noticed by a man called Alfredo Azzopardi. A Maltese gangster that controls prostitution in London. A thoroughly unpleasant man that exploits young girls for money. Ruins their lives. This Azzopardi could have any number of the girls he keeps in his brothels, but he wanted Joyce. Not to whore for him, although that might have come later. I imagine he wanted her as a trophy. A symbol of respectability, or perhaps celebrity. He let Spelthorne know this. Told him to arrange it. Spelthorne didn't think twice about offering his favourite starlet to this man. He got his man Giordano, who moonlights as one of Azzopardi's ponces, to fix it. Or at least he tried to. Why? Because Azzopardi was one of Spelthorne's backers, a director of a company called Primipilus Group. Primipilus launders the dirty money from Azzopardi's brothels, via a property company called Mayho Estates, and funnels it into Centurion Pictures. You see Azzopardi and Spelthorne are old friends. They go way back. Back to the days when Spelthorne went by his real name, Carmelo Portelli. The Bentley that went up, the one with CP1 on the number plate? I bet you thought that stood for Centurion Pictures. It stands for Carmelo Portelli, a little nod to Spelthorne's roots in the Saffron Hill Maltese community.'

He saw small tears welling in Yvonne's tired eyes. She wiped them away with her sleeve and shook herself, as if disgusted by her own emotions.

'It killed her didn't it?' said Calloway. 'Being offered to a gangster as a tribute. Whether her death was deliberate or accidental, Joyce died because of these men. Spelthorne, the self-made mogul, Azzopardi, the gangster, Giordano, the ponce, even Ivor Cole, the publicist who turned a talented young woman with drive and ambition into a performing puppet for his publicity campaigns. It wasn't the gin, or the pills, or the betrayal, or the feeling of utter hopelessness that killed your sister. It was these men, and every man like them in the dirty business we call pictures.' He took another gulp of the wine. 'And you came back from France intent on doing something about it.'

Yvonne looked up at him. 'Did I?' she said. 'Why do you think that? You've got no proof.'

He nodded to the framed photo of Yvonne in uniform. 'The cap badge. I recognised it. The First Aid Nursing Yeomanry. The FANYs we used to call them. It explained everything. The explosion, the damage to the studio equipment, the fact that you carry a time pencil in your purse and keep a Welrod pistol in this underground lair you now call home.'

She smiled and put the wine bottle to her lips to drink. It was his moment. He summoned all the strength he could muster and sprang up from the bed. He threw the tin mug at the woman's head. She ducked by reflex, dropped the wine bottle, then raised the pistol from her lap. Calloway was faster. He pulled the Welrod from her hand and pushed her back into the chair. He returned to the bunk and sat, pointing barrel of the ugly weapon in her direction.

'Now you tell me your story,' he said.

TWENTY-EIGHT

A major in The Buffs called Selwyn Jepson had recruited Yvonne personally in late 1943. He had been lunching at the Granchester Hotel where Yvonne's parents worked. They had pulled strings to get her work as a waitress, after she'd proved unsuitable for a succession of jobs - secretary, telephonist, shop assistant in a florist - mostly through her seeming inability to take any instruction she disagreed with. Her sister Celeste was the agreeable daughter, she went out of her way to please. Yvonne could be most disagreeable when she wanted to. And she was proving a poor waitress. She came to Jepson's attention quite suddenly when she stumbled and spilled oxtail soup into his lap. Jepson, to her relief, didn't make a fuss. He quickly gathered up the serviette from his lap and screwed it into a ball before the sticky brown liquid had a chance to stain the trousers of his uniform.

'No harm done,' he said, smiling at Yvonne. He had an oval face with dark, piercing eyes, mischievous caterpillar eyebrows and a head of wavy hair. He friends told him he looked like Claude Rains. Yvonne thought he looked kind and she was grateful for his understanding. She had no love for the waitressing job, but this was the hotel her parents had worked at most of their lives. It was their reputations at stake as much as hers. Jepson's lunch guest, a Frenchman in a civilian suit, was less understanding. He made disparaging comments in French, suggesting that the girl should be sacked. Yvonne, conscious the head waiter was by this point looking very much in her direction, started to apologise in fluent French. Jepson raised a mischievous eyebrow and listened with interest. He sat back in his chair, his smile broadening with every word she spoke.

'Do you speak any other languages?' he asked.

'Some German,' she said, swiftly adding, 'my mother is Alsace French' to avoid arousing any suspicion from the stranger in uniform.

'Do you enjoy your job?' he asked.

She gave an embarrassed smile and looked over at the head waiter, who was scowling at her, gesturing that she should withdraw from the table at once.

'I'm not sure I'll have a job for much longer if I carry on like this,' she said, scooping up the soiled serviette. Jepson unbuttoned the breast pocket of his uniform jacket and pulled out a calling card. He checked to see if the head waiter was looking before giving Yvonne a conspiratorial wink and saying, 'Call me on this number. I may have some work for which your abilities might be better suited.'

She had assumed Jepson had singled her out for some kind of administration or translation work. But after a series of interviews, the first by Jepson himself, she realised that what the kind-looking major had in mind for her was both top secret and dangerous. His plan was to drop her, along with others like her, into occupied France to subvert and sabotage the enemy war effort. She would be part of a unit called the Special Operations Executive. At first she thought he was joking. Some test perhaps for something altogether more prosaic. This SOE sounded like something a writer of thrillers had dreamt up. (She was unaware that in addition to his military role, Jepson was indeed a well-known writer of thrillers.) The idea of training men, and more to the point, women, to pose as French civilians while secretly carrying a pistol in their knickers and a stick of dynamite god knows where sounded too fanciful to be true. But Jepson was serious. In fact, he had lobbied Churchill personally to be allowed to recruit female agents, considering them better than men for the task due to their greater capacity for what he called 'cool and lonely courage'.

She was reluctant at first. The work sounded foolhardy and by no means assured of success. Female SOE agents operated outside the protection of the Geneva Convention and fell within the Nazi's Nacht und Nebel law, which permitted execution without trial. Once deployed she would have an estimated life expectancy of six weeks, a fact she did not learn until much later and which may have swayed her ultimate decision.

She had been brought up to consider herself as much French as English. She and Celeste had spent many summers with their grandparents during the school holidays and she considered France a second home, with not a little pride and a fair degree of patriotism. She was in time brought around to the idea that she could play a meaningful role in ridding Europe of the Nazi scourge, for the sake of her family in France. Before long, she became impatient to do her bit, something that Jepson, an enthusiastic sponsor of Yvonne's, had worked hard to encourage.

She joined the First Aid Nursing Yeomanry. It was the parent unit for female agents of the Special Operations Executive, essentially a cover that would allow them to move in military circles without giving away their true role. Anyone one who met her in her new, and to her mind rather frumpy, uniform would assume she was probably a driver, or something equally dull.

She was sent for training to a succession of stately homes in remote locations that had been requisitioned by the War Office. At each location she learned the skills of clandestine warfare. Coding, close combat, even silent killing. There were a series of schools, some with names Yvonne considered ridiculous. There was parachute school, which was fair enough, but 'toughening up school' and 'finishing school'? There was something childishly Baden Powell about it all.

Some parts of her training seemed dull and pointless. Other parts were either gruelling or quite disturbing. She'd be woken in the middle of the night and dragged off for interrogation by instructors dressed as Nazis. Or she'd be hectored by overzealous instructors into crossing the 'slack-ropes' between what appeared to be two of the tallest trees in a Scotland as the finale of the assault course.

‘I can’t see the point in that,’ she’d said to her instructor. ‘We’re fighting Nazis, not bloody monkeys.’

This earned her the nickname Guenon, French for monkey, for the remainder of her training.

She attended ‘finishing school’ at Beaulieu House, an overbearing and draughty old pile in the New Forest. At Beaulieu she met a young lieutenant in the Coldstream Guards called Leonard Howes. At first she knew him only by his codename, Renard. By this stage in their training only code names were used. Born to an English father and French mother, he was educated in France while his father, a civil servant with the foreign office, was attached to the British Embassy in Paris. Unlike other civil service brats, he was spared boarding school in England. This was at his mother’s insistence. Despite their differences in background, the attraction between the Leonard and Yvonne was obvious. Relationships between trainees were strictly discouraged, the risk being pregnancy and birth in the field. But by the end of finishing school, Leonard and Yvonne were secretly engaged. He had proposed on one knee with the ring of a dummy hand grenade. Their compatibility had been noticed by their instructors, though not their love affair, which was strange considering the extent to which their every behaviour was scrutinised. Perhaps this was testament to the clandestine skills they had developed. As a result they were paired for their first operation: Leonard as circuit leader and Yvonne - by this time codenamed not surprisingly Guenon - as courier. Their wireless operator was a female agent they knew only by the codename Souris. The fox, the monkey and the mouse. Their clandestine network would be known by the codename Menagerie.

Menagerie’s first operations was to organise the resistance in a part of west-central France to sabotage French factories producing machinery for the German war effort. Yvonne’s role as courier would be to liaise with the leader of the local Maquis, briefing him on targets and arranging for the supply of finance and arms.

Yvonne was dropped into France by parachute after four

extremely cold hours in a modified Halifax bomber of the RAF's 138 (Special Duties) Squadron, during which she tried to keep warm with the help of a thin sleeping bag and a flask of weak coffee. She trembled throughout the flight, whether through nerves or cold she couldn't tell.

'Five minutes,' the co-pilot shouted down from the cockpit above the engine noise. 'I'm putting the red light on.' He flicked the switch and she was engulfed in a glow the colour of blood. If she'd wanted a bad omen, this was undoubtedly it. She knew it was merely the way to allow her eyes to adjust to the darkness of the night she would be dropping into. But she couldn't help but be discomfited by it as she shivered in the cold, coffin-like fuselage of the noisy aircraft.

Her RAF dispatcher, who had sat beside her for most of the flight without saying a word, save for offering her some curled-up sandwiches, now gestured upwards with a flattened hand and shouted, 'Red on.' A demonic crimson eye bore into her. The dispatcher opened the circular hatch in the floor. A gust of icy air blew upwards into her face. She could see the ground below. There was France. Her second home and now her battlefield. She reached into her jumpsuit to reassure herself that the Llama .38 calibre automatic was still in her jacket pocket. She couldn't imagine using it, despite being the best shot on the training course. Right now it was more like a lucky charm.

'Drop your legs over the hatch, miss,' the dispatcher shouted. She eased herself towards the hole and dangled her legs over the edge. The freezing air bit her ankles like a snarling German Shepherd. Her nerves turned to fear. An ice-cold fear that surged through every vein in her body, numbing her from head to toe.

'Remember the drill, miss. Tuck your chin in when you jump. You don't want to lose your teeth.'

She nodded, not sure that she'd heard or understood. She felt a reassuring hand on her shoulder.

The dispatcher leaned into her and spoke quietly into her ear. 'It'll be alright, miss.'

An estimated life expectancy of six weeks.

She felt a sudden urge to vomit.

The red eye closed, the green eye opened.

'Green on. Go!' the dispatcher shouted.

She gritted her teeth, eased her backside over the rim of the hatch and fell feet-first into the darkness.

TWENTY-NINE

The rush of night air sucked the breath from her lungs. Her parachute opened for what seemed like only a few seconds before she hit the cold ground hard in her civilian shoes. She rolled by reflex. The still-inflated chute dragged her before she grabbed the straps and wrestled it to the ground like a great billowing beast. Then she stopped, crouched on her haunches, perfectly still in the quiet. No broken bones. She ran her tongue over her teeth. Still there. She let her eyes adjust to the light of the full moon. The faint sound of the Halifax's engines faded to silence. She felt entirely alone.

She realised now that she had been blown off course during the drop and missed her reception committee. Leonard should have been there with members of the Maquis to take her into town to a safe house. But there was no one, neither friend nor foe. She concealed her parachute and jumpsuit like she'd been taught, picked up the suitcase that had been dispatched thought the hatch after her, and made for the woods at the edge of the field. She would have to rough it tonight and contact Renard by letter box tomorrow. She did her best to burrow into the mossy ground at the foot of a tree, but she didn't sleep. Every breath of wind through the trees, every rustle of leaves conjured images of Germans, their jackboots stamping through the dense woodland in search of her. But no one came. Her arrival still seemed to be a secret.

Before dawn she walked the eight miles to her final destination. The small shabby town with its worn-down flagstones and peeling walls was waking up. She could hear the sounds of early morning. The clang of milk churns, the clank of last night's wine bottles, a church bell striking six. She caught the reassuring smell of a bakery. As she passed it, she saw through its open door the baker, wearing only underpants and an apron as he shovelled perfectly formed parcels of dough into the glowing oven. It made her laugh and forget her fear, at least in that moment.

She walked to the railway station, navigating by the map she had memorised. She checked the timetable pinned to the wall and noted the time and destination of the first train. Limoges, 06.10h. If asked she would say she was waiting for the train, using the cover she had been given by her French Section handlers. She was a sales representative for a cosmetics supplier, travelling the west-central region visiting retail clients.

At eight o'clock she made her way to the cafe in the town square to send a message to Renard via the letterbox. The cafe was open but empty. She sat at one of the tatty chairs with a good view across the square. The letterbox was in reality a surly waitress called Marie-France who, she had been told, was the niece of a resistant. What she lacked in grace she made up for in discretion, apparently. Yvonne used the agreed password, which Marie-France acknowledged with a bored look. Yvonne ordered coffee and tartine and waited.

Around ten minutes later Yvonne got her first sight of the enemy. A German patrol was crossing the square towards the café. Her heart started to thump in her chest. Her mouth went dry and her limbs went weak. Then she felt a surge of adrenalin-fuelled anger. Could Marie-France have betrayed her? Was that sulky little bitch an informer? She ran her hand over the outline of the automatic in her pocket. But what use was that against four Wehrmacht soldiers with machine pistols and rifles? She looked to the rear of the café, wondering if she should make a run for it through the back. But there could be more soldiers there, waiting. She pictured Marie-France sitting on the knee of her Gestapo boyfriend, smoking a German cigarette and tucking a fifty-franc reward into her stocking top.

The patrol stopped in the middle of the square. One of the soldiers unbuttoned his fly as he walked into the little round pissoir. He stood behind the pissoir's half-screen, his boots visible below, his head bobbing up and down above them like something from a Punch and Judy show as he stood there pissing. Splashes of urine spattered his boots. His comrades laughed and made obscene gestures. Yvonne's beating heart slowed and she felt a wave of relief. It was just a routine patrol and a young soldier cut short. She needed to get a grip of herself. This was her life now.

Marie-France brought the coffee, bread and jam and placed it on the table with the merest hint of a smile. Yvonne felt a pang of guilt for the bad thoughts she'd had about the girl. Then she heard a wonderfully familiar voice.

'It's a beautiful morning.'

She fought hard against the urge to fling herself into his arms. She wanted him badly, right there and then. Fear had turned to a desperate passion, as her overwrought mind played with her emotions. Instead she did her best to give the most casual of nods towards the chair opposite, inviting him to join her. She looked into his eyes for a moment and couldn't resist a smile, and the tiniest, most provocative of pouts.

That night he stayed with her at the safe house. It was contrary to his orders but neither of them cared. They made desperate love, like the final wish of the condemned. Tomorrow they might die.

The safe house was a one-room bedsitter above a shabby, disreputable-looking bar opposite the railway station. It had a cold-water sink, a gas ring and tatty, but comfortable furniture. The privy, bizarrely she thought, was in a makeshift cubicle on the small balcony that overlooked the street. The next door flat had the same arrangement, meaning the sound of bodily functions was frequently shared between neighbours, somewhat to Yvonne's discomfort - although this should have been the least of her worries. There was one other tenant in her building, a worn-out prostitute who would take clients she'd picked up in the bar downstairs to the room above Yvonne's. Her clients were French, not German - Leonard had done his homework - and the frequent comings and goings made it easier for Yvonne's movements, and those of visitors like Leonard, to go unnoticed. This was welcome. What was less welcome was the nightly sound of drunken Frenchmen fucking to the unenthusiastic encouragement of a veteran whore. Yvonne knew France well, but this was an experience she'd thus far been spared.

She spent the coming weeks making visits to a town twenty kilometres away, taking messages from French Section in Baker Street, via Renard and Souris, to contacts in the Maquis. She was the go-between, arranging for the supply of cash and equipment to be used for sabotage. Plastique explosives, detonators, Sten guns, silenced pistols and ammunition, dropped by parachute in long metal canisters onto remote drop zones that had been reconnoitred by Leonard, who would travel many miles by bicycle using a Michelin tourist map to identify suitably remote locations.

Yvonne would travel by train in the third-class carriages, sitting on the hard wooden bench seats next to men who smelled of sweat that were carrying live geese by their necks to market. In third class she didn't need to make conversation, as she would have done in second. This meant less chance of her cover being compromised.

She suffered gut-wrenching nerves on every trip, with the foul taste of fear in her mouth, bile in her gullet and bowels fit to burst. Her papers were forgeries and only good enough to withstand cursory inspection at the frequent police checkpoints. If she were ever taken in, the Gestapo would discover her identification number was fake. She had been briefed on what would happen next. They would interrogate her, most likely torture her, so that she would give away the members of her circuit, their resistance contacts and their mission. Then she would be sent to a concentration camp, where death would follow through maltreatment, starvation or execution. The only way to avoid this fate was to swallow the death pill concealed in the lipstick she carried with her everywhere.

She saw Leonard more frequently than was safe from an

operational perspective, but true to form she believed that some rules were meant to be broken. And anyway, she thought, it was her life at risk here, not the top brass back home who made the rules. If she could find some solace from the daily routine of anxiety, she was damn well going to take it. On the nights he stayed they would make love nosily and with abandon, their cries lost among the insincere moans of the whore upstairs.

Two months into the operation, the Menagerie circuit received new orders from Baker Street. They were instructed to scale up the Maquis's activities to prepare for the Allied invasion of Europe. The objective was to sabotage road and rail routes to disrupt German military supply lines and to equip resistance groups to support allied troops in their push through France. Yvonne approached this new assignment with confidence. She had excelled in the explosives and demolition course during her training. Supply drops increased, now with heavier weapons like Bren Guns and anti-tank rifles, together with thirty thousand francs to finance operations. And the circuit needed more SOE agents to coordinate resistance. Leonard, as circuit leader, was charged with identifying landing zones capable receiving the small Lysander aircraft that would bring new agents from London. He and Yvonne instructed members of the Maquis to serve as reception committees, using hand-held torches as landing lights on the improvised runways, in reality flat fields in remote locations, their fences pulled up and other obstructions removed.

Yvonne took part in these night-time operations with Leonard, leading the reception committees and driving newly arrived agents to their safe houses in an old truck powered by an improvised charcoal burner, the kind that had become a necessity due to the shortage of petrol for civilian use.

One such operation proved disastrous for the Menagerie circuit.

It was a clear night with a full moon. The wind was moderate and the ground conditions good. The pilot of the Lysander had no trouble making out the two rows of improvised landing lights. He put the small aircraft down without a hitch. His passenger, a twenty-four-year-old SOE agent codenamed Blaireau, slid back the plexiglas hatch at the rear of the cockpit. As he stepped onto the fixed ladder on the port side of the aircraft's fuselage, the sound of gunfire cut through the night above the din of the Lysander's engine. Blaireau fell to the ground with a thud. His body lay motionless. Yvonne heard Leonard shout 'Christ.' He pointed towards the edge of the landing field where a dozen armed men were running towards them. They wore oversized berets, belted tunics and baggy trousers tucked into high-laced boots. By the light of the moon Yvonne saw that the uniforms were blue, not the field grey the Germans wore. They carried Berthier carbines and captured Sten Guns. They were Milice, French fascist paramilitaries loyal to Vichy. They were viscous bastards. Yvonne knew this. The Milice were easily more feared than the German Wehrmacht. They were said to be more ruthless than the Gestapo. You didn't want to get captured by the Milice.

Leonard dropped to one knee and raised his Sten Gun. He fired at the advancing Miliciens in short, controlled bursts, then gestured to the Lysander to leave. Yvonne heard the rapid fire of a light machine gun as a Milicien FM 24/29 tore into the cockpit of the aircraft. She saw the pilot slump. The Lysander continued to taxi across the landing field towards a copse of trees at the edge of the field, the dead pilot at the joystick. Gunfire echoed around her. She was disorientated. The sudden surge of adrenalin made her head spin and her knees weak. A bullet buzzed like a hornet past her ear, close enough for her to feel its heat against her flesh. It snapped her back to attention. She looked around her for cover, but there was none. The landing field was flat, the trees that surrounded it too far away. There was no chance of running. The Milice were too close. She remembered her training. She drew the Llama .38 from the waistband of her trousers, gripped it with both hands and raised it to eye level, bending her knees as she'd been taught. She selected her target and loosed off two rounds, double tap. The Milicien fell. He lay on the ground clutching his belly and screaming obscenities. A tremor of satisfaction shot through her body. Almost sexual. She selected another target and again fired twice. The shots went wide. She heard Leonard shout, 'Guenon. Run. I'll cover you.' He was gesturing towards the truck. 'Go to Souris and send a message that Menagerie is blown.'

She shook her head. 'I'm not leaving you.' She raised the .38 and fired all five of the remaining rounds in the magazine towards the militia soldiers. She pulled the spare magazine from her jacket pocket and snapped it into the grip of the pistol. She heard Leonard shout, 'Just fucking go, will you. Contact London.' He was right. If she stayed she would die and London would continue to send agents, only to be captured, tortured and killed. The circuit would be rounded up, Souris would be found and forced to send false information back to Baker Street. Many would die. But love fought with duty. A part of her wanted to die right there with him. Not leave him. Be there, together, as they gasped their last breaths, their bloodied bodies intertwined in one last embrace.

An explosion lit up the night sky. The Lysander had hit the copse. Its fuel tank was ablaze. The Milice were distracted. She saw Leonard throw down the Sten Gun. He ran for the cover of the woods behind them. He shouted, 'I'll be fine. Get to the truck. Go to Souris. We'll regroup at the fallback.' Their fallback location was a farmhouse nine kilometres from the town, owned by an old farmer who had two sons in the Maquis.

Yvonne ran towards the truck. She pressed the starter and prayed. The starter motor rasped and spluttered. She heard gunshots. Rounds pinged off the rusting bodywork of the old truck.

She swore at the motor, pushing the starter button over and over. A round pierced the windscreen, which shattered like a sudden hailstorm. Glass shards lodged in her clothes and her hair. She felt pinpricks of pain on her face. She pressed the starter button again and again. She heard the engine rumble into life, slammed the truck into gear and pushed the accelerator pedal so hard her foot might break through the rusting chassis. She swung the truck towards the road. The Milice were just yards away, raising their weapons. Two of them fired in her direction. A round glanced off the truck's bonnet. It sent a shower of sparks into the night. She looked back and saw one of the Miliciens turn and aim his weapon towards the woods behind her. She saw Leonard running, still on open ground, only a few yards from the cover of the trees. A single rifle shot cracked. Leonard jerked and fell. Yvonne gasped. She lost control of the truck. She wrestled with the wheel, only just managing to pull the lumbering old vehicle back onto the farm track that led to the road.

She looked back once more and saw two Miliciens dragging Leonard's limp body across the ground.

A Milicien sat on the bed. An officer with an 8mm Lebel revolver in his hand. The revolver was pointing at her belly as she stood frozen in the doorway of her room. Bundles of French francs lay beside him. The thirty thousand destined for the Maquis. She'd come back to collect it. It was a big risk, but without that money, she would not have been able to fund Maquis operations. That was her plan. Escape to the countryside, team up with one of the more remote resistance units and lead sabotage operations against German supply lines, as per Menagerie's orders. This was to have been Leonard's role, but Leonard was dead. She would take his place. She would instruct the resistants in the use of explosives and blow up railway lines. If the circuit was blown and the location of Maquis hideouts discovered, they would just have to fight it out with the enemy. It was worth a go. But that wouldn't happen now. The Milice officer was a step ahead of her.

He said, 'Come in. Close the door.'

He nodded towards the bulging hip pocket of her jacket. 'Don't think about reaching for the pistol.'

She complied. He would have shot her before her hand had touched the pocket.

'If you're going to shoot me, then do it,' she said.

She'd rather be shot than taken to the Gestapo for interrogation. The officer smiled. It was a smile with intent.

'I'm not going to shoot you. For one thing, you're far too pretty.'

So that was the deal. He intended to have her. He'd bank on her thinking compliance would save her skin. She wasn't that stupid. He'd have her and shoot her.

'And for another?' she said.

He considered his answer. 'And for another thing, I'm going to keep this money. No point handing it to the Gestapo.'

'So shoot me and take it,' she said.

He made a face. He waved his head from side to side, as if considering this option.

'It's not quite that easy,' he said. 'There's a problem you see. My men will be outside now. If they hear a shot they'll come running in and they will see the money. Then I'll have no choice but to hand it in. Instead I'm going to give you enough money to disappear and let you go. You can leave through the back. It will give me time to conceal the bundles of cash inside this loose and rather unflattering uniform. I'll go down to my men and tell them that you weren't here. No one will be any the wiser.'

'So toss me one of those bundles and let me go.'

He stood up from the bed and crossed the room towards her, the gun still pointing at her middle. She didn't move. She thought of the Milicien she'd shot in the guts. She heard his curses and screams in her head. She wasn't going to go that way if she could help it.

The officer stood facing her. He leaned in close. She smelled cognac and tobacco on his breath. She felt the barrel of the Lebel pressing into her abdomen. The officer raised his free hand and stroked her cheek. He kissed her lightly on the forehead.

'We have a few minutes,' he said.

She gritted her teeth. 'I'll break your neck before you're all the way. I know how.'

She did. She'd excelled in silent killing techniques during

training. She never thought she'd need it under such circumstances.

He laughed quietly to himself. He pressed his lips against her ear and whispered, 'If you do, you'll never see your boyfriend again.'

Her stomach tightened. The veins at the side of her head pounded.

'He's alive,' the officer said. 'Your agent Renard. He's hurt but he'll live. I've not reported his capture to the Gestapo yet. If you're nice to me I'll let him go.'

He was clever. He knew she wouldn't strike a bargain for herself. But for her lover? That would be different. Her head reeled. She couldn't think straight. She knew she should reject him. Sacrifice Renard. Not submit to the enemy, not least to this crooked French collaborator. But the urge to save her lover's life was strong. To see him one more time at least. To hold him in her arms.

She pressed her lips against the foul-breathed Milicien and kissed him.

'Let me make myself nice for you,' she whispered. He put his head to one side, as if weighing up her suggestion. Then he smiled, satisfied. She felt the barrel of the revolver pull back from her stomach. The officer stepped back.

He nodded towards the gun in her pocket. 'Take off that jacket first and throw it into the corner.'

She did as he asked. She unbuttoned her blouse so that he could see the silk of her underwear beneath. She had dressed for Leonard. Now she was baiting this animal. She stepped towards him and looked into his eyes. They were lustful and aggressive. She held his gaze and pursed her lips. She slipped her hand into the pocket of her trousers and drew out her lipstick. She pressed its blood red tip against her lips and traced seductive lines. The Milicien smiled. A wolf's smile. The gesture excited him. His hungry jaws opened. She leaned into him, pushed the lipstick into his mouth and slammed his jaws shut with the flat of her hand. The lethal pill cracked. Cyanide gushed into the Milicien's mouth. His face contorted. His lips bubbled. His eyes rolled like a rabid dog. He spasmed and fell to the floor with a thud. She put the heel of her boot into his groin, ground it down hard and heard the last breath of life seep from his from his pale, dead mouth.

THIRTY

'Leonard died in Dachau concentration camp. That's where they sent captured SOE agents. They told me when I returned to London after the Allies had liberated France. Vera, the French Section's intelligence officer, met me at Victoria station and bought me tea and a slice of fruitcake at the buffet. That was all the welcome I got. She asked how I was, told me what had happened to the rest of the Menagerie circuit and then said goodbye. Just like that. It was the last I saw of her or anyone else from the section. I'd served my purpose. I was no longer needed. I suppose they thought I would just settle down to civilian life and make some young chap a pretty young wife.' She laughed. 'A wife that could kill with her bare hands, fire any infantry weapon you cared to hand her and blow up a railway line, should the need arise.'

Her face tensed. She bit her bottom lip. She picked at her nails and shifted in the chair.

'I could have saved him,' she said. 'Not a day has passed that I haven't wished I had chosen to go along with that pig Milicien. Given him what he wanted, taken the money and gone to Leonard.'

'Chances are he was spinning you a yarn,' said Calloway.

'Perhaps. I'll never know, will I?'

'What happened then?'

There was a pack of cigarettes and a lighter on the table next to her. She nodded towards them and said, 'May I?'

'Alright,' said Calloway. 'But slowly.'

She did as he asked. She took a long drag on the tobacco and blew a plume of smoke upwards towards the dim bulkhead light above them. The light flickered.

'I looked for Celeste. She was all I had. Mother and father were dead. I had no other family in London. I tried all of the film studios and found her at Centurion. She was doing well. My little sister a film actress. Just bit parts at that time, walk-ons, but I could tell she would amount to something special. She had it in her. Something pure. Something magical. We spent some time together. We talked about old times and future plans. She told me about the charm school and I told her the little I could about what I'd been up to, which was little more than a cover story. The one contact I'd had from the War Office since Vera left me at the station was a letter reminding me that I had signed the Official Secrets Act. It was lovely to see Celeste doing well, but it was clear there was no room for me in her new life. I didn't resent that. I was pleased for her. There was nothing else keeping me in London and I had no idea what I was going to do with my life, so I went back to France. To Paris.'

'What did you do there?' he said.

He didn't like Paris. He'd been on leave there once. It seemed to him like a city living off a reputation it didn't deserve. A colourful myth, but a miserable reality. Perhaps that was just the effects of the war.

'I fell in with a bohemian crowd. Writers, poets, artists. You know the type. They were outsiders. It suited me. I'm not sure I'll ever be able to live what you'd call a normal life. Not now. Not since the war. I started writing poetry as a distraction and it turned out that I was actually quite good. One of the crowd I went around with knew a publisher in London who was interested in new British poets. He was starting a magazine. He was a pretentious and conceited arse, in truth. Called himself Mephisto.'

'I've met him,' said Calloway. 'He didn't take to me.'

She laughed. 'No, I don't imagine he did.'

She drew on the cigarette and blew another wisp of smoke towards the bulb. It flickered again.

'The power down this end of the shelter is not so good,' she said. 'Most of it's disconnected. I fiddled with some of the wires and managed to get some of the lights working. It's a bit hit and miss though.'

'What is this place?'

'It's a deep-level shelter. Built during the war for civilians to escape the air raids. But it proved too expensive to run so it was never used. At least not by civilians. The Americans took it over and billeted a signals unit here. Most of it is still in military use. This section of the tunnel was sealed up as surplus to requirements.'

'How did you know about it?'

'I came here during the war. The Americans were putting Jedburgh teams together to drop into France and carry out similar operations to ours. Some of the agents from French Section acted as liaison with them before we were deployed ourselves.'

He gestured with the pistol. 'Carry on with your story.'

She stubbed the cigarette out in an empty Spam tin. The hot tip made the leftover fat hiss.

'Mephisto published my work under an English-sounding pen name. He wanted his magazine to feature exclusively English poetry. I wrote to Celeste and asked her to send me some copies. You couldn't get them in Paris. Celeste and I started writing to each other regularly. We were both building new lives and we had a lot to tell each other. Her letters were a joy to read. She was so excited. Full of ambition, loving the life. Her dreams were starting to come true. But the letters started to change. The joy went out of them. It was when Spelthorne's friends showed up. She became more and more uncomfortable with that side of the job. You know, putting on a pretty face for her boss's financiers. But it didn't stop at a pretty face, did it? She told me what happened. With that bastard Azzopardi. And the drink. And the pills. Her last letter arrived a week after they found her dead.'

She lit another cigarette without asking him and took a long, desperate drag.

'So you decided to kill Spelthorne.'

She shook her head. 'Not kill him, destroy him. Destroy

what he held dear. His empire, his money, his backers. Sabotage and intimidation. That was my plan. I went back to the region I'd operated in during the war. We'd buried a cache of arms and I knew they might still be there. Guns, explosives, detonators. I smuggled what I needed back to Britain and got myself a job as a cleaner.'

'Using your pen name.'

She laughed. 'I thought that was a nice touch.'

'So you set about sabotaging the studio equipment and worked your way up to a bomb under Spelthorne's car. On the night of the annual Producers Club dinner, when you knew all his backers would be there. You could have killed everyone.'

She shook her head. 'But I didn't. I knew what I was doing. I'd had enough first-hand experience with detonators in the field to time it just right. When everyone was half cut and stuck into their sherry trifle.'

The light flickered again. The room went blank for a full two seconds before coming back on. The light flex was buzzing.

'What are you going to do?' she said.

'I should take you in. Hand you over to the police.'

He'd be off the hook then. He'd keep his job, Bernie would leave him alone and Special Branch could close their file. It would be the best result for him.

Again the light flickered. The flex buzzed louder.

Then he heard the bulb pop.

The room stayed dark this time. It was pitch black. He couldn't see a thing. He heard the legs of Yvonne's chair scrape on the ground. He heard the door open and the sound of running. He stumbled through the darkness towards the noise. His shin slammed into something hard. He heard the clang of metal and the rattle of springs. He fell forwards over one of the old iron cots. His head hit the hard concrete of the floor. Light flickered, this time behind his eyes. Then it went dark.

He came to an hour later. His skull buzzed with pain. He flipped open his lighter. The tunnel lit up like a Dickensian scene from a better class of film than Centurion made. He scanned the floor. The Welrod had gone. She must have come back and taken it when he was out cold. He pulled himself to his feet, stepped between the abandoned cots and headed for the staircase in the half light of the lighter's flame.

It felt cold in the street. He shivered and pulled his jacket tight around him. His ears were ringing. His eyes couldn't adjust to the street light. He felt like throwing up. Concussion. Nothing he could do about it. He flagged a taxi and told the driver to take him to the studio. He slurred his words. The cabbie thought he was drunk. He gave him the once over, deciding if his fare was going to vomit in his cab. He satisfied himself and swiped the taxi meter. The engine tick-ticked as they headed east.

Old Arthur was asleep in his watchman's hut. Calloway left him to it. Better that way. He headed for the administration block. He wanted the purse and the detonator from his desk drawer. It was evidence. It corroborated the real story. He saw that the lights were on in Studio B. He crossed the courtyard and pushed open the big double doors. The Irish pub set was lit. Giordano sat at the table pouring champagne. It looked incongruous. He had company. She couldn't have been more than seventeen. She was dolled up. One of his swanky nights out, Calloway thought. Show her the high life. Play the movie mogul to impress. Give her a late-night tour of Centurion. Champagne on set. Fill her head with notions of movie glamour. She'd be upstairs at Curzon Street before the year was out.

'You need to leave,' Calloway said to the girl.

Giordano bristled. 'You need to fuck off,' he said.

Calloway ignored him. He stepped onto the set and took the girl by the arm. He led her towards the door. He said, 'Wake up the old boy in the hut and get him to call you a cab. The studio will pay.'

The girl looked back at Giordano confused. 'Gio, what's going on? You said we'd make a night of it.'

Giordano shrugged and smiled at the girl. It was the kind of smile that said he couldn't have cared less.

'Maybe next time,' he said. 'I'll call you.'

The girl walked towards the exit doors in quick uppity steps. Her heel caught a cable that snaked across the floor to one of the cameras. She tripped. She steadied herself and shot Giordano a backwards look.

The big Maltese rolled his eyes. He knocked back his drink and poured himself another.

Calloway waited until the girl had left. 'Does she know you're a ponce?'

Giordano rocked on the back legs of his chair and lit a cigarette. 'Not yet. The penny will drop sooner or later. By that time she'll be a busy girl. Fifteen quid a go, I reckon. They pay more for the young ones. She's good for a ton and a half a night.'

Calloway pulled a chair up to the table. 'Enjoy your work, do you?'

Giordano smirked. 'It has its benefits.' He made an obscene gesture. 'And it pays well,' he said, stroking the lapel of his jacket with the back of his thick, manicured figures. 'I don't see you wearing a suit like this.'

'Clothes maketh the man, that's what they say, don't they?' said Calloway. 'In which case you're made of something loud and very vulgar.'

The goon snorted through his flat boxer's nose. 'I should skin you for that.'

He pulled the knife from his pocket, the one he'd used in Spelthorne's car, and stabbed it into the tabletop.

'Careful,' said Calloway. 'You might need that later, if your boss wants another cigar. He gets you to run around him all day long doing all the little jobs. He knows a lackey when he sees one.' The big goon's face stiffened. 'I bet you'd wipe his arse if he asked you.'

Giordano heaved his big frame out of the chair and grabbed Calloway by the lapels. He threw back his head to butt him. Calloway slammed his flattened hand upwards and deflected the blow. Giordano's jaw crunched. Calloway grabbed the lapel of his wideboy suit and spun him around. He rabbit punched the back of his thick neck before grabbing a mop of oily hair and slamming his head down hard on the tabletop. He punched his kidneys and threw him back in the chair.

'Don't ever think your anything special, son,' he said. 'You're the shit on my shoes. You're a gangster and a ponce. No better than the villains you work for, just cheaper and more obedient. Like a dog at their heels.'

Giordano lifted his head and spat blood from his mouth. He reached for the knife. Calloway had been a fool to leave it stuck in the table. He'd let anger cloud his judgement. He went to bat Giordano's hand away, but the gangster was quicker. He grabbed the knife in his big hand and slashed at Calloway. The blade ripped through his jacket. It drew blood. Calloway made to grab the big Maltese's wrist. His foot snagged a cable. He stumbled. The gangster had him by the throat, one hand pressing his windpipe into his spine, the other pushing the blade into his solar plexus. Calloway felt the cold metal puncture his skin. It was heading for his heart. He flailed his arms. He punched the air. He choked. He heaved his chest, trying to draw air into his lungs. His windpipe was shut tight. The big gangster's thumb had it sealed. He felt faint. He felt nauseous. His heart pounded, fit to burst. He forced his hand between their two bodies and balled his fist. It stopped the blade going further. Giordano gripped the knife and pushed harder. Calloway tensed his arm and squeezed his fist. He tried to push the goon away. Giordano put the full force of his weight behind the knife. He lay on Calloway. He sandwiched him between his body and the tabletop. Calloway felt dizzy. Bright white light engulfed him. He gasped and gasped but couldn't draw a breath. Suffocation summoned unconsciousness. He started to fade out. The bright white light was turning to darkness. The gangster pressed harder. The blade was easing its way towards Calloway's heart. He felt Giordano's lips against his ear. He heard his voice.

'I ain't shit on no one's shoes.'

There was a violent spitting sound. White heat singed Calloway's ear. The gangster jolted. He went limp. He lay on

Calloway like a dead weight. Calloway summoned strength and pushed back. The gangster rolled to the floor. He landed on his back. The crash echoed around the studio. Calloway looked down at him. Black-red blood trickled from a perfect hole in his temple. The left side of his face was missing. Brain and bone oozed onto the studio floor.

Yvonne Leclerc stood in the doorway, knees bent, arms outstretched, gripping the butt of the Welrod in both hands.

'The bastard deserved it,' she said.

THIRTY-ONE

She lowered the pistol.

'You came back for the detonator,' he said.

She nodded. 'I tried before, but you caught me in the act.'

'I've still got the bruising.'

He saw something catch her eye.

'You're bleeding,' she said.

The gash in his sleeve was wet with blood and a deep red stain was forming on his shirt front. They were flesh wounds. No blood vessels cut.

'I'll live,' he said. 'Have you got the detonator on you?'

She tapped her hip pocket. He saw the glint of the lamé purse protruding from the pocket flap.

'Give it to me,' he said.

She laughed. 'Why the hell would I do that?'

He looked down at Giordano's body. The gangster's head lay in pool of vivid red that glinted under the studio lights.

'Because you and I are in more trouble than each of us has ever been. I can fix that if you give me that detonator. You've got to trust me.'

'Why would I ever trust you?' she said.

'We're cut from the same cloth, you and me,' he said. 'We've lived the same lives. We know what war does. We know what loss is. We know the value of happiness, especially when it's ripped from us, and from those we loved.' He nodded at the body on the floor. 'We know good from evil. We fought gangsters. Gangsters in uniforms. People like him, but smarter and more powerful. We've killed and we've maimed and we might even have enjoyed it sometimes. We've done terrible things. In some ways we're just as guilty as him and his bosses. The difference is that somewhere deep inside us we know right from wrong. That earns us the right to live. I've cheated the hangman's noose by the skin of my teeth. You can too. Just trust me.'

She stood silently, thinking, then slipped the pistol into the waistband of her trousers.

'I need a cigarette,' she said.

He tossed her his cigarette case and lighter. She lit up and took a long hard drag.

'I've not finished with him,' she said.

'Meaning you've not destroyed Spelthorne?'

She nodded.

'I can do that,' he said. He looked around him at the studio. 'I can bring his empire tumbling down. I can reduce him to nothing.'

They stood in silence in the glare of the lights. Up close the film set looked as fake and flimsy as Spelthorne's ill-gotten grandeur.

She reached into her pocket and brought out the purse.

'Here,' she said, holding it out for him.

He snapped open the clasp, took out the pencil and unscrewed the barrel. He slid the time pencil into his hand. He passed the purse back to her.

'You'd better lose this,' he said.

She nodded and pushed it back into the pocket of her jacket. Calloway knelt beside the body on the floor. He slipped the time pencil into the pocket of Giordano's suit.

'Did the night watchman see you arrive?'

She shook her head. 'He was asleep in his hut. I slipped past him.'

Good old Arthur, thought Calloway. He could be relied on for something.

'You need to get away from here. Away from London. Tonight. And you need to be out of the country tomorrow.'

'That's easier said than done,' she said.

'Come with me,' he said, walking towards the door.

She took a last look at the body and followed him. He killed the studio lights on their way out. He didn't want old Arthur waking up and being suspicious. If Giordano's body was found while they were still on the premises, they were in even deeper trouble.

They crossed to the administration block and climbed the stairs in darkness. The lock on his office door was broken. There was a size-five boot mark on the door panel.

'That's one way of doing it,' he said.

She shrugged and said, 'Needs must.'

He switched on his desk lamp. The top drawer of his desk was open. No lock picking tools this time. Just jemmied, good and proper. He opened the lower drawer and pulled out the bottle of Black & White and two glasses. He slid them across the desktop.

'Pour us two large ones,' he said.

She took the bottle, poured the drinks and downed hers in one. Then she poured herself another. He picked up the phone and dialled a number. He knocked back his scotch while he waited for an answer. It rang for a good half minute before he heard a male voice, woozy with sleep.

'Johnny, it's Cab. I know it's late but listen. I'll do that job. The one you told me about at the baths. But I need a favour in return.'

He explained what he wanted.

Suskind said, 'Alright, Reg, I'll be there in thirty minutes. I'll bring Solly. He's a good man.'

Calloway thanked him and put the phone down. He put his hand in the desk drawer. Yvonne saw him slip a package into his pocket. He reached in the drawer again and pulled out a newspaper. He rifled through it and ripped out a page. He took a big bunch of keys from a row of hooks behind his desk and said, 'Where's your passport?'

'I have it on me,' she said. 'When you've lived in an occupied country, you get used to carrying your papers everywhere.'

'Good,' he said. 'You're going to need some other things too. Follow me.'

He took her to the props store and picked out a suitcase.

'This do?' he said.

She nodded and smiled. It was Joyce's smile, from the first reel of her home movies.

'I've travelled with less,' she said.

Their footsteps echoed down the corridor. He pulled out the keys and unlocked the door of the wardrobe department. He flicked on the lights.

'You need to pick out some clothes. I've no idea what's where. You'll have to poke around but be quick. We've got less than thirty minutes.'

'I know my way around. I used to clean in here. It's how I knew where to find the dress I wore for the gala dinner. It's back on the rails now.'

He'd not thought that she might have borrowed her ball gown from the studio.

'The purse too?' he said.

She nodded.

'Put it back then. Take your personal effects out first.'

She emptied the contents into her pocket and put the purse with the others that were lined up tagged and numbered in a row along one of the shelves.

He watched her pack clothes into the case. Two dresses, a suit, trousers and a jacket. A belted mac. Heeled shoes, flats and sandals. Silk underwear and stockings. A handbag, two berets and a handful of scarves. She was a fast shopper, he thought. Not that he'd really know. He'd never been shopping with a woman. Never been close enough, at least not in peacetime. The woman he'd loved hadn't survived the war.

She pushed the lid of the suitcase down hard and snapped the clasps shut. She patted the bulging lid and said, 'Ready.'

He pointed to the Welrod in her waistband. 'You'd better give me that,' he said.

Arthur was still asleep as they passed the watchman's hut. Johnny was waiting in a taxi outside the main gates. Solly, the cabbie who had transported them from the last dust-up with Hamm's fascists, was at the wheel. He gave Calloway a nod of recognition.

Calloway introduced them to Yvonne. He called her Eve. Best she kept her real name out of this. Johnny held the door for her. He said, 'Solly and me will take you to the coast tonight. I've got a mate in Deal you can hole up with until first light. He'll take you to Dover. You can get the first boat the France.'

Suskind handed Yvonne a small roll of bank notes. 'Don't worry,' he said, with a wink. 'Reg says he'll pay me back.'

'There's enough there to get you to France and buy you a fortnight in a hotel. The rest is up to you,' said Calloway.

Yvonne climbed into the cab. Johnny noticed the blood on Calloway's clothing.

'Do you need that looking at? I know a doctor. He's discreet.'

Calloway shook his head.

'I can fix it. Drop me at my place on the way.'

The taxi rumbled over the cobbles. Its diesel engine tick-ticked through the silence of the night. It was past one o'clock. The streets were empty. They passed a row of shop fronts. A baker, a delicatessen, a kosher restaurant. There were fascist slogans daubed on the restaurant's shutters. Fresh paint ran from the points of a swastika.

'Bastards,' Johnny muttered under his breath.

Solly parked the cab outside Da Costa's factory.

Calloway said, 'Keep the engine running, Solly. I'll be right back.'

He returned with the case full of mementoes he'd found in Joyce's flat.

'You should have this,' he said. He slipped his hand into the pocket of his jacket. 'And this.' He put the first reel of Joyce's home movies into Yvonne's hand. She looked at the film reel, confused at first. She opened the case and saw the letters and photographs and the copy of the poetry magazine. He saw a small tear well in her eye. She leaned out of the window and kissed him on the cheek. She put her lips against his ear and said, 'Destroy him. You promised me.'

He clapped Johnny on the back and said, 'Over to you.'

Suskind gave him a mock salute. 'I'll see you later, Reg,' he said. 'I'll let you know the time and place.'

Solly turned on a sixpence and headed back up to Shoreditch High Street. Calloway saw the two red tail lights glare at him, like the eyes of a devil taunting him. He'd struck two deals tonight. Made two promises. He would enjoy keeping the first. The second he wasn't so sure about.

He walked the length of the factory floor in the semi-darkness. A lone street lamp outside cast a web of shadows through the metal window frames onto the worn wooden floorboards. Sewing machines stood in rows on one side, cutting tables along the other. Dressmakers' forms stood sentinel. They reminded him of the straw-filled dummies he'd used in the army for bayonet practice. He felt his chest. The blood stain on his shirt was damp but the bleeding had stopped. He pulled a key from the fob in his pocket and opened the door to Da Costa's office. As caretaker he had keys to all the doors in the building. He switched on the desk lamp. He took a telephone directory from the shelf behind the desk. London A to E.

He slid the directory into the rectangle of light under the desk lamp and leafed through the pages. He reached the Ds. He ran his fingers down the dense column of names until he found the Daily Sketch. It was a populist conservative rag. It abhorred immorality. It revelled in lurid tales of villainy. He noted down the address. He took a foolscap envelope from Da Costa's drawer and on it wrote the name of the journalist whose byline had appeared on the articles about the death of Joyce Rose. He reached into his inside pocket and pulled out the papers Ndungu had passed him. The Companies House files and the Land Registry lists. He ringed names in red ink, blew on the ink to dry it, then slipped the papers into the envelope. He took a sheet of Da Costa's note paper, ripped off the letterhead and slipped it onto the roller of the typewriter on the secretary's desk adjacent to Da Costa's. He cranked down the roller and two-finger typed. Then he slipped the finished note into the envelope with the cutting he'd ripped from the newspaper, the story about Azzopardi and the vice charges. He reached into his pocket and pulled out the final reel of Joyce Rose's home movies. He stuffed it into the envelope and sealed it.

It was two a.m. The roads were empty as he drove east towards Fleet Street. The night was damp. Mist hung in the air. Street lamps cast a putrid, smog-yellow glow. He pulled the car over. The Daily Sketch offices were lit like a fairground. There was life in every window. He heard the printing presses rumbling from the rear of the building. He walked up the steps and into the foyer. It was decked out like a grand hotel. A rugged-looking commissionaire with a row of campaign ribbons sat behind a reception desk the size of the Queen Mary. He glanced at the clock on the wall and gave Calloway an inquisitorial look.

Calloway put the envelope on the desk and jabbed the name of the journalist with his finger.

'See this gets to him will you,' he said. His tone had authority. The commissionaire deferred. He gave Calloway a respectful nod and said, 'Right you are, sir.'

He left the car where it was and walked south towards the river. While the rest of London slept, this small quarter of the city was alive. He could hear the shouts of print workers as they loaded bundles of newspapers into the liveried vans that waited at the loading docks of the big newspaper buildings. Early editions heading for the hotels and railway stations. Closer to the river it was quieter. He did his best to blend into the mist and shadows. He crossed the street and walked towards Blackfriars Bridge. He stood at the centre of the bridge and leaned on the railings looking down onto the blackness of the Thames. He smelled the damp, rotten smell of the river. He slipped his hand inside his jacket, pulled out the Welrod and dropped it into the dark waters below.

THIRTY-TWO

It had hit the papers. Calloway sat in the canteen reading the headlines.

Film mogul linked to gangland murder

Vice ring profits fund Centurion productions

Studio car bombing was 'gang feud' revenge

Marge pulled up a chair and joined him at the table.

'How terribly exciting,' she said.

'I expect we'll all be out of a job soon,' he said.

'I'm not so sure. Rumour has it that J Arthur Rank is already circling.'

He leafed through the pages of the paper. Joyce Rose's face stared out from the centre spread.

Maltese 'ponce' drove starlet to suicide

'Poor Joyce,' she said.

You should speak to your pal, Tony, he thought. There was no mention of him in the story.Or of Ivor Cole or any other movie Mephistos that worked behind the scenes trading dreams for souls. They sullied the young and innocent for publicity and profit. Underneath the gloss and the glamour they were as viscous and corrupt as any gangster. Joyce was the leading lady of an un-filmed epic. Romance, melodrama, tragedy. And no amount of pills could take away the hurt and no amount of soap could scrub away the filth.

He left these thoughts unvoiced. He wanted out. Bryant and Belcher had their man. McCaffrey was off the hook. Bernie was off his case. He had one thing more to do.

'I'll be taking a holiday, Mr Da Costa,' he said. They stood on the factory floor amid the locust-clicks of a dozen sewing machines. Plumes of smoke rose from cigarettes that hung from the lips of the seamstresses. It was past eight p.m. They were pulling a night shift on time-and-a-half. Da Costa had a big order to fill. A radio played dance band music above the din.

Da Costa gave Calloway a knowing look. 'A holiday is good. You are tired, young man.' Calloway caught a twinkle in the old boy's eye. 'Will you be holidaying alone?'

Calloway shrugged. 'Maybe not.'

'Then maybe not is also good.' He frowned and thought for a moment. Then he looked up and smiled. 'I can spare you for a week or two. My nephew can keep an eye on the place. That lazy schlemiel needs something to do with himself.'

Calloway packed a case. He didn't pack for a holiday. He packed everything. Then he pulled the flex of the telephone out of the wall. He took a last look at the attic room. He thought of Marjorie naked in the orange glow of the fire.

He left the building and dropped the case onto the back seat of his car. He walked to the call box on the corner of the street, pushed tuppence into the slot and dialled Marjorie's number.

'Marge, it's Reg.'

'Reggie, darling. I hear you're going to be a very brave boy tonight.'

'I'm doing that job for Johnny. I thought we could meet afterwards.'

There was a pause. He heard a voice in the background. A man's voice.

'I'm so sorry, Reg, darling, but I'm busy tonight. A friend of mine is visiting and he's taking me to Mirabelle for dinner.'

He felt stupid. Why did he think he had some claim on her? They'd slept together. Once. No dinner beforehand, no dancing, just an opportunistic fumble on sweaty sheets by the light of a spluttering gas fire.

'Of course,' he said. 'I'm sorry.'

He put the phone down. He felt empty and alone.

Johnny was waiting for him at the corner of Ladbroke Grove and Arundel Gardens. A stocky man with tight black curls and a heavy brow stood next to him. He wore a grey demob suit with a black shirt buttoned to the collar.

'This is Dai the Dairy,' Johnny said.

The stocky man turned to Johnny and said, 'Fuck off.' Calloway recognised traces of a rich Valleys accent from just those two syllables. He'd known a lot of Welshmen in the army. It was that or the pits for most of them, just like it was for him. Calloway nodded at the stocky man and said, 'Why's he call you that?'

'Because I'm a Welshman and I run a dairy.'

He aimed a cuff at Suskind's head. The ex-paratrooper ducked then grinned. The stocky man grinned back and offered Calloway his hand.

'I'm Gruffydd,' he said. 'You can call me Griff.'

Johnny said, 'Griff's family have been delivering our daily pint for generations. He's an honorary East Ender.'

Griff nodded. 'I moved to London when I was demobbed and took over my uncle's business. I'd been dairy farming with my father in Wales before the war.'

'Griff could have missed the whole shout if he'd wanted to,' said Johnny. 'He was in a reserved occupation. He could have avoided service altogether.'

Griff sneered. 'I wasn't having that. On the first day of the war I took the bus into town, told a few fibs and signed up. Royal Marines.'

He rolled up his sleeve and showed his tattoo, a winged anchor crossed by a Tommy gun, the emblem of Combined Operations.

Johnny said, 'Griff was a commando.'

Griff reeled off names of famous raids. 'Lofoten Islands, Bruneval, St Nazaire...'

In other words, a right tough bastard, thought Calloway.

Johnny went over the details of the plan. He pointed to a house on Arundel Gardens. A tall townhouse, typical of Notting Hill, shabby and smog-blackened.

'That's the Union Movement headquarters. Jeffrey Hamm has an office and flat on the fourth floor. He lives there with his bodyguard. He's been shitting himself ever since we stepped up operations. Don't forget boys, they're more scared of us than we are of them.'

Griff nodded. He puffed out his barrel chest. His muscles bulged in the sleeves of his jacket. Calloway doubted he needed reassurance.

Johnny continued. 'You need to get in there, sort out the bodyguard and teach Hamm a lesson he won't forget. Then grab as many files as you can and get the hell back here.'

He nodded to a taxi parked at the corner of the street. Calloway recognised the driver.

'Solly will get us clear before Hamm and his boyfriend have noticed you're gone.'

Calloway saw Griff slip a knuckle duster onto his muscular fist.

They knocked at the door. They heard heavy footsteps on the stairs. The door opened and the bodyguard blocked it with his oversized frame.

'Who the hell are you?' he said, in heavily accented English.

It was the German from the rally. The Nazi POW who'd shouted his battle cry before tasting Calloway's boot. He showed no signs of recognising his erstwhile opponent.

Griff clicked his heels, gave the fascist salute and said, 'Hail Mosley!'

The bodyguard looked bemused.

Calloway said, 'We need to speak to Hamm. We have an urgent message.'

The two of them pushed past the bodyguard and ran up the stairs.

Hamm was in his office. He sat at a desk reading papers. Calloway took in the scene. Fascist heraldry. Flags, shields and posters. Slogans screamed at him.

Mosley speaks! Tomorrow we live! Keep out alien Jews!

Hamm read their faces. He looked alarmed. He stood up and said, 'What the hell do you want?'

Griff shut him up. He slammed brass knuckles into the fascist leader's face. Hamm went down. Griff struck again. Hamm whimpered. He spat blood through loosened teeth. Griff hit him twice more, good and hard. Hamm was out cold.

A piss stain spread across the trousers of his suit. Behold the master race, thought Calloway. Griff grabbed files. Calloway rifled the desk. He found a book. A big ledger. He flicked through it. Names of every Union Movement member. Johnny's going to love this, he thought. He stuffed the book into his waistband. The two men headed for the stairs.

The bodyguard was blocking their way. He gripped a lead pipe in his hand. He swung at Calloway. Calloway parried the blow. Pain shot through his arm. The bodyguard spat obscenities and swung again. Calloway side-stepped this time. He kicked at the bodyguard's legs. The bodyguard buckled. He teetered on the top step and lost his footing. Calloway grabbed his lapels. He channelled his anger and summoned strength. He lifted the big German off the ground and heaved him down the stairs. Bang, bang, bang. The bodyguard hit every step. He smashed through the stair spindles. He sent the bannister flying. Calloway picked up the lead pipe and piled down the stairs after him. Griff followed close behind. The bodyguard lay on the ground, his limbs contorted. He raised his head and sneered. Calloway swung the pipe. He heard the snap of bones. The bodyguard squealed. His jaw jutted sideways like a gargoyle. Calloway fell on him, full weight. The bodyguard looked up at his two attackers. All three men had fought the same war. Two had driven fascism into the ground. One was trying to revive it. Calloway grabbed the Nazi by the hair and yanked his head up. He leaned in and whispered, 'Wir kommen wieder.'

We will be back.

THE END

About the author

DDC Morgan lives in South East London. He has written professionally as a journalist and consultant for more than thirty years. Crime writing fills the rock'n'roll-shaped hole in his life left by no longer playing in bands.

You can follow him on Twitter @DDCMorgan

More great books from Fahrenheit Press…

Abide With Me by Ian Ayris

Abide with me is the story of two boys forced to walk blind into the darkness of their shattered lives and their struggle to emerge as men. It's also a story of loyalty, of community, and of powerful friendships shaped by adversity and celebrated on the football terraces of England.

With power, sensitivity and wit, Ian Ayris has crafted one of the most authentic snapshots of working class life you will ever read.

Black Moss by David Nolan

In April 1990, as rioters took over Strangeways prison in Manchester, someone killed a little boy at Black Moss.

And no one cared.

No one except Danny Johnston, an inexperienced radio reporter trying to make a name for himself.

More than a quarter of a century later, Danny returns to his home city to revisit the murder that's always haunted him.

If Danny can find out what really happened to the boy, maybe he can cure the emptiness he's felt inside since he too was a child.

But finding out the truth might just be the worst idea Danny Johnston has ever had.

Find more amazing books

www.Fahrenheit-Press.com